home again

home again

MELISSA GRACE

Also by MELISSA GRACE

Home Is Where You Are

For Nicole,
Because some friends are our soul mates. Love you always.

"Storms make trees take deeper roots."
—*Dolly Parton*

ONE

Ella

"CAN SOMEONE PLEASE TELL ME WHY I'M NOT SITTING poolside with a hot cabana boy serving me cocktails on the eve of your wedding?" I whined and slammed the trunk of my SUV. "I should be sipping Mai Tais and working on my tan, but no. I'm about to do physical labor. *On a farm.*"

"Honestly, Ella, it's goat yoga," my best friend Liv Sinclair reminded me as though somehow that fact made this unfortunate situation any better. I grumbled to myself, shoving the brand new yoga mat I'd purchased solely for this occasion under my arm.

"Mom," my daughter Grace chided me. "It's going to be *fun.*"

"Fun," I echoed with a snort. "It's all fun and games until someone gets shit on."

Liv gave my arm an encouraging squeeze. "Besides, we're getting brunch with Katie and Antoni afterward."

I narrowed my eyes at her. "Why didn't *they* get to come be crapped on by goats?"

"Because," Liv said, "this is one of the last days the

1

three of us get to be together before Grace runs off to England with Sam."

She sang his name, and I felt a knot form in my stomach at the thought of my nineteen-year-old daughter leaving the country. It was a gorgeous Friday morning in the second week of June, and not to be dramatic or anything, but this was going to be the last day of life as I knew it.

The changes had started a year and a half before when Liv met her soon-to-be husband, Jax, who just so happened to be a rockstar. It was wild to think that not that long ago, the guys from the band Midnight in Dallas were celebrities to us because in just a few months' time they'd practically become family. And in less than twenty-four hours, Jax *would* be family.

Out of the corner of my eye, I saw a girl about Grace's age sneak a photo of Liv. That was one part of having a famous best friend I didn't think I would ever get used to. She couldn't go anywhere without being recognized since she'd become a celebrity.

I watched as Brady, Liv's security guard, observed the young girl who turned seven shades of red once she realized she'd been noticed. She was probably embarrassed because that was *so* not a Nashville thing to do, but also because Brady was kind of a hottie with his beefy chest and tatted arms. I liked Brady a lot. He'd become a friend and a warm presence I'd grown to appreciate, but I had to admit, I missed the times when it was just us.

Of course, I was happy for Liv, but I did feel a sense of impending doom that after she and Jax said 'I do' things would never really be the same. This doom was amplified by the fact that come Monday morning, my daughter, my only child and star of my life, Grace, was leaving the country. The previous summer, Grace had started interning as an assistant for Cash Montgomery, CEO of Carrie On Records, the very same label that housed Midnight in Dallas, Liv and Jax's duo, and the heartthrob pop star from England, Sam Corbyn. Grace had done so well that when Sam needed a temporary personal assistant while his gal was on maternity leave for the summer, Cash suggested Grace for the position. She would fill in on her break and be back in time to return to school at Belmont University in the fall.

I groaned. "I don't even want to think about you leaving me."

"You're going to be fine, Mom." Grace looped her arm through mine as we trudged up the gravel drive to the gated entryway of The Nashville Goat.

The sound of a shrill scream pierced the air from just beyond the wooden gate, and I stopped dead in my tracks. "Oh my God! Did you hear that? I bet someone got bit. I told you this was a bad idea."

Grace and Liv exploded into hysterical laughter.

"That's not a person," Liv said between giggles. "It's a goat."

"Well, are they stabbing it?" I asked in horror. I didn't particularly want to be there, but I didn't wish bodily harm on the little shit factories either. "Why is it screaming?"

Grace shook her head. "That's what goats sound like, Mom. It's called bleating."

I pouted. "Like the string of expletives that are going to fly out of my mouth when one of those goats shits on me?"

"Not bleeping." Liv laughed, twisting her long chestnut hair into a messy bun on top of her head. "*Bleat*-ing."

"This is bleating bullshit," I said, reluctantly resuming our trek toward the sound of the goat screams. *Ahem. Bleats.*

"So help me God, if one of these goats poops on me, you're both dead."

We proceeded to the wooden gate and checked in for our torture. *Class. I mean class.* I bolted toward the grassy area furthest away from the instructor with Liv and Grace on my heels. My nose scrunched involuntarily at the scent of eau de goat shit as I unrolled my yoga mat.

Liv settled in next to me, and Grace dropped her mat on the ground before running off in search of one of the little screaming creatures.

"So, how was last night?" Liv asked, looking like a fitness model as she stretched in her sleek black leggings and sports bra.

I returned my gaze to Liv and grimaced. In anticipation of my entire life being upended, I'd done what any sane woman would do and joined the wonderful world of internet dating. "Caleb was sufficiently boring."

Liv tilted her head in confusion. "I thought his name was Kyle."

"Same difference," I said with a wave of my hand. "He's a financial advisor, and that's literally all he talked about. But hey, I should now be able to retire an entire five years earlier based on his advice."

Liv chuckled. "Well, that's something. What about Will? The guy you're bringing to the wedding?"

"About that." I sighed. "Will reunited with his ex-wife, so I had to call an audible and invite someone else." Will and I had really just been friends. Most of our 'dates' were wine drenched outings where he talked about missing his ex. I wanted to help him reconnect with her because I could see how much he still loved her, but my advice had worked so well I'd lost my wedding date.

"Who's the lucky guy?"

4

"Ryan."

"Wait, isn't he the football coach? I thought we didn't like him."

I shook my head. "No, that was Bryan, and we definitely don't like him." Bryan had coffee breath and was still reliving his glory days as a high school quarterback. Perhaps that would have been cute in my early twenties—endearing even. But at nearly forty, I would have preferred to have a pap smear than talk about sportsball of any kind. "Ryan is the guy who works for Gibson Guitar. I went to dinner with him last week."

Her eyes widened. "The one that looks like Matthew McConaughey who took you to Kayne Prime?"

I flashed her a salacious grin. "That's the one."

Liv gave me an approving nod. "We love a man who skips the coffee date and takes you right to a steak dinner."

"That we do," I agreed. "And he's hot. Like fry an egg on his chest *hot*. He was perfectly nice and super respectful, but there's something missing. The chemistry just isn't there for me."

"Sometimes it takes a while for love to bloom into something amazing."

I snorted. "Says the woman who fell in love at first sight with a fucking rockstar. Excuse me if I don't believe you, Cinderella."

"Yes, there was an instant attraction with Jax," Liv said, "but love came with time."

"Like two weeks," I challenged.

She opened her mouth as though she were about to say something but closed it.

"Even after all these months, your eyes still turn all gooey like the center of a fucking cinnamon roll any time you talk about Jax." I smiled at my best friend looking all

5

glowy and happy. "I want to be a cinnamon roll again. Actually, maybe I just want a cinnamon roll. I'm starving."

"You know you don't *have* to bring a date. I don't want you to feel like you have to bring someone you're not excited about," Liv said gently.

I knew I didn't have to, but the idea of going to Liv's wedding alone and being offered a pity dance by one of the guys was more than my pride could bear. Ryan was cute enough, and hey, maybe Liv was right about love blooming and all that. *Probably not, though.*

"Mom, I'm getting a goat." Grace saved me from my thoughts as she approached with a tiny brown and white goat in her grasp. "Isn't he cute? His name is Ralphie."

Liv's eyes turned even mushier as she cooed and made over the disgusting animal.

"I'm pretty sure you can't sneak that on the plane." I gave her a pointed look, and Ralphie screeched in agreement.

Grace laughed. "Don't you want to pet him, Mom?"

"Absolutely not."

"Alright, everyone!" The perky yoga instructor right out of a Lululemon catalog clasped her hands together at the front of the class. "We're going to get started now." Grace placed Ralphie on the grass, but he stayed glued to her side as she unfurled her yoga mat beside me. I side-eyed the little shithead as the instructor continued on. "We're going to start in Child's Pose and focus on our breathing. We want to find our center today. And some cute goats, of course."

The class giggled, and a couple of the goats screamed. I watched Lulu contort her body, her legs tucked beneath her as she extended her arms, and I did my best to emulate her. I watched while Ralphie chewed on the tip of Grace's ponytail as she stretched her arms to the top of her mat.

Ralphie stopped mid-chew as though he were assessing me with his beady little eyes.

"Listen here, Ralphie. You better keep your bleepin', bleatin' ass over there," I whispered loudly.

Liv swallowed a laugh beside me.

"Wonderful," the instructor said. "Now, we're going to transition into Tabletop, but we're still concentrating on our breathing. Breathe in through your nose and out through your mouth."

"The last thing I want to do right now is breathe," I muttered, following Lulu's lead.

I got on my hands and knees, flattening my back. I was focusing my energy on *not* breathing in the scent of the barnyard when I suddenly felt four little hammers on my back. My body tensed as I felt something tugging on the fabric of my tank top and a cold snout on my shoulder.

"It's on me! Grace! Liv! Get it off me! Please!" I squealed as they both broke their Tabletops, collapsing on their mats in heaps of giggles. The air smelled even more fowl than it had seconds before. "I smell poop! Why do I smell poop?" I screamed, and the goat squealed in response. His hooves poked me in the back as he began to chew on my ponytail.

Liv's eyes widened in my direction. "Oh sh—"

"SHIT," I cried.

Grace jumped to her feet, prying the little demon off my back. She attempted to stifle a laugh, but she, along with several of the other class attendees, dissolved into hysterics. I scrambled to my feet and gagged, shaking the shit from my back.

"Uh-oh," Lulu said, looking up at me from her Tabletop pose, her voice chipper as though I had not just been the victim of a drive-by pooping. "Sorry about that!

7

On the bright side, you get a free shirt. Can someone please grab the lady in the back a T-shirt?"

"Sorry, Mom," Grace managed to choke out between laughs as a lady in a hot pink tank top with 'The Nashville Goat' printed on it approached, handing me a rolled-up grey shirt.

"Sorry about that." The lady smiled but backed away quickly because I smelled like the inside of a goat's ass. I ripped my shirt off, not even caring that everyone in the class had started to watch. I pulled the new shirt over my head and huffed.

Liv took one look at me and collapsed once more. This time, Grace and the entire class joined her. I looked down at my chest and was both annoyed and amused by the words written across it: *I got shit on by goats, and all I got was this t-shirt.*

I shook my head and laughed, looking from Grace to Liv. "Can we go now? Please?"

"NORMALLY, I WOULD GIVE YOU SHIT ABOUT SOMETHING like this, but it appears you've had your fair share already, honey," Antoni quipped, raising one perfectly arched eyebrow at me. He gave Grace a furtive nudge with his elbow. Though Antoni served as the manager for both Jax & Liv and Midnight in Dallas, he had become a treasured member of our found family. Grace worked closely with him at Carrie On Records, and she'd come to think of him as her cool uncle. He was brutally honest, loyal to a fault, and the only person I knew who could rock sequins at any time of the day.

"Ha. Ha." I rolled my eyes and took a sip of my mimosa. "Very funny."

"But why not tease her one more time anyway?" Katie piped in conspiratorially. "For *shits* and giggles." She beamed at me, and I swatted at her with my napkin.

Katie was the head pastry chef at Livvie Cakes Bakery and Cupcakery, the business Liv started several years before she became a famous pop star. Liv brought me on to handle the business and marketing side of the bakery even though my only job experience at that point consisted of retail and changing diapers. I busted my ass figuring out how to do the job, and it must have paid off because we were starting renovations to expand the store in a few days.

One of the best decisions Liv and I ever made was to hire Katie Kelley. She came with about as much experience as I did, but what she lacked in experience, she made up for in moxie. The best part about Katie, though, was what a precious friend she turned out to be. If we were in trouble or sad or sick, Katie was always there with a homemade dish and a hug. She was a little younger than both Liv and me, but she was totally our mother hen.

For Liv's bachelorette brunch, Katie had booked a table at Milk & Honey because of their adorable southern vibe and their penchant for fresh pastries like the giant cinnamon roll I had on my plate. I cut into the gooey bun as big as my head and savored the way the sugar melted on my tongue.

"You guys are regular comedians," I said, my mouth bursting with the comfort of carbohydrates. "But enough about me. How about we talk about this one getting married tomorrow?" I squeezed Liv's shoulder.

"How are you feeling, honey?" Antoni directed his

attention to Liv from across the table. "Are you getting nervous?"

I watched as a pretty dark-haired girl with her phone out made a beeline in Liv's direction, but she was quickly intercepted by Brady. A few of the other patrons took discreet photos, undoubtedly sharing them on Instagram.

Liv shook her head, completely oblivious to the spectacle happening around her. "Honestly, no. In a lot of ways, I feel like Jax and I are already married. Especially after going through foster parent training together."

Katie smiled. "I'm so excited for you guys, and I can't wait to be Auntie Katie."

Liv's face had that lit-from-within appearance I always heard about in makeup tutorials I found on YouTube. *I guess that's what happiness does to a person.*

"Are you excited about the honeymoon?" Grace's eyes went all hazy as she took a bite of her french toast.

"I am. After the foster training, the tour, the wedding planning, and finishing the next album, it's going to be nice to have a couple of weeks to ourselves." Liv let out a dreamy sigh. "I'm ready to do nothing but order room service and lay on the beach with Jax."

"You're gonna have to lay there 'cause you won't be able to walk once Jax finally gets to be alone with you." I grinned at her, popping another bite of the cinnamon roll in my mouth.

"Mom!" Grace laughed, rolling her eyes. She was used to this kind of talk from Liv and me.

I looked into my daughter's blue eyes, not at all dissimilar from my own. She had the softness of her dad's features and the same rounded tip of her nose, but her pale blue eyes and golden hair were all mine. After Craig passed away, it was just Grace and me and Liv. I still had my mom, but soon after we lost Craig, she was diagnosed with early-onset Alzheimer's. As her disease progressed, I wasn't able to go to her for advice the way I always hoped I'd be able to. I didn't have anyone to tell me if I was screwing up this parenting thing, so I did the best I could.

"I know that's right, honey," Antoni said. "That boy is chomping at the bit to get you alone and spoil you rotten. We should all be so lucky to have a Jaxon Slade in our lives."

A twinge of jealousy gnawed at the edges of my heart, and I immediately felt like a jerk.

"Thank you guys for pitching in and helping us plan this wedding." Liv glanced around the table to each of us before settling her gaze on Katie. "Especially you, Katie, for making the most gorgeous wedding cake I've ever seen."

It was true. The five-tiered cake could have been ripped directly out of *Southern Living* magazine. The statuesque confection looked like beautiful ribbons stacked upon each other and was adorned with tequila sunrise roses Katie had crafted herself.

Katie reached across the table and grabbed Liv's hand. "I just want you to have the most perfect day. You deserve it."

Liv's phone rang, and as she plucked it from her bag, a puzzled expression flashed across her face. "Huh. That's the social worker. I better take this."

"Of course," I said, and we all grew quiet as she answered the call.

"Hi, Ms. Ross." Liv smiled into the phone. "How are you?" She paused for a moment. "Yes, the wedding is tomorrow. We're so excited." She fell silent once more, but her face grew pensive, and her eyes widened. "I'm sorry. I can't possibly be hearing you right." Liv's eyes glossed over with tears.

Antoni flashed me a worried glance, and Grace hung on every word Liv said. Katie instinctively placed a comforting hand on Liv's arm.

"Yes," Liv choked out, and I watched her intently, waiting for any clues she might give. "Yes, of course. Jax and I will come to meet you right away. Thank you so much, Ms. Ross. Thank you. Yes, I'll see you soon." Liv pulled the phone away from her ear and stared at it as though she were a squirrel who'd just darted in front of a semi-truck. "I… I have to go. I have to call Jax. We have to go meet the social worker."

I touched her arm. "Is everything okay?"

Liv turned to me with tears streaming down her face as a smile formed on her lips. "We got a placement."

"Oh, babe," I cried. "That's wonderful!" Liv's struggle with infertility had already led her and Jax to start the process of becoming foster parents with hopes of adopting, so this was amazing news.

Katie's eyes welled up with tears, and Grace squealed with excitement.

"Yassss, honey!" Antoni cheered. "You just tell me what you guys need, and I'll help you get everything taken care of while you two are on your honeymoon."

"There won't be a honeymoon. We'll have to go to Knoxville to get the kids on Sunday." Liv chewed her lip.

"What?" I asked louder than I intended. "That's—wait. Did you say *kids*?"

"As in plural?" Katie asked.

Liv nodded. "Siblings. A two-year-old and a five-year-old."

"Hot damn, yes ma'am!" Antoni dabbed at the corners

of his eyes with his napkin. "Oh, Liv, I'm so happy for you!"

Liv grabbed my hand, her eyes filled with joy and hope. "I'm going to be a mom, Ella."

"I... honey, I'm so happy for you." I pulled her into my arms.

And I was happy for her. But as I held my best friend on the brink of a brand new family and some of the best days of her life, I couldn't help but feel that all of my best days were behind me.

TWO

Cash

"Cash, can you help me with this?" Jax asked as he fiddled with the peach-colored tie. "I'm so damn nervous that my hands are shaking."

I chuckled. "Sure." I placed the tumbler of scotch I'd been drinking on the credenza and set to work on forming Jax's tie into a crisp Windsor Knot.

I remembered those wedding jitters well. About fifteen years ago, I'd been in a little white room a lot like the one we were standing in, sweating profusely as I awaited the moment I got to say 'I do' to the love of my life, Carrie Davis. Of course, I was just becoming a husband that day, unlike Jax who was about to become a husband and a dad all within twenty-four hours of each other.

"I still can't believe this is happening." Jax's eyes were as big as saucers. "This is really happening, right?"

"It is." I smiled at him. "It really is." I clapped him on the back and gave his shoulder an encouraging squeeze.

Jax's expression grew wistful. "I wish Carrie was here to see it."

Working with Midnight in Dallas had been one of the greatest blessings of my life. The guys had become my own ragtag band of brothers. It was only natural that they ended up spending a good bit of time with Carrie too.

"She's here in spirit," Dallas, the band's drummer, said as he pulled Jax and me into a hug. "I'm proud of you, Jax."

"We all are," I agreed.

"You guys are such sentimental saps." Luca, the lead guitarist, entered the room and downed the last of his scotch. I narrowed my eyes at him, wondering how many refills he'd already had. He took a look at all of us and gave an approving nod. "You look great, gentlemen. And we all know I look great."

"And you call *us* sentimental," Dallas quipped as his cousin and bass player, Derek, appeared in the doorway and snapped a picture. Derek was also an amateur photographer, though his skills were anything but, and he'd insisted upon taking a few photos of the big day.

"I just saw the girls, and they look amazing." Derek placed his camera back in its case. "It's almost time, but before we go out there, I have something for you, Jax."

"Here we go," Dallas said, pretending to be annoyed. "I have a feeling my wedding gift is about to become a lot less cool."

Luca snorted. "What did you expect? It's a fucking serving platter."

"It's from Tiffany's." Dallas crossed his arms in mock indignation. "What did *you* get them, asshole?"

Luca beamed proudly. "The gift of my presence."

"Can it, jokers." I laughed as Derek plucked a small box from his camera bag and handed it to Jax.

Jax untied the black satin ribbon and lifted the top off

the box to reveal a shiny gold pocket watch. "Wow, Derek. Thanks, man. This is awesome."

"Open it," Derek insisted.

Jax opened the clasp to reveal a photo as the face of the watch. I recognized the picture immediately. It was from the meet and greet where we met Liv, Ella, and Grace for the first time. The guys were all smiles, smushed into the frame with the girls. Jax's eyes misted over.

"My only regret was that Cash wasn't in the picture," Derek said, "but that was only because he was the one taking it."

Jax smiled down at the photo.

"I want this to serve as a reminder that no matter how much time passes, no matter where we are, you'll always have this family to come home to." Derek pulled Jax into a hug. "And now that family is growing, and I couldn't be happier for you, man."

"Thanks, Derek," Jax choked out. "This means a lot, brother."

Luca made gagging noises as he moved in to take a look at Jax's gift.

"Oh, shut up." Dallas laughed, throwing his arms around me and Luca. "I think we need to have a group hug."

"For fuck's sake." Luca rolled his eyes, but his mouth stretched into a wide grin.

"Bring it in here," Dallas said as Derek and Jax piled in.

"Aw, what a tender moment," Antoni's voice interrupted from the doorway. Antoni was equal parts fire and ice, one of the best managers in the business, and an even better friend. "Now, who's ready to get married?"

Everyone smiled except for Luca whose face screwed up into a pained grimace.

"I ain't even talking to you, Mr. Luca-I'm-Dead-Inside-Sterling. Everybody already knows there's no hope for you, honey." Antoni pursed his lips in Luca's direction, and we all laughed. Even Luca. "But I digress. Are the rest of you fools ready?"

Glancing over at Jax, I raised my brow at him in an unspoken question. He gulped in a deep breath and nodded.

He was moments away from some of the most important days of his life. He was on the cusp of becoming a husband and a father. In a lot of ways, his life was just beginning.

My chest tightened, and I felt a lump form in my throat. I missed Carrie all the time, but I especially missed her on the big days—the ones that reminded me that part of my life was over.

"INTRODUCING, FOR THE FIRST TIME AS HUSBAND AND WIFE, Mr. and Mrs. Jaxon Slade!" A voice boomed over the speakers of the courtyard. Jax and Liv entered to the wild approval of their two-hundred-and-something waiting guests. "If you'll turn your attention to the dance floor, the new Mr. and Mrs. are going to kick off the reception with their first dance." The band started to play "Can't Help Falling In Love."

The ceremony was beautiful, taking place at the picturesque East Ivy Manor, with cascading chandeliers and a winding staircase straight out of Cinderella's castle. Liv looked like a princess, and for all the ways she looked like a princess, Ella looked like a queen with her golden hair falling in soft waves around her shoulders and her gown stretching down into a v, perfectly showcasing a little tanned cleavage.

Because she and Dallas were the maid of honor and best man, I'd had the distinct privilege of watching her glide down the aisle as I stood between Derek and Luca at Jax's side. It was the first time I'd seen her all day, and I had to pry my eyes away as Liv made her entry.

After the ceremony, the wedding party had been swept away in a flurry of flashbulbs. Ella, Grace, and Katie all wore coordinating peach dresses, while Antoni was decked out in a peach tuxedo made entirely of sequins. Jax, Dallas, Derek, Luca, and I all wore navy tuxedos with peach ties and boutonnières. Even though Brady was still stuck handling security, he'd gotten a matching tux so he could join us in some of the photos.

I found myself at a table, looking across the dance floor to the entryway of the courtyard for Ella. As I glanced around, I noticed Katie join Dallas and Derek who stood off to the side watching Jax and Liv spin around the floor.

Antoni sighed as he plopped down beside me. "I just love weddings, honey. The cake, the dancing, the feeling of love in the air, the free booze—it all makes me feel like I'm in a fairytale."

I chuckled. "I don't think there's alcohol in fairytales."

"Well, there should be."

"Speaking of love being in the air, where's your date?"

"He's over at the bar getting me a Cosmopolitan." He pointed over to his new boyfriend, Nate, who caught Antoni's eye and winked. Nate looked like he could have easily walked off the pages of an Armani advertisement. I'd only met him a couple of times, but he was sharp and sophisticated and gave off an air of confidence without being arrogant. "Mmmmmm. Isn't he delicious? I'd sip his bath water with a straw."

I choked on a laugh as the song came to an end, and the band started playing a more upbeat tune, inviting everyone out on the floor.

"Look at her." Antoni clutched his hands to his chest, his eyes landing on the entryway. "Doesn't she look stunning today?"

I turned to follow his gaze and watched as Ella floated into the courtyard looking like a walking daydream. She was a vision draped in peach chiffon with her tanned skin peeking out from beneath the high slit of her dress. A broad smile spread across her face as her eyes settled on something I couldn't see, causing my heart rate to pick up speed. Before I could even think about what I was doing, I was on my feet. I didn't have a plan. All I knew was I had to ask her to dance.

But before my legs could carry me in her direction, I watched as Ella walked into the waiting arms of a guy who was a dead ringer for Matthew McConaughey. As if it wasn't bad enough that Nate made all of us guys look bad.

He kissed her on the cheek, and it felt like someone had punched me in the gut. My eyes followed her as they smiled and giggled their way to the bar. I wondered what they were talking about. There was no way he could be that good looking *and* funny, right? My mouth suddenly felt dry, as though it was full of cotton. I grabbed a glass of water from the table and nearly drained it in one gulp. I stretched awkwardly, clearing my throat before returning to my seat.

"And she's got herself a hot date," Antoni purred as Nate joined us at the table, two cocktails in hand. Nate and I nodded a greeting to each other, and Antoni took a long pull from his drink. "He's cute, but I wouldn't peg him for being Ella's type."

"Who?" Nate asked. "The Matthew McConaughey guy? I'm pretty sure he'd be everybody's type."

I take it all back. Nate is the worst.

"Why do you say that?" I asked Antoni, decidedly desperate for there to be some reason, *any* reason, as to why this thing with Ella and Matthew McConaughey couldn't work.

"Oh, I don't know," Antoni said. "I'm probably just being silly."

"Tell me," I urged. "Why do you think he's not her type?"

Antoni shrugged. "I guess I always thought you two would end up together somehow... or at least I hoped you would." My hands involuntarily loosened my tie in a futile attempt to cool the burn I felt rising in my chest. Antoni drained the rest of his cocktail in one fell swoop and laughed. "Anyway, if you'll excuse me, I believe I hear the sweet sound of Beyoncé calling my name. Nate?"

He reached for Nate's hand, and they set off toward the dance floor, leaving me alone with the grenade of truth Antoni had just hurled at me.

"ARE YOU GOING TO SIT HERE BY YOURSELF ALL NIGHT?" Grace's voice interrupted my thoughts. I'd been trying to distract myself by watching Antoni and Nate swing each other around on the dance floor. Somehow my eyes always ended up on Ella and Matthew McConaughey. Ella only stepped away from him long enough to help with the cutting of the cake, beaming as Liv smushed white buttercream into Jax's face. After the cake had been served, I noticed Ella and her date take a seat at another table across the courtyard.

"Just enjoying some people watching," I said with a smile as the band transitioned from "Uptown Funk" to the opening notes of "Stand By Me." "I saw you out there dancing with Sam a while ago. You guys seem to have fun together."

A soft blush crept onto her cheeks as she glanced over to where Sam Corbyn stood talking to Dallas. Sam's eyes seemed to instinctively find Grace's, and his mouth broke into a goofy grin. "He's okay." She shrugged, but her face betrayed her with a smile.

"I think he's taken a shine to you."

She studied him for a moment, appearing to consider my statement before turning her attention back to me. "Come dance with me."

"Me? I'm sure Sam is itching to get back out there with you."

"That may be," Grace said matter-of-factly. "But I asked you."

"Well, how can I turn down an invitation like that?" I asked, rising to my feet and offering her my arm.

Her smile glittered up at me as she slid her arm through mine. "You can't."

I led her onto the dance floor, and she looped her dainty hands around my neck. An overwhelming sense of pride came over me—a pride I wasn't sure I had a right to feel. Gazing at her in her elegant peach gown with her blonde hair piled atop her head, I became aware that Grace had transformed into a young woman right before my eyes.

I didn't have the honor of watching her grow up, but in

the time I'd known Grace, I'd gotten to watch as she took her last steps out of high school and her first into college and the professional world. Her presence was unassuming and sweet, and everyone who got near her soft glow couldn't help but love her and feel uplifted by her gentle spirit. Myself included. Sure, she'd been an asset to the label, but more than that, she'd snuck into my heart and turned the light on in some of its darkest corners. She'd become like family.

"I'm very proud of you, Grace," I said. " You've really come into your own the last year at the label. Starting Carrie On Records was a huge undertaking, and I couldn't have done it without your help."

After getting a behind the scenes look at what the music industry was like through Liv, Grace wanted to pursue a career in the music business, and I was happy to teach her everything I could.

"I appreciate you taking a chance on me. I've got a lot to learn, but you've taught me so much already."

"You'll always have a place at the label," I promised. I thought about how empty the office would feel once she left for England. "It's not going to be the same without you this summer."

Her mouth twitched into a grin. "I'm going to miss you too."

"I want you to promise me you'll be extra careful while you're gone, and you know I'm only a phone call away if you need anything."

"Look at you getting all protective on me." She laughed, but her face softened.

I nodded. "Damn right I am. People prey on beautiful young ladies traveling alone."

"I'm not traveling alone," she insisted. "I'll be with Sam and the crew."

"And they all know they're to protect you with their lives, or I'll fire every last one of them." I chuckled, but I absolutely meant it. "About Sam…"

"Uh-oh." Grace feigned indignation. "My mom has already told me I'm not allowed to date till I'm thirty. Are you about to tell me you agree with her?"

I shook my head. "No, not at all. I just want you to be careful is all. Take your time. You're so young, Grace. You have the whole world ahead of you and so many beautiful things left to experience."

"I know." Her gaze turned to where Jax and Liv danced nearby. Their foreheads touched, and they swayed to their own beat as though they were in their own little world. "Trust me, I'm not looking to get married anytime soon. I just… I look at Aunt Liv and Jax and see how in love they are, and… I know I want that one day. And maybe I'll get my heart broken, but I think it might be worth it to know what that kind of love feels like." My chest twisted as I thought about the innocence of her words—words that were tainted with the dark blue of losing someone you love. Grace knew a thing or two about unspeakable loss and the echoes that death left behind. Losing a parent at an early age was something we had in common. "That's why I'm so proud of my mom for getting back out there, and Ryan seems like a pretty cool guy."

I raised my brow at her. *So, Matthew McConaughey has a name.* "Does this mean you approve of him?"

"I didn't say that," she amended quickly. "I don't think it's serious with him or anything. I just think she's ready to give the whole dating thing a try. After she lost my dad, she really dedicated her life to me. She deserves to find someone that makes her happy."

I swallowed hard. "Yes," I agreed. "She does."

The song faded to an end, and a Black Eyed Peas song began to play. Our swaying came to a stop, and Grace looked at me earnestly. "So do you, you know. You both deserve that." She threw her arms around me and kissed my cheek. "Thanks for the dance. I'm going to go find Sam."

She tossed a smile at me from over her shoulder, leaving me wondering if maybe she was right. If Grace could still have hope even after the loss she had experienced, maybe I could too.

THREE

Ella

I GULPED DOWN MY THIRD GLASS OF CHAMPAGNE AND sighed. At least I thought it was my third. It could have been my fifth or seventh for all I knew. The party had been going strong since about seven-thirty. If there was one thing consistently true about musicians, it was that they knew how to throw down.

For the first part of the reception, I'd stayed busy making sure everything went smoothly for the cake cutting and the toasts. After that, I found myself holding down a table next to the dance floor with Ryan who apparently was *not* a dancer. I felt a pang of jealousy as Dallas and Katie swept by us, which was only made worse when I saw Sam dip Grace as though they were on *Dancing With The Stars. I mean, who actually dips people? Calm down, Fred Astaire.*

"Are you sure you don't want to get out there?" I asked, flashing Ryan a flirtatious grin as the band started to play "Unforgettable."

"I'm not much of a dancer, sweetheart," he drawled. He wasn't much of a talker either. When I found out he worked for Gibson Guitar, I assumed that meant he would be a musician, and as far as I was concerned, all the musicians I knew were pretty fun. Ryan, however, worked in Accounting. He'd never picked up a guitar in his entire life, and he was decidedly un-fun.

Ryan checked his phone for the twenty-seventh time in an hour and a half. Perhaps I wasn't as interesting as I thought I was. *Fuck that. I'm a peach.*

"Hey, Ella." I looked up at the sound of Derek's voice. I smiled as he turned his attention to Ryan. "I don't believe we've met. I'm Derek."

"Ryan," he replied. "Nice to meet you."

At twenty-nine, Derek was the youngest member of Midnight in Dallas. Upon first glance, you'd think he was a California surfer with his blond hair and tanned skin, but in reality he was a tender-hearted guy who loved photography and motorcycles.

"You guys should go dance." Derek motioned toward the sea of dancing bodies. "I don't think I've seen you two out there all night."

Ryan shrugged. "I'm not much for dancing, but I'm having a lovely time." He clicked the button on the side of his iPhone, lighting up the screen. I rolled my eyes, and Derek shot me a sympathetic look.

"On that note, would you mind if I asked Ella to dance?" Derek asked.

Ryan's face flooded with relief. "Actually, that's a great idea. I really need to be heading out anyway. It's getting late."

"It's ten o'clock on a Saturday night," I blurted.

Ryan stood from his seat. "Yeah, but I'm doing a ten-mile hike bright and early tomorrow."

I wrinkled my nose. "On purpose?"

"You're a trip, Ella Claiborne." Ryan chuckled and leaned down to kiss my cheek. "I'll call you. Give my best to the bride and groom." Before I could remind him that he was supposed to be my ride home, he was gone.

"So, about that dance?" Derek extended his hand to me.

"Just so we're clear, I know this is a pity dance." I took his hand and allowed him to pull me to my feet. "But I'm so bored I don't even care."

"It's not a pity dance," Derek assured me, "but anyone with eyes could see how... not exciting Ryan is. I couldn't stand to see you sitting there in misery anymore."

I laughed. "I'm pretty sure you just defined what a pity dance is, but I'm grateful nonetheless." He guided me to the dance floor, and we fell into step with the slow tune.

"I have to ask the obvious question," Derek said. "Where on earth did you meet that guy?"

I grimaced. "We met online. We had one date, but I didn't quite grasp the full extent of how boring he actually was. He said he worked for Gibson, so I assumed he might be fun and cool. You know, like you guys."

Derek beamed. "You think we're cool?"

I shoved him playfully in the arm. "You drive a motor-cycle for fuck's sake. I'm pretty sure they won't even sell you one of those if you aren't cool. Anyway, I didn't realize how... dull he would be."

"It's okay to call it like it is. That dude is a dud."

I snorted. "Don't I know it." My heart suddenly felt heavy.

My face must have reflected the sadness I felt because Derek's eyebrows had knitted together with concern. "Everything okay?"

I chewed my bottom lip thoughtfully for a moment. "It's

just… it's times like this that I miss my husband. I mean, there's not a single day I don't miss him, but on days like today? I really, really miss him. Honestly, sometimes I don't think I'll ever find love like that again."

"You will," Derek said gently. "But you won't find it with a guy like Ryan. He's not your type. You deserve a lot better than that dude."

"Oh, really?" My curiosity was admittedly piqued. "What kind of guy do you see me with?"

Derek gazed at me for a moment, a contemplative expression on his face. "You deserve someone who lives out loud, a guy who would dance with you even if there wasn't any music playing."

"Derek Knights, that might be the nicest thing anyone's said to me in a long time."

"You also deserve someone who says nice things to you all the time… someone who is happy to be with you and not glued to his phone."

"Hmm," I mused. "Perhaps I should get a dog. They're always happy to see you, and they don't even use phones. It's a win-win situation."

Derek laughed. "That's true. I never had a dog, but my neighbor did when I was growing up. They kept her outside and pretty much neglected her, but I loved that damn dog. I used to sneak food out to her all the time, and I even taught her how to sit and shake hands."

"Aww." I tilted my head up at him. "I had no idea you were a dog whisperer."

Antoni strutted to our side, shimmying to the beat of the new up-tempo song the band had begun to play. "Excuse me, but may I cut in? I saw that Ella finally got her tushie on the dance floor, and I just *have* to take her for a spin."

"Of course." Derek grinned. "Thanks for the dance, Ella." Derek disappeared into the crowd as Antoni and I moved in unison to the beat.

"This is the most unsolicited male attention I've received in a long time," I joked. "Please continue fawning over me."

"Honey, your date should have been falling over himself." Antoni bumped my hip with his. "Have you seen yourself? You're a vision." He gestured approvingly at my legs. "And those gams, girl! God really does have favorites."

I laughed. "I think I could have been naked and Ryan wouldn't have noticed."

"Well, Ryan's dick must be broken or something, honey. Because I'm pretty sure every other man in this joint can see how gorgeous you are."

I choked on a giggle. "I highly doubt that."

"When you walked into this courtyard, Cash looked like he'd been touched by an angel, honey," Antoni purred. "That man's jaw hit the floor."

"What?" I asked incredulously. "Cash? No way." I had to admit, I'd always had a bit of a crush on Cash, but I'd never really thought he'd look at me in that way. I mean, I knew I was a catch, but I also knew I came with a little baggage. Besides, he was Grace's boss, and technically he was Liv's boss too.

Antoni pressed his lips together. "I probably shouldn't have said anything."

"You're not serious." I pressed him further.

He stopped dancing and huddled close to me. "Lord, forgive me. I turn into such a loose-lipped Lucy when I've been drinking." Antoni's voice dropped low in my ear. "When Cash saw you walk your pretty self over to ole

29

what's-his-name, I thought the man was gonna come unglued."

"What did—" I started to ask what he'd said when Grace appeared at our side.

"It's time," Grace said. "Aunt Liv wants us to meet her in the bride's room."

"I better go grab Nate and get outside," Antoni said breezily, as though he didn't just tell me one of our friends thought I was hot. He gave my shoulder a squeeze. "Toodles!"

I reached for Grace's hand, and a wistful smile spread across her face. We started across the courtyard toward the room where Liv waited for us, and my chest tightened. The heaviness in my heart gave me a silent nudge to remind me it was still there. I knew this would be the last moment the three of us would be together for a long time, and the winds of change felt as though they might blow me away.

IT WAS ALMOST ELEVEN P.M. WHEN GRACE AND I ENTERED the bride's room to find Liv buzzing around the room like some sort of erratic bumblebee. Makeup, clothes, and undergarments sailed through the air as she appeared to be looking for something. That, or trashing the place.

"Are you okay?" I asked cautiously.

"I can't find my phone." Her voice was frantic and at least an octave higher.

"I have it." I crossed the room to the dressing table, grabbing my purse off the back of the chair. "Remember, I held onto it for you earlier when we were at the salon."

She smacked her palm to her forehead and sighed with

relief. "I'm losing it, you guys. I can't keep track of anything."

"You've had a lot on your mind, Aunt Liv." Grace gave her a reassuring smile. "Besides, it's your day today. It's our job to keep track of things for you so you can relax."

Liv looked anything *but* relaxed as she collapsed on the puffy white sofa in a heap of tulle and lace. "How will they ever give me a kid, let alone two kids, when I can't even keep track of my phone?" She burst into tears, her shoulders shaking as she buried her head in her hands.

"Liv…" I moved to sit beside her on the couch, pulling her into my arms as Grace hurried to her side with a box of tissues. "Sweetheart, you've got this."

"What if I mess this up, Ella?" Her words were a warbled mess. "What if I'm a terrible mother?"

There were a lot of things I wasn't sure of in the world at that moment, but this wasn't one of them. "Honey, you are going to be an amazing mother, and Jax is going to be a great father."

"Yes you are," Grace agreed, squeezing Liv's hand.

Liv looked at me through glossy eyes. "How do you know?"

"How the hell do you think I've survived this long?" I asked. "You've always helped take care of me and Grace. If it weren't for you, I don't think I would have made it after Craig died. You held me together." It was true. For months, I barely moved from the safe cocoon of my bed. Liv cooked, cleaned, took care of Grace, paid the bills, made sure I showered and brushed my hair. "You've always made sure I eat well and take care of myself because you know if I were left to my own devices I would exist solely on take-out and pizza rolls."

A soft smile crept onto her face. "You know those things are loaded with sodium."

I felt a lump form in my throat. Liv had been my rock, and I had been hers. But now she had her own rock in Jax. As selfish as it was, I had kind of hoped that after Grace grew up Liv and I would have some time together that just belonged to us—time where we could travel and do all the things we'd wished we had time for when we were younger.

"See? Without you, I would eat all the sodium," I said matter-of-factly. "Actually, I still eat it. I just hide the evidence."

"Just like a teenager," Liv teased.

I smiled and squeezed her shoulder. "And you say you won't be a good parent."

"Thank you," she said, hugging me tightly. "I'm sorry. I guess everything is finally starting to hit me, and I'm kind of freaking out."

"I'd be worried if you weren't freaking out," I assured her. "This is a lot for anyone to process, but you can do this."

She nodded, dabbing at the corners of her eyes with a tissue. "I've got to pull myself together so Jax and I can get out of here. We can at least have one night of wedded bliss before we become parents."

"It's going to be the best twelve-hour honeymoon ever." I kissed her on the cheek. "Grace and I will make sure you've got everything packed up here and get you to your man."

I flitted around the room and gathered Liv's belongings, putting them into the appropriate bags until everything was ready to go. Liv was touching up her lipstick in the mirror when there was a knock at the door.

"Liv?" Jax's voice called. "Are you ready, baby?"

Liv took a deep breath and looked at me, her face full of a million questions—the kinds of questions you ask every day of your life as a parent.

I gave her an encouraging nod. "You've got this."

"Heck yeah, you do," Grace agreed.

I slung her weekender bag over my shoulder. "I'll hand your bag off to Brady so he can go ahead and put it in the car for you."

"Thank you." She started toward the door before stopping abruptly and spinning around. "Oh! How was your date with Ryan?"

I couldn't tell her the truth. She had enough to worry about without feeling sorry for her best friend who had a dud for a date. I plastered a smile on my face. "It was really great."

Liv's face lit up, and she reached for my hand. "I can't wait to hear about it."

"Soon," I promised.

Liv looked from me to Grace before throwing her arms around us both. And for a moment, the three of us held each other, just like we had hundreds of times before.

"I love you guys," Liv cried. "So much."

"We love you too, Aunt Livvie," Grace's soft voice replied.

Tears burned my eyes. "You bet your ass we do."

"Babe? Everything okay in there?" Jax's voice called again.

I cleared my throat and answered for her. "Come in, Jax. She's ready."

The door swung open to reveal Jax waiting with a smile on his face. With one last hug, I let her go, and she walked through the door to her new life.

Grace grabbed my hand and squeezed it. "Are you okay, Mom?"

"I'm good. Just happy for Liv." *And sad for me.* I folded Grace in my arms, breathing in the familiar lavender scent of her hair as I kissed the top of her head. The time had come for me to encourage my best friend in this next chapter of her life, even if it meant she fell off the pages of mine.

FOUR

Cash

GUESTS BEGAN TO TRICKLE OUT OF THE COURTYARD JUST after eleven, a little wobbly on their feet as they went in search of their Ubers. I watched as Luca downed yet another scotch before whisking away one of the pretty cocktail waitresses. I rolled my eyes when he threw a wave at me from over his shoulder before disappearing into the night. Dallas, Derek, and Antoni had already left, but I'd hung around for another drink in hopes I might get to talk with Ella.

The clean-up crew had already started clearing things away, and I watched Ella talking to the wedding coordinator, making sure everything would be returned to its rightful place the next morning. I took a sip of my scotch and lost myself as I watched her talk, her hands fluttering in conversation.

I hadn't seen Ella's date since earlier in the evening, but I had noticed her out on the dance floor with Derek and Antoni. It was impossible *not* to notice her. I'd only wished it were me she'd been dancing with, but Grace had whisked her away before I had the chance to try.

The wedding coordinator waved at Ella and set off toward the bar. Ella's smile faltered a bit until she noticed me standing near the table I'd been holding down most of the night.

"Hey, Cash." She glided over to me and wrapped her arms around me, enveloping me in the sweet scent of lemon and sugar. "I feel like I haven't gotten to see you all day. You look so handsome."

When she pulled away and I finally got to look at her up close, I was speechless. Looking at Ella Claiborne was like trying to look directly at the sun. She was arrestingly beautiful, so much so that her light was almost overwhelming at times. Her smile radiated a warmth that you felt from the inside.

"And you look…" I swallowed hard, raking my hand over my mouth as I attempted to find words eloquent enough to describe her beauty. "Wow… just wow." *Great job, Cash.*

"What? This old thing?" Her voice was sarcasm and cotton candy. "Did you have a good time tonight?"

"I did." I left out how unnerved I'd been when I saw her with her date. "It was a beautiful wedding."

"It was," she agreed. "Did you bring anyone?"

"I went stag tonight," I said, leaving off the part about how much I'd wished it was me she'd been walking toward with that smile and those legs for days. "What about you? I thought I saw you with someone earlier."

She rolled her eyes. "Yeah. His name was Ryan, and he was far more interested in his phone than he was in me, so he left a while ago. Which is just dandy seeing how he was my ride."

"I'd be happy to dri—"

"Mom, I'm heading out. I've got to run inside and grab my things," Grace's voice interrupted as she bounded up to her mother.

"Already?" Ella placed an arm around her daughter. "Are you sure you want to spend your last Saturday night in town with Lexi and not with your mother who birthed you? And yes, I am trying to guilt-trip you. Is it working?"

Grace giggled. "We'll have all day tomorrow, Mom. I promise. I'll be back in time for us to go see Grandma."

"Fine." Ella pouted. "I'm done here, so I'll call us an Uber and drop you off."

"Actually, Sam offered to drive me there." She looked at Ella hopefully. "His place is on the way to Lexi's."

Ella propped her hand on her hip. "Sam, whom you will be working ever so closely with the next two months in another country? That Sam?"

"That's the one," Grace said. "Is that okay?"

"Fine. Just leave your poor, pitiful mother to watch TV alone in her sweatpants." Ella sighed heavily before hugging Grace and kissing the top of her head. "How about now? Did *that* guilt trip work?"

"I love you, Mom." Grace kissed Ella on the cheek. "I'll see you in the morning."

Ella laughed. "I'll take that as a no."

Grace moved to hug me. "Good night, Cash."

"G'night, Grace," I said as she started toward the mansion.

"You have your phone, your house key, and all of that?" Ella called after her.

"Yes, Mom," Grace replied before disappearing inside.

I felt like I'd been handed a huge stroke of luck. Maybe

it was the scotch giving me courage, but I wasn't going to let it pass me by.

"I guess I'll call my Uber. I foresee a date with *Gossip Girl* and a pint of Jeni's ice cream in my future." She started to walk away.

"What flavor?" I asked.

She shot me a grin that splashed across my face like cold water, waking up my insides. "Probably some Salty Caramel."

"Hmm. This is quite the predicament, you see," I said. "You can't really go home for Salty Caramel. Brown Butter Almond Brittle, maybe, but not Salty Caramel." Her laugh surrounded me, and I pressed on. "Why don't you let me take you out for a drink instead?"

She raised her brows. "You want to have a drink with me?"

I nodded. "I want to have a drink with you."

She took a step back in my direction. "I didn't bring a change of clothes. Don't you think we're a little overdressed?"

"I think you look perfect."

She tilted her head and chewed her lip thoughtfully. "I have to admit, this reception did make me want to go out for a night on the town. I haven't been dancing in ages."

"So, let's go dancing," I said.

"Seriously?"

"Seriously." I offered her my arm. "I'll call us a car right now."

"What the hell. Let's do it." She looped her arm through mine. "But there's one place I want to go first, if that's okay."

"And where's that?" I asked, suddenly aware of my own heartbeat, thundering in my ears.

Her smile grew as she looked over at me. "You'll see."

"I CAN'T BELIEVE YOU'VE NEVER BEEN TO SANTA'S PUB before," Ella said over the sound of a man in a cowboy hat singing some very off-key karaoke to "Don't Stop Believing" by Journey. "It's basically a rite of passage."

I glanced around the doublewide trailer at the quirky Christmas decor and twinkle lights that decorated the packed bar. We'd manage to score a small table in the back near the cash-only bar where we'd ordered the only thing on the menu—beer. Cigarette smoke formed clouds around us so thick you could almost grab them. I spotted a man that looked a lot like Santa Claus if Santa Claus happened to be Willie Nelson's brother.

Ella must have read my mind because she pointed right at him. "Oh, and there's Santa himself."

I chuckled. "They take this Christmas business seriously."

Ella nodded. "That and their no cussing on stage policy." She pointed to a sign to the left of the make-shift stage with the words 'NO CUSSING' scrawled across it.

"Are you going to get up there?" I asked, unable to contain the smile that spread across my face.

"Hell yeah, I am." She leaned in close to me, her breath sending tingles all the way through my fingertips. "The real question is, are you?"

"It would take a *lot* more of these to get me on that stage." I held up my beer for emphasis. "I'm not a very good singer."

"I didn't say I was any good," she countered, taking a drink of her Miller Lite. "You aren't going to be discovering any talent tonight, Mr. Record Executive. That started and ended with Liv."

She leaned on the table, propping her head on her hands. "Something just occurred to me."

"What's that?"

"Is this the first time since we met that we've hung out as just the two of us?"

"I guess it is." My mind flashed back to the night we first met. It was a year and a half ago when Liv, Ella, and Grace walked into one of our meet and greets in Nashville.

Jax had been taken with Liv immediately, and if I was being honest, he wasn't the only one who saw something he liked that night. But I wasn't even able to consider the prospect of being with someone. At that point, Carrie had only been gone about a year, and the little crush I'd developed on Ella since then was hard enough to wrap my mind around.

I already felt guilty for all of the moments I spent with her when we were together with the group or when she stopped by the office to see Grace. This was the first night I'd shoved that shame aside.

Maybe it was the alcohol. Maybe it was Antoni's words still echoing in my mind. Or maybe it was Grace's poignant reminder that I deserved some happiness too.

Ella laughed to herself and took a swig of her beer.

"What?" I asked curiously.

"Nothing," she chirped, grabbing a golf pencil and two scraps of paper from the stack in the center of the table. She hummed to herself, a goofy grin growing on her face as she scribbled something she shielded from my view.

I made a show of trying to peek over her hand. "You mean you're not going to tell me what song you're going to do?"

She flicked the pencil back on the table and clutched the papers to her chest. "Nope." She disappeared to the small table beside the stage where she handed in her requests, leaning in to say something to the karaoke host. The guy looked to be about thirty and definitely seemed interested in Ella. I noticed the way he laughed at whatever she'd said, and when she turned and wove through the crowd, his eyes didn't leave her backside.

I felt a twinge of jealousy bubble at my core as I watched her stop by the bar, and yet another man started chatting with her. He complimented her dress, and she took his words in stride. His gaze lingered on Ella, and she seemed oblivious to her growing fan club as she returned to our table with two more beers. It appeared I needed to take a number.

I raised my brow at her. "If I didn't know any better, I'd think you were trying to get me drunk."

She smirked. "Maybe I am. You need a little fun in your life, Cash Montgomery."

"And who says I don't have any fun?" I found myself leaning closer to her involuntarily.

"Grace," she replied.

I laughed. "My secret's out, I see."

"Mmmhmm," Ella said knowingly. "She's said you work till all hours. She might have even suggested that she came in one morning to find that you'd fallen asleep at your desk."

"That happened one time!"

She narrowed her eyes at me.

"Okay," I relented. "It happened twice. I'm going to miss Grace, but maybe I should be glad she won't be around to tell on me."

"Don't worry," she said with a wave of her hand. "We

already set up the indoor security cameras so she can spy on you from afar."

I chuckled, feeling my body relax as I started to work on my next beer. "I'm really going to miss her."

Ella's expression softened. "Grace adores you. Thank you for taking her under your wing the way you have. You've given her opportunities I never could have provided for her."

"I'm happy to do it. She's a bright young lady. If I could have been lucky enough to have a kid, I'd have wanted them to turn out just like her."

"She's pretty great, isn't she?"

I nodded. "You've done an amazing job."

She flipped her hair with one hand and clutched the other to her chest. "Thank you, but I can't take all the credit. Her dad definitely made an impact on her, even at an early age. He was a doe-eyed romantic, and that quality seems to have been passed down to Grace."

"You're not a romantic, huh?"

"Maybe not in the conventional sense," she answered. "Craig believed in love at first sight and fairytales. I guess I used to believe in them, but it's hard to have faith in happy endings when your ending wasn't happy. That's not to say I don't believe in romance, but for me romance isn't in the big gestures or the flowers and theatrics anymore. It would just be nice to have someone to wake up next to, someone who knows how I take my coffee in the morning."

"How do you take your coffee in the morning?" The words flew out of my mouth before I even realized what I was saying.

She bit back a smile. "More cream than coffee and not before seven-thirty. I am so not a morning person."

"Me either."

"Probably because you're sleeping at your desk." She looked at me from beneath her fluttery lashes. "How do you take your coffee?"

"I believe I'd take it any way that was available if it meant I got to have coffee with you." I gulped dry air and mentally smacked myself. *What the hell are you doing, Cash?*

Before she could respond, the song that was playing ended, and the host's voice boomed in the mic. "Next up, we're going old school with a little Sinatra from Cash Montgomery!"

Ella grinned wildly as the color drained out of my face.

I felt a smile twitch on my lips. "You did this."

Her smile was so dazzling it was intoxicating.

"You don't have to if you don't want to," Ella promised. "I figured they would call me up first. We can just pretend you're not here."

"Cash... where is Mr. Cash?" The host looked out into the crowd, shielding his eyes from the lights of the small stage.

I chewed my lip a moment before throwing back the rest of my beer. "What the hell. Why not?"

"Are you serious?" Ella squealed as I rose to my feet.

"If you want some Sinatra, then honey, I'm going to give you Sinatra." Perhaps it was the beer talking and all the scotch I'd had earlier in the evening. Or maybe the liquid courage was giving me the push I'd needed for months.

I maneuvered my way to the stage to the sounds of a few errant cheers and applause. I leaned down to see that she had submitted me for "Fly Me To The Moon."

"Hey, man," I said to the host. "Mind if I switch Sinatra songs?"

"Sure, dude," he answered. "Whatcha want?"

He shifted so that I could see the song list on the screen of his laptop. I saw the one I wanted and pointed. I took a deep breath and shook out my shoulders as the opening notes to "The Way You Look Tonight" began to play.

FIVE

Ella

CASH AND I EXITED OUR UBER AT THE ENTRY OF PRINTERS Alley in downtown Nashville. It was the only part of downtown proper I went to on the rare occasion that I had a night out. Broadway was home to the honky-tonks and the bachelorette party invasion, but Printers Alley was a former publishing industry hub turned nightlife dream. With its twinkly-lit cobblestone alleyway, speakeasy-style bars, and robust music scene, it was a true testament to the diversity that made Nashville so much more than the country music capital of the world.

"Ho*ly* shit," I said, looking over at Cash, my face still veiled with shock. "I still can't believe you did that."

He chuckled softly. "I blame being under the influence of alcohol and a certain beautiful blonde who put my name in for me." Despite the evening breeze, I felt a heat rise to my cheeks at the sound of him calling me beautiful.

"I didn't know you sang!"

"I don't," he insisted. "Not usually, anyway. Not unless I'm in the shower."

"*And* you sing in the shower? I'm learning so much about you tonight, Cash Montgomery." The heel of my stiletto slid on the cobblestone, and Cash wrapped his arm around my waist, steadying me. I looked into his hazel eyes, and for a moment, the twinkle lights strung above the alley seemed to circle around us. I cleared my throat, shifting my eyes ahead again. "You had quite the stage presence too. You would have given ole blue eyes a run for his money. I'm pretty sure that lady in the front row was ready to stuff a couple of twenties in your belt."

Cash choked out a laugh. "I'm pretty sure the lady in the front was so drunk she didn't know where she was." He looked around as we neared the bars and businesses with small groups of people scattered in the alley. "Where is it we're going?"

"It's this new*ish* speakeasy I heard about called Dirty Little Secret," I explained. "It's even got a super-secret entryway." The lights of Skull's Rainbow Room and Bourbon Street Blues and Boogie Bar beckoned us closer.

"So, how do we find it?"

"Oh, I know where it is," I said with a wave of my hand.

He broke into a laugh. "That doesn't sound like much of a secret."

"Here we are," I exclaimed, stopping in front of the All Saints clothing store.

He shot me a quizzical glance. "It's a club inside of a store?"

"It's a club with *an entrance* inside of a store." We flashed our IDs to the bouncer who pointed beyond the clothing racks to a door that could have easily been a storage closet. The sounds of music with a heavy bass made the ground vibrate beneath our feet.

Cash stepped ahead and opened the door for me, revealing colorful strobe lights dancing across the small sea of people in the shadowy nightclub. We squeezed our way to the bar where the bartenders were all clad in crisp white shirts and ties.

"What would you like?" Cash asked.

"A vodka tonic."

A young woman to my right got shoved by someone trying to access the bar, sending her sailing into my side. I collided directly into Cash's chest, and he caught me, preventing me from hitting the floor. Cash had always been handsome, but had this muscular chest just been existing under my nose all this time? *Get a grip, Ella. He's your daughter's boss. He's your best friend's boss.*

I studied him as he ordered our drinks. He had a perfect square jaw that was outlined in a five o'clock shadow, and his aftershave smelled of sandalwood and jasmine. His dark, whiskey-colored hair was just long enough to make me wonder what it would feel like to run my fingers through it. My eyes traveled down his torso, and I thought about what else was hidden under that tuxedo. *Slow your roll, Ella.*

"Here you go." He turned back to me with a broad smile, his eyes creasing in the corners as he handed me my drink. He licked his lips slightly before taking a pull from his glass of what looked like bourbon.

"Thanks," I said, turning my gaze to the dance floor to keep myself from wondering what it would feel like to kiss him. We were surrounded by beautiful people, all dancing so close to one another. My cheeks felt like they were on fire as I imagined dancing with Cash like that. I threw back my drink in three swallows, placing the glass on the bar. "You know what we need? Shots."

"Shots?" Cash echoed. "Are you sure about that?"

I flagged down the bartender. "Two shots of Patron please."

Cash's eyes widened. "I haven't done shots in ages."

"Me either. Not since my thirty-fifth, and I made it a new rule to never do shots again. But rules were made to be broken."

"Ella Claiborne," Cash said my name slowly and deliberately. I noticed the faintest southern accent begin to peek through. "You really are trying to get me drunk." He knocked back the rest of his drink, returning the glass to the counter just as our shots were delivered.

"I do believe I promised you a fun night, Mr. Montgomery," I said, plucking my Visa card from my small purse and sliding it across the bar. "Actually, bartender, let's go ahead and get another round of these. We're celebrating."

"You've got it," the bartender said before disappearing once more. Cash and I each took one of the shot glasses in our hands and held them up.

"To Jax and Liv," I said.

Cash's warm eyes settled on me. "And to us on our first night alone together."

"Cheers," I said, gulping down my shot. The liquid burned its way down my throat, loosening my limbs almost instantaneously. I watched as Cash tossed back his shot and the way his Adam's apple bobbed ever so slightly. I had no idea that could be so sexy, but on him, it was.

The bartender came back with our next round, which we quickly downed.

"Now, we dance." I reached for his hand and guided him through the throng of people to a spot near the center of the dance floor.

THE TWO SHOTS WERE EXACTLY WHAT I NEEDED TO LOOSEN me up and get me out of my own head. My body fell into rhythm with the Rihanna song that was playing, my hips shaking to the beat.

It turned out Cash's moves extended beyond Frank Sinatra, and I was entranced by how sexy he looked, his face glistening with sweat. He'd rolled up the sleeves of his tux—enough to expose a set of toned forearms that seemed to flex just to taunt me.

With each song that played, our bodies got closer, another layer of self-consciousness peeled away by the tequila. The room and my heart thudded as Cash's hands made their way to my waist, pulling me in. We moved together, our hips in sync in a way that had me thinking about all of the other ways our hips could work together. Admittedly, the thought had crossed my mind before, but those times I'd been sober enough to not actually fling myself at him. *Stop it. He is off-limits.* Yet my hands managed to slide around his neck of their own accord.

His eyes locked with mine in an intense stare, and suddenly it felt hot. Unbearably hot, as though the club was on fire and Cash was on fire and I was on fire from these thoughts about a man I should most definitely not be thinking about. My mouth went dry, and I licked my lips— partly because they were so dry and partly to give me some-thing to do so my tongue wouldn't find its way into Cash's mouth. As we swayed together, I wondered what that mouth would feel like all over my body. *Seriously, Ella.*

The strobe lights seemed to swirl around us, and all of that tequila started to seem like a really bad idea, especially when I remembered how little I had eaten all day. My entire body tingled with warmth, and the way he was looking at me wasn't helping with the whole remembering he was off-limits thing.

His grip around my waist tightened, and if his eyes were laser beams, my clothes would have melted right off me. I recalled that old Usher song, the one that talked about wanting to make love in this club, and I realized I finally understood what he meant. Because I wanted all these people to disappear. I needed to feel the heat of his body over mine. I needed...

"I need water." I leaned into his ear so he could hear me over the music. I really did need water, but I also needed to do something to break this trance before I climbed him like Mt. Everest in front of all these people.

He nodded, and I started weaving my way toward the bar. Cash's hand slipped from my waist to my hand, his fingers lacing through mine in a way that felt like foreplay. *Jesus be a Xanax. What am I doing?*

I pressed up to the bar with Cash behind me, and I found myself leaning into him as I waited for the bartender to notice me. Why did this feel so good... so natural?

After I ordered, I noticed the raised voices of the couple standing next to me. At least, I assumed they were a couple based on the way he gripped her. Then I remembered how closely Cash and I had been dancing and reminded myself that making assumptions makes an ass out of you and me. *I wonder what Cash's ass feels like. Focus, Ella.*

The girl beside me wore a pained expression, and her body language was screaming for this guy to get off of her. Every time he leaned in, she leaned away. She was pretty with a spray of freckles across her face and blonde hair. She reminded me a little of Grace, so my Mama Bear radar was on full alert. With his popped collar, the guy looked like a douche—like his dad probably bullied some school to let him into a fraternity.

The bartender returned with our glasses of water, and I turned to face Cash, handing him his.

"Do you mind if we stand here a moment?" I asked. I moved in closer so that he could hear me. "I think there's something going on with these people standing beside us."

He nodded, his face wrinkling with concern. Why were all of his facial expressions so sexy? I pretended I was peering off into the club, but I was really trying to listen to the conversation taking place next to us.

"Come on, baby," the douche said. "We'll have a good time."

"No, thank you." The pretty girl looked as though she were praying for the floor to swallow her whole. "I want to leave with my friends."

He pushed his way into her space even more. "They can come too."

Pretty girl looked to be a little tipsy, but she also looked uncomfortable as hell. "I don't think so. I had fun, but we're just going to go home."

"So, why have I been buying you and your little friends drinks all night? You need to come home with me. It's the nice thing to do. Your friends will understand."

The girl looked like she was ready to cry. "I really just want to go home." The guy opened his mouth to say something, but I was faster on the trigger.

"She said *no*," I stated firmly. "You need to back off."

"Who the fuck are you?" The douche turned his attention toward me. "Her mother?"

Cash zeroed in on him. "Watch your mouth."

"I'll be whoever the fuck I need to be to get you to go away," I countered, looking up at him. He had at least a foot on me and probably a good hundred pounds, but I didn't care.

"Mind your business, old lady. This conversation has nothing to do with you." He puffed out his chest in what I assumed was an effort to scare me.

"I'm gonna need you to take a step back, young man." Cash took a protective stride toward me, holding his hand out toward the jerkface to prevent him from advancing any further.

"Okay, gramps." The guy rolled his eyes. "Are y'all out on a field trip from the old folks' home?"

Cash started to say something again, but I placed my hand on his chest, stopping him.

"It's okay. I've got this," I said to Cash before turning my attention to the pretty girl. "Hi, sweetie. Do you want to go home with this man?"

She shook her head vehemently.

"Would you like any further contact with this absolute dumpster fire of a human?" I asked.

"No ma'am," she answered.

I placed a protective arm around her. "What's your name, sweetheart?"

"Brooke," she replied.

"I'm Ella, and this is Cash." I gestured to where Cash stood with his arms crossed, staring the guy down. "And we're going to make sure you find your friends and get out of here safely."

"Thank you so much." Brooke looked up at me with gratitude.

"I don't know who the fuck you think you are, you old ass bitch." The douchebag stepped toward Brooke and reached for her arm, but I pushed my way between them, poking my finger in his chest.

"Listen here, *Chad.*" I plastered a smile on my face. "Is that your name? Because you look like a Chad. My *old ass,* as you so eloquently put it, is your worst fucking nightmare. Because I'm not her mom, but I am *a* mom, and that means I know what pain feels like. Have you ever pushed a seven-and-a-half pound human out of your vagina with no painkillers? No? Cool. Well, let me tell you why that's important information for *you.* It means I'm not scared of *anything,* least of all a little pissant like *you.* So, I'm going to give you a tip for free-ninety-nine. Go home, Chad. Unless you want me to inflict some vagina-ripping pain on you."

Chad's nostrils flared, and for a moment, I thought he might actually hit me. "Fuck both you bitches." With that, he turned on his heel and disappeared into the crowd.

"Brooke, we've been looking all over for you," a girl with long black hair shouted, gripping Brooke by the arm. "Lacey even went to one of the bars next door because she thought maybe that weird guy convinced you to go."

"Thank God. No, that guy was a total psycho." Brooke flung her arms around her friend before turning back to me and giving me a hug. "Thank you, Ella."

"Don't mention it, sweetie." I smiled. "Do you girls need anything? Do you want me to call you an Uber?"

"We're okay," she said. "Our other friend drove."

I raised an eyebrow. "Is your other friend sober?"

She nodded. "She is. I promise."

"Okay then." I patted her on the arm. "Y'all have a good rest of the night, and be careful."

"We will," Brooke said as she and her friend disappeared into the crowd.

When I turned back to Cash, his eyes were wide and his mouth hung open slightly, and I suddenly felt self-conscious.

"What?" I asked.

"That was just… " Cash trailed off as he moved closer to me, his hand finding mine.

With that little Chad diversion out of the way, my thoughts drifted back to the way Cash's hand felt on my skin.

"Do you want to get out of here?" I raked my teeth over my bottom lip. *What are you doing, Ella? He is off-limits. He is—*

"Yeah." He nodded slowly, slipping his other arm around me. His mouth was so close to mine I could feel the warmth of his breath on my lips. "Yeah, I do."

SIX

Cash

THE UBER RIDE BACK TO ELLA'S PLACE WAS SHORT, AND OUR driver, a young fellow named Dean, tried to keep us entertained with stories about his organic vegetable garden. To be honest, I wasn't listening. No offense to Dean—it was just hard to pay attention to anything when Ella was sitting next to me with her golden hair framing her face like the crown of some sort of sun goddess.

I stole glances of her in the passing street lights, and I wondered what she was thinking. She reached over, placing her hand on my thigh, and my pulse began to thud in my ears. Our eyes met, and we seemed to be stuck in a wordless conversation of are we or aren't we. I wondered if she could see through me. Could she see how unnerved she made me?

We'd both been drinking, though, I had to admit the alcohol was starting to wear off. I felt like I was caught somewhere between reality and a fantasy world... lost in those first couple of moments of waking up after a really good dream, except that dream was sitting right next to me.

Her clear blue eyes peered at me from beneath her lashes as Dean pulled to a stop. I should do the right thing. And the right thing was to drop her off at her house and take the Uber back to my own place. I still had things I was working through. It hadn't even been three years yet...

"Here we are," Dean chirped.

Do the right thing, Cash.

"Do you want to come in?" Ella asked before I could decide if I was, in fact, going to do the right thing.

I felt like I was swallowing dry air. "I'd like that."

We climbed out of the Uber, and Ella wished Dean good luck with his garden. My heart slammed against my chest as though it were a sledgehammer in the hands of one of those *Property Brothers* on demolition day.

"I guess we're lucky this night didn't end with you having to bail me out of jail for beating Chad's ass." Ella's voice broke the silence as we walked up the stone path to her dusty-blue, Craftsman-style house in the heart of the Melrose neighborhood.

I laughed. "I would have been sitting in that jail cell right next to you. There's no way I wouldn't have gotten in a punch or two. After you whooped him, of course." We reached the door, and she dug in her tiny purse for her keys. The bright yellow of the door glowed beneath the porch light. "When you told me you had this and you railed on that guy? That was hot. You don't need anyone, and that's incredibly sexy to me." *What are you doing, Cash?*

She stuck the key in the lock before turning her gaze to me. "Just because I don't need anyone doesn't mean I don't want anyone." She grabbed my tie and pulled me into her, closing the distance between us.

Her lips grazed mine, softly at first, as she guided me over the threshold and slammed the door behind us. She gently tugged on my lower lip with her teeth as her hands climbed my chest.

"Ella…" I broke our kiss, and her lips landed on my neck, soft and warm like a cashmere scarf. "Are you sure this is okay?" My jaw clenched, desperate to retain what little self control I had left.

Her laugh vibrated against my skin before her eyes met mine again. "I did ask you to come in, didn't I?"

My cheeks burned beneath the heat of her gaze, and I gave her a bashful nod.

She leaned in as though she were about to kiss me, but stopped. "So, it's settled then."

I felt any resolve I'd had burst into flames. We were a tangle of kisses and arms as I leaned her against the door, sliding the deadbolt until it clicked. With one hand tangled in her hair, I let the other travel down her body, the silky material of her dress sliding beneath my fingertips.

"Bedroom," Ella murmured as she kissed her way down my jawline. "Down the hall. Now." She guided me through the dark to a room toward the back of the house lit only by the moonlight filtering through the blinds. "So many clothes. Aren't you hot?" She shoved the door closed behind us with her foot while her hands tore at my jacket.

"You have no idea." I wasn't sure if the beads of sweat that formed along my hairline were due to too many clothes or the fact that these clothes were keeping my skin from hers. She set to work on my tie while I unzipped her dress, relishing the way my fingertips felt against her skin as I sent the peach chiffon falling to the floor.

"If I'd known this was going to happen tonight I might have picked something a little sexier." Ella laughed, but her voice dripped with confidence. And for good reason. The nude contraption she had on beneath her dress hugged her every dip and curve, and her breasts threatened to spill out over the top.

"God, you're beautiful," I said softly. She kicked off her heels and stepped out of her dress, her tan skin glowing in the moonlight. I took in a shallow breath as she unbuttoned my shirt, sliding the fabric down my arms.

My fingers wove into her hair, trembling slightly. She unfastened my belt, sending it sailing across the room. I blinked hard, certain that when I opened my eyes again I'd find myself back at the wedding—that this had all been some vivid daydream. Her hands slipped down my bare chest and stilled just above my waistband, confirming that this was actually happening. I couldn't deny how much I wanted Ella. Or how long I'd wanted her.

"Cash," Ella whispered my name as I trailed my fingers lightly along her arms. "Are you okay? Your hands… they're shaking." She wrapped her arms around my waist.

"Yeah." I swallowed hard. "It's just that this is the first time since…" I didn't finish the sentence. I didn't have to because I knew she understood.

"It's okay. We don't have to—"

I tucked a piece of hair behind her ear. "No, it's not that. I want to. I want *you*." I hooked a finger under her chin.

"I promise to be gentle with you," she said as she placed open-mouthed kisses along my chest.

"I hope you won't be." Her eyes flickered up to mine, and she held my gaze for an eternity locked inside a moment.

"I was hoping you'd say that." She backed me up until I was against the bed, and she pushed me onto it, falling with me. Her hands found the button on my pants and she tore at it until she managed to break the snap.

"Ella, what are you doing to me?" It was a rhetorical question, of course, because what she was doing was making me come undone. She took her time pulling my pants off, teasing me with kisses along my chest and down my thighs. My hardness pressed against her thigh as she straddled me, causing my eyes to squeeze shut.

When she decided she'd tortured me enough, she placed a long, deep kiss on my lips. "I don't know. What *am* I doing to you?"

"Your turn." I rolled her over until she was laying on the bed and began pulling at the straps on the skin tight jumpsuit looking thing. I pried and clawed but the fabric barely gave. "What is this thing? It's like air-tight Tupperware but for your body."

"They're called Spanx." Her hands covered mine, guiding them over the spandex. "Have you ever opened canned biscuits before?"

I snorted. "What do biscuits have to do with Spanx and Tupperware?"

"Contents under pressure." Her giggle sent goosebumps dancing all over my skin.

Finally, I pulled the torture device down to her waist, freeing her soft breasts, which I teased with my thumbs. A whimper escaped her that immediately registered at my core. For as sexy as her confidence was, it was her vulnerability that nearly pushed me over the edge.

"Cash," she moaned, stroking me slowly. It had been so long since I'd had a woman's soft hands on me. I gritted my teeth and put my focus on the material separating us so as not to explode from her simple touch.

With renewed conviction, I wrenched the Spanx down her hips with such force that it sent me flying off the foot of the bed, landing with a thud.

"Oh my God, are you okay?" Ella asked, and I could see the outline of her silhouette peering over the edge of the bed through the darkness.

"Aside from the fact that I got my ass kicked by a tiny piece of Lycra Spandex, I'm great." I laughed despite my bruised ego and soon-to-be bruised tailbone.

Ella dissolved into peels of laughter. "Come here. But please be careful. I'd hate to have to explain a sex injury in the emergency room."

I got to my feet and climbed over her, both of us still shaking with laughter. "Now, where were we?"

Ella's voice lowered as she ran her hands through my hair. "I believe you were about to make me feel really, really good."

"Was I?" My fingers traveled from her neck down to her folds, and I wasn't sure who it turned on more.

She took my hand in hers, pressing me into her. "More of that."

I slipped one finger inside her, gliding it slowly in and out. She wriggled beneath me, a soft gasp on her lips. Adding a little pressure to her clit with my palm, I eased another finger in this time, picking up speed.

"Yes. Like that," Ella purred in my ear, a sound that was my own personal kryptonite. She raised her hips to meet my hand. "Please don't stop."

My fingers became drenched in her as I moved them faster, and she bucked beneath me, greedy for my hand. The tempo of her breathing quickened, and I was lost in what it sounded like to please her.

When her panting finally slowed, she raised her lips to meet mine. She kissed me tenderly at first, while her hands explored my body. By the time her journey led her to my cock, we were both breathless.

"I want you. Now." With one quick movement, she had me on my back and straddled me. She grinded against my shaft.

"Damn it. I don't have a condom," I groaned, feeling myself start to tumble from the high we'd built together.

"Me either," she said, "but the few times I've had sex I've used protection, and I'm on the pill. I'm clean."

"Me too," I said as she leaned down and kissed me, her breasts grazing my chest.

"Well, thank fuck." She raised her hips, took me into her hand, and sank onto me. My hips instinctively rose to meet hers as I filled her. Our eyes locked for a moment, and for the first time in a long time, everything felt exactly right.

My hands slipped around her waist as she rode me, and our hips found a rhythm together just as they had on the dance floor. Watching her with her head thrown back was enough to make me want to come undone. It had been so long, I was afraid I would have to start reciting all of the presidents to keep from coming.

Ella's soft cries of pleasure got louder as our pace quickened. When I felt her walls shudder around me, I let go too. I let out a moan that sounded almost primal, and she sagged against me as we rode out our aftershocks together. I kissed her cheek and rubbed my hands up her back.

She let out a satisfied laugh. "God, I can't tell you how long I've wanted to do that."

"What?" I asked, completely stunned. "You mean the sex or the sex with me?"

She kissed me softly, a mischievous smile playing on her lips. "Want to go again?"

THE MORNING SUN POURED INTO THE ROOM, WAKING ME with a vengeance. My head throbbed a steady reminder of what a bad idea shots were at forty-two. The shots may have made my head feel as though it were going to explode, but luckily they didn't mess with my memory. I rolled over to see Ella still sleeping soundly beside me, and I couldn't help but smile. I'd made at least one good decision the night before.

I closed my eyes, thinking about the way Ella had moved on the dance floor and then the way she looked at me on her doorstep, all smolder and silk. For so long, my crush on Ella had been just that—a crush—but that infatuation had crossed into uncharted waters. I heard her words echo through my mind. *Just because I don't need anyone doesn't mean I don't want anyone.*

Since I lost Carrie, I thought I hadn't even wanted anyone—not in any meaningful sort of way. Sure, I could admit when I found a woman attractive, but wanting someone else while I still missed Carrie felt... wrong. Yet here I was, wanting Ella.

Her lashes fluttered slowly, her eyes framed with soft black smudges.

"Good morning," I said softly, my fingertips grazing over her bare shoulder. For a moment, I thought she might drift back to sleep, until her eyes flew open and an alarmed expression spread across her face.

"Holy shit," she said, bringing her hand to her forehead.

I chuckled. "I'm sorry. Didn't mean to scare you."

"You... you didn't." She clutched the sheet to her chest, looking from me to the clock on the nightstand that read nine-thirty a.m. "I just... wow. That really happened last night, huh?"

"That really happened." I laced my fingers through hers, and her mouth stretched into a seductive smile. "You know, you never did answer my question last night."

"What about?"

"You said you couldn't tell me how long you'd wanted to do this."

"Shit." Her eyes widened. "I said that out loud?"

"And I asked if you meant the sex or the sex with me."

She chewed her lip, not answering the question.

My stomach sank. "I'm sorry, Ella. I shouldn't ha—"

"No," she interjected quickly, placing her hand on my arm. "I wanted to… *with you*. I just can't believe I said it quite so bluntly."

I burst into laughter. "Have you met you?"

"You have a point there." A mischievous grin stretched across her face, and she leaned in, pressing a kiss to my lips. "But as great as this has been, Grace will be home soon."

"I should probably go ahead and call an Uber." Reluctantly, I pulled away from her warmth, reaching for my pants that were haphazardly laying on the floor. I extracted my phone from my pocket and quickly flipped to the Uber app, ordering a ride. "Alright. We've got about twenty minutes until Charles shows up in his black Lexus." I tossed my phone back to the floor.

Ella's eyes sparkled. "I could think of something we could do for twenty minutes."

"Mmm." I wrapped my arms around her, pulling her into me. "What did you have in mind?"

She began trailing kisses down my neck. "I was thinking we could start—"

Ella was interrupted by the sound of a soft thud echoing through the house, followed by Grace's voice. "Mom, I'm home. I brought coffee and bagels."

"Shit," Ella cursed, throwing the covers off of us. "You've got to get dressed. You've got to get out of here. She can't see us like this."

I almost fell as I scrambled to my feet, pulling my pants on. I threw on my shirt and jacket, not bothering to button either one of them.

"They were out of the blueberry, so I got you a cinnamon raisin," Grace's voice continued.

"That's okay, honey," Ella called, snatching a fluffy pink robe off of the hook on the back of the door and wrapping it around her. "Set them in the kitchen, and I'll be right there. I just woke up." Her voice was shrill and definitely didn't sound like she'd been asleep moments before.

"How am I going to get past her?" I whispered, shoving my feet into my shoes.

"You're not," she replied. "You have to go out the window."

"What?" I asked louder than I intended, picking up my socks and belt from the floor.

"Shhh," she hissed, holding out her hands as though she could somehow stop the sound of my voice with her fingers.

"Did you say something, Mom?" Grace's voice shouted.

"Uhh no." Ella's face was flustered. "I just... uh... stubbed my toe." Ella quickly crossed the room and unlocked the window, prying it open.

My eyes widened. "Oh wow, you weren't kidding."

She opened the screen on the window with one push and gestured from me to the outside.

"I'm sorry," she said, "but Grace can't find out. We should probably talk about this, but—"

"Do you want cream cheese?" Grace shouted.

I moved to the window and breathed a sigh of relief that it was only about a five-foot drop to the ground.

"Yes, please," Ella chirped, giving me a sympathetic look. "This was…" She trailed off, grabbing my shirt with both of her hands and tugging me down to kiss me.

I slid my arms around her waist, wanting to savor every last second of this time with her. "I'll call you later today?"

She smiled and nodded as the sound of footsteps filtered down the hall. A look of panic settled on Ella's face, and I crouched down until I was sitting on the window frame.

"I'm sorry again," Ella said.

With that, she gave me a shove, sending me headfirst into a bunch of azaleas.

SEVEN

Ella
___

I LOWERED THE BLINDS JUST AS GRACE PUSHED OPEN THE door with a takeaway coffee cup in her hand. "Everything okay, Mom? I thought I heard voices in here."

"I just stubbed my toe," I said nonchalantly, crossing over to her. *That whole no boundaries parenting thing is great until you're trying to sneak your daughter's boss out the window.*

Grace laughed, handing me the cup of coffee. "On the window?"

"On the bed, on the way to the window," I explained. "I was so exhausted when I came in last night that I crashed with the window wide open."

Grace made a face, scrunching up her nose. "No offense, Mom, but you stink."

Shit. It was at that exact moment when I remembered we'd gone to Santa's Pub before going to the speakeasy. But I couldn't tell Grace that I had been out with Cash. She would ask a lot of questions, and she'd certainly make it into some big *thing.*

Wait… Is this a thing? I shook my head in an attempt to shake the thought from my mind.

"Oh yeah," I said with a wave of my hand, feeling like a teenager who had just been caught redhanded with a boy in her bedroom. "My Uber driver basically chain-smoked the entire ride here."

She eyed me suspiciously. "Why didn't you just take a shower?" Her gaze shifted to the floor where my dress was piled in a heap. *Does it smell like sex in here?* I prayed that the scent of Santa's ashtray overpowered any additional smells that may be lingering.

"I was so exhausted. It was like something came over me the second I walked through the door." *Well, that's partially true. Something did come, or more accurately, someone. Multiple times.* "How was Lexi?"

"She's good." Grace bent to grab the pile of peach chiffon and hung it in place of my robe. "She just got a job at Molly Green Boutique for the summer."

I took a sip of the coffee, willing it to give me the energy of someone who slept more than three hours. "How's her mom doing?"

"Uh, she's fine. You know, same ole same ole." Grace fluffed the dress on the hanger, attempting to smooth the wrinkled fabric. She turned back to me with narrowed eyes, and I held my breath. "I'm going to go take a shower before we leave to see Grandma. Your bagel is waiting for you on the counter."

"Right." I nodded so hard I shook my entire body, causing droplets of hot coffee to jump from my coffee cup.

Grace cocked her head and crossed her arms. "Why are you being weird?'

"I'm not being weird," I said defensively.

"You're awfully jumpy for someone who's not being weird."

"I think I still have a little emotional hangover from yesterday," I said. *And a real one.* My head and heart pounded.

Grace's face softened. "Everything's going to be okay, Mom." *Except that I just slept with your boss. And I liked it so much that I'd like to do it again.*

"It's not too late for you to change your mind on England," I teased. "You can spend the summer with your poor, lonely mother. Who needs to go to England? Stodgy bunch of blokes."

"Mom." She laughed at my pitiful attempt at a British accent.

"You know it rains there like all the time, and they don't even have air conditioning."

"Come on." She rolled her eyes and started toward the door. "We've got to get ready to go."

"When we get home, we can watch *Gossip Girl* reruns while I help you finish packing." She paused in the doorway allowing me to pull her into a hug. "I'm going to miss you so damn much, kid."

"Mom?" she said, leaning her head against mine.

"Yeah, sweetie?" I asked.

She pulled back so that she could look me in the eyes. "You really, *really* stink."

BY THE TIME WE ARRIVED AT RICHLAND PLACE NURSING Facility to visit my mom, Betty, it was nearly lunchtime. We brought her a vegetable plate from Arnold's Country Kitchen and a vase of fresh daisies. Grace and I busied ourselves by cleaning up around her room a little, breaking in between to remind her about the plate of food in front of her.

Some days were good days—ones where she remembered who we were, where she'd ask questions and even remember little details we'd told her during some of her lucid moments.

This wasn't one of those days.

I pulled my phone out of my back pocket and discreetly checked to see if I had any messages from Cash, but there was only a text from Liv letting me know they were on the way to pick up the kids. I replied to her with several shooting stars and heart-eye emojis before stuffing the device back in my pocket. *Focus, Ella.*

"James should be here to pick me up any minute now," Mom said nervously, looking at the large digital clock on the wall. "He's never late. I'm so sorry to keep you two here." My chest tightened. James was my dad, and punctual as he may have been, he wasn't coming. Because he'd been dead for nearly eight years.

"You're not keeping us," I assured her.

Mom looked at me through uncertain eyes. She was especially nervous, glancing back and forth from me to Grace. "Are you girls from the church?"

"No, Mama. We're just here to visit," I said.

"I'm going to miss you, Grandma." Grace smiled over at her grandmother as she fussed with the daisies in the vase, arranging them perfectly. "But I'll be back soon, and Mom will be visiting you every week, just like always."

We tried to stick to a routine when visiting my mother. For Alzheimer's patients, a routine was extremely important. We generally came on Thursday evenings, but with

Grace leaving the next day, we had to move our visit to Sunday.

"You're such a sweet girl," Mom said to Grace. "What's your name again, dear?"

Grace's face fell. I knew she had been hoping for one of those good days before she left for England, but those good days had become few and far between.

Before she could answer, Mom had turned her attention back to the clock. "My James will be here soon. He's always on time. Have you girls met my husband?"

I nodded. "We have. He's an amazing guy. You're so lucky to have each other." And they had been. My mother's Alzheimer's had started early. She was only fifty-two when she'd gone to the store one morning to pick up some milk and forgotten how to get home. She'd panicked, but luckily remembered her phone number that she had the cashier call. That day was the day that changed everything.

"We're lucky," Mom replied. "So lucky. James will be here shortly. He's always on time."

I sighed and watched as my mother stood and used her walker to maneuver to the window that overlooked the parking lot. Her once blonde hair was now white and kept in a bob that grazed her shoulders. Her skin was thinner than it used to be, and the disease had aged her beyond her years, but she was still beautiful.

"Why are there so many cars here?" Mom started to panic, clutching at the wool of her cardigan. "My husband should be here by now. James should be home." I nodded a silent request to Grace who quietly picked up the room phone to call the nurse's station.

"Mom," I said softly as I approached her. "It's okay. Come finish your lunch." I placed a gentle hand on her shoulder, but when she looked up at me, I knew it was a mistake.

"Who are you? Where is my husband?" Her voice was shrill and panicked, and I could see that she was breathing harder.

The door opened, and her favorite nurse Nicole strolled in. "Hey, Miss Betty," she greeted. She looked to me with an empathetic smile. Mom didn't always know who Nicole was, but when she got like this, it was Nicole who was able to calm her. "You've had some good visitors this afternoon, huh?"

Mom looked to Nicole with relief. "Can you help me find James? He should be here by now."

"Why don't you come have a seat over here in the chair, and let me take a look at you?" Nicole asked. "I understand you're worried, but I'm here to help."

My mother looked at her with uncertain eyes for a moment before allowing Nicole to guide her over to the armchair.

Mom grabbed Nicole's hand. "James should be here. He was picking up Ella from daycare."

I blinked back the tears that threatened to form in my eyes and swallowed down the lump that lodged itself in my throat.

"Don't you worry, Miss Betty," Nicole said. "I'm going to take care of everything. Alright? You just breathe in real deep for me. In and out. Good." I watched as Nicole calmed my mother before turning on the television, flipping the channel until she landed on an old showing of *Breakfast At Tiffany's*. In moments, she was immersed in the movie, and James and baby Ella were forgotten.

Nicole patted my mom on the shoulder before turning to Grace and me.

"She's having more days like this, isn't she?" I asked. "She's getting worse."

Nicole pressed her lips together and nodded. "I'm so sorry. I wish there was something I could say or do to make this better. I watched my own grandfather go through it too. I know how hard it is to see her like this."

"We couldn't do this without you," I told her, and I meant it. Nicole had been our saving grace ever since Mom had been placed at Richland. "You take such good care of her. And us."

"I hate that she doesn't know who we are anymore." Grace chewed her bottom lip.

Nicole placed a hand on Grace's arm. "She knows, sweetheart. Deep down she knows. The part of her that's still Betty loves you both more than anything in this world. The rest of this? That's the illness talking. You've got to remember that."

I cleared my throat, suddenly desperate to get out of the confines of the room. "We should probably head out." I turned to Grace. "Let's go home and get you packed."

"That's right. You're about to be leavin' on a jet plane." Nicole smiled. "You travel safe, and we'll see you when you get back. And I'll see you next week, Ella."

I nodded, and Grace glanced back at my mom with a wistful expression on her face. Mom was deeply involved in the movie, seemingly oblivious to our presence anymore.

I put an arm around Grace and steered her from the room as she leaned into me. After difficult visits like this one, we would spend the rest of our evening together trying to take our minds off of it. We'd curl up on the couch and watch reruns of our favorite shows in quiet appreciation that we still had each other.

I knew there was nothing I could say to make her feel

better about my mom's condition because there wasn't anything that could make me feel better. Grace was my rock, the one constant in my life, and she was about to be thousands of miles away. I'd still visit weekly, but instead of going home to Grace, I'd be going home to an emptiness that only seemed to be growing.

As we got into my SUV, I checked my phone, hopeful there would be a message from Cash waiting for me. When I saw I had no unread messages or missed calls, annoyance pricked at the inside of my chest, and then I felt the heaviness in my heart begin to close in.

"I don't care what anyone says. Dan Humphrey is a turd." I flopped on Grace's bed after binge watching several hours worth of *Gossip Girl* and helping her pack. "He never deserved Serena."

Grace zipped her large plaid suitcase and rolled it over to where her carry on bag was propped near her bedroom door. "You are entitled to your wrong opinion." She crawled in the bed, curling up next to me. She pulled her phone from her pocket, seeming to check something and gave a discontented sigh.

"What's wrong?" I leaned my head against hers.

"I texted Cash earlier to tell him goodbye, but I never heard anything back from him," she said. "I hope he's not regretting suggesting me for this job."

My chest tightened, and that annoyance I'd felt earlier in the day started to grow. "I'm sure he's just busy."

I'd checked my phone no less than twenty times and still had no messages or missed calls from Cash. Finding out he wasn't responding to Grace either was enough to make my blood boil and my Mama bear claws come out. Though to be fair, I had nobody to blame but myself. I knew getting involved with Grace's boss was a bad idea, but I guess I'd expected more from him.

This was Cash we were talking about. Cash was thoughtful and considerate. He wasn't like Ryan who ditched a date early to go hiking the next day. It was par for the course when the Ryans of the world didn't text or call, but when it was Cash, it felt all wrong.

When he'd left, or more accurately, when I'd pushed him out the window, things had felt... different? No, I didn't exactly know where we stood at that moment, but I'd thought there might be a very real conversation about what happened. Or at the very least a text. His silence had begun to feel like its own answer to the question hanging over my head of what we were or weren't. I knew I had to reach out and make sure he didn't shut Grace out over a mistake we had made. *That's what it was right? A mistake?*

"I wonder how Aunt Liv and Jax are doing with the kids," Grace said, wrapping her arms around me.

I shifted my focus to soaking up these last few moments with Grace. "I haven't heard from her since earlier. I wanted to give them a little space to get settled in before I called."

"I can't believe I'm going to miss all of this while I'm gone." Her voice was small as she nestled closer to me. "It kind of makes me wish I wasn't going."

"Are you having second thoughts?" Selfishly, I hoped she was, but I also knew that Grace needed this. She needed to step out on her own a little.

She shook her head. "I just wish I could be there and here at the same time. I feel like I'm missing out on so much."

"We'll all be here when you get back," I promised.

"Are you going to be okay?"

"Me?" I asked. "What are you worried about me for?"

"This is going to be the first time you've been alone in a long time."

"I'll be fine," I said with as much conviction as I could muster. "I'll be busy at the bakery with the renovations, and you know I'll be calling to bug you all the time. These three months are going to fly by. And if Sam steps even the slightest bit out of line, I'm going to hop on the Hogwarts Express and make a trip to jolly ole England just to whoop his ass."

She laughed. "Sam's a good guy, Mom, and don't worry. He keeps things very professional."

"He better."

"I'm going to miss you, Mama." My heart swelled. She hadn't called me 'Mama' in years, and suddenly I longed for the days when she was small enough for me to fold her in my arms and keep her safe.

I blinked away the tears that attempted to form in my eyes. "I'm going to miss you too, honey. I better let you get some sleep. You've got a big travel day ahead tomorrow, and we've got an early start." I kissed the top of her head and pulled out of her grasp.

"I love you, Mom," she said as she climbed under the covers.

"Love you too." I made my way to the door, flicking off the light. I looked back at Grace one more time before shutting the door, and my heart felt heavy again.

As I padded back to my room, I pulled my phone out of my pocket and illuminated the screen. There was still no message from Cash. I huffed and threw myself back on my bed, scrolling through my contacts until I landed on Cash's name.

I cleared my throat, preparing myself for the call I knew I had to make. I had to nip this in the bud. *We'll just pretend it never happened, and everything will go back to normal.*

I wondered how I could ever go back to normal again, knowing how good he could make me feel. I pictured how sexy he'd looked the night before, glistening with sweat as we danced and how good his lips felt on my—*Stop! Pull yourself together, Ella.*

This was exactly why I had to put a stop to this nonsense right now. I was already too involved, and it had only been one night. Who gets this up in arms over *one* night? *One perfect night.*

I sucked in a deep breath as I tapped his name and pressed the phone to my ear. As the call connected, an unfamiliar phone ring echoed through the room causing me to jump. Frantically, I searched for the source of the factory setting ring.

I crouched down, tearing at the dust ruffle, and just as the voicemail picked up, my eyes landed on Cash's phone under my bed.

EIGHT

Cash

From the moment I got shoved out of Ella's window, I'd felt disjointed. That probably had a lot to do with the fact that I'd managed to leave my phone somewhere on her bedroom floor. I'd wanted to call or text her no less than a dozen times since I'd left. I'd even been half tempted to go back to retrieve my phone, though, I knew if I were being honest with myself what I *really* wanted was to see Ella again. But I also knew this was Ella's last day with Grace for a while, and they needed that time together. So, I'd decided to busy myself by running errands and going to the gym. When I had nothing left to do but sit with my thoughts, I'd opted to try to go to bed early.

I set the old fashioned alarm clock by my bed so I could get up early enough to get to Ella's in time to see Grace off and retrieve my phone. I'd helped Grace book her flight, so I knew she'd be leaving for the airport around eight a.m. I laid there in the dark for a few minutes before finally flicking on the lamp that sat on the nightstand. The room was bathed in a soft glow, and Carrie's smiling face beamed back at me from the dresser. She was smiling at the camera, a perfectly wrapped package on her lap. It was a photo from our last Christmas together—right before the headaches started.

A flurry of emotions rained over me as I looked at the face I knew by heart. I still missed Carrie every day of my life, and I couldn't imagine a day when that would stop. A wave of guilt crashed over me as I thought about what happened with Ella. Carrie had been gone almost three years, but somehow I felt like I was cheating on her.

My love for Carrie lived on, but in so many ways I had not. I'd been going through the motions and just getting by for so long now that it felt like second nature.

But this? These feelings I had for Ella were all new, yet familiar somehow. How could I feel like this for Ella when my heart still belonged to Carrie?

I scrubbed my hands down my face and threw the covers off of me, rising to my feet. I shuffled over to the dresser and picked up the picture, smoothing my thumb over the cold glass.

"I wish you could tell me what to do," I said out loud to Carrie's photograph.

You already know. I could hear Carrie's voice as clear as a bell in my head.

When we found out what Carrie's fate would be, she'd forced me to talk about it. And just when I thought she was done, she made me talk about it some more. She wanted me to promise her I would move on and be happy—that I would find love again. But how could I promise something like that when I was still coming to terms with a life that no longer had her in it? How could I promise her something I didn't know was possible?

I gently returned the picture to its place and turned out the light before crawling back into bed.

Truth be told, I still didn't know if it was possible. All I knew was that for the first time since I'd lost Carrie, I wanted to try.

I PULLED MY RANGE ROVER TO A STOP IN FRONT OF ELLA'S house early the next morning, cut the ignition, and strolled to the door. A cocktail of anxious energy sloshed through my veins—a nervousness that felt both foreign and familiar at the same time. I suddenly wished I'd taken one last glance in the mirror to make sure I looked okay. *Get it together, Cash.*

I rolled up the sleeves of my crisp navy-blue button down in an attempt to look casual, realizing the amount of thought I was putting into my clothing was anything *but* casual. I took a deep breath and raised my hand to knock on the door, but before I could, the door flung open.

"Cash... what are you doing here?" Grace asked, her head cocked to the side and her voice laced with confusion. She was standing next to a bulging suitcase that looked as though it may erupt with a river of clothes, makeup, and whatever else a nineteen-year-old girl traveled with. A smile slowly spread across her face, and her eyes lit up. "Did you come to take us to the airport so you could see me off?"

I caught a glimpse of Ella's shocked face from where she appeared behind Grace and flashed her an apologetic glance. I knew she probably wanted these last few minutes with her daughter, and as much as I wanted to see Ella, I hadn't intended to intrude on their ride to the airport.

"You're the best. I'm really going to miss you." Grace

flung her arms around me. "I knew something was up when I didn't hear back from you yesterday. Mom acted like she had no clue what was going on, but I knew she was up to something. She was acting weird all day yesterday and checking her phone constantly."

"Nothing gets past you." Ella's face flushed as she pressed her lips together and shook her head.

Grace pulled back and poked me in the chest. "So *that's* why I never heard back from you yesterday. You knew you'd ruin the surprise."

I chuckled and held my hands up in surrender. "You got me. I knew you'd probably want one last latte from that Frothy Monkey coffee shop you like so much."

"It's a little known fact that they only serve tea in England, so you better enjoy it," Ella teased.

Grace giggled and rolled her eyes. "I've got to go grab my phone and my purse, but then I'm ready to go."

"Don't forget your passport," Ella and I said at the same time. We exchanged a look of surprise, and a smile curled on Ella's lips.

Grace snickered. "You two are clearly in sync today."

"Make sure you have your boarding pass too," Ella reminded her.

"How could I forget?" Grace beamed. "I'm flying first class, baby."

"I'll go ahead and load up your suitcase." I grabbed the handle of the behemoth and swiveled it toward me.

"I'm going to uh… help Cash," Ella called after Grace as she bounded down the hall. "Turn the lock on your way out."

After we'd made it a few steps down the walkway, Ella reached into her purse and pulled out my phone, discreetly passing it to me as though Grace might have somehow developed x-ray vision and be able to see straight through the walls of the house. I quickly slipped it in my pocket.

Ella smirked. "Nice save."

"I'm so sorry," I said as we reached my SUV, and I popped the trunk open. "I hope this is okay. I was thinking I would just stop by to tell her goodbye and try to sneak my phone back from you."

"It's fine." She waved me off. "I'm sorry I didn't realize I had your phone sooner, and I'm sorry I was mad at you all day yesterday for not calling." She caught my eye as I hoisted the suitcase in the trunk. Her grin was smooth like Kentucky bourbon.

"I wanted to call you so many times," I admitted.

She leaned into me, her blue eyes shimmering in the glow of the morning sun. My mouth felt as though it were being pulled to hers involuntarily, but before I could attempt to kiss her, Grace came bounding down the walkway.

"We may have to skip the coffee run," Grace said, tossing her carry-on bag in the trunk. "Sam texted and said he and the band just got to the airport, and they're waiting for me outside security."

I nodded, slamming the trunk closed. "Straight to the airport then."

I moved to open the back door on the passenger side, and Ella started to climb in before Grace swooped in and cut her off. "You sit up front, Mom," she insisted.

"Okay then," Ella said as I closed the door behind Grace.

"My lady," I joked, as I opened the passenger door for Ella.

She stuck her tongue out at me, and I couldn't control the smile that spread across my face. I strolled around to the driver's side and climbed in. Before I had even closed the door, Grace was chattering animatedly, ticking off a laundry list of things she'd packed. She did most of the talking while Ella piped in with occasional questions and reminders as we made the short drive to Nashville International. I forced myself to keep my eyes on the road when all I wanted to do was steal glances at Ella.

"I mean it, Grace," Ella warned as we pulled into the parking garage. "You have no business out at night without Sam or one of his security guards or one of the people on his team. You're a beautiful young woman in an unfamiliar place. You've got to stay aware of your surroundings."

"I know, Mom. I will," Grace promised.

"Your mom's right," I added as I parked the car. "And you know if you need *anything*—day or night—all you have to do is call me."

Ella looked over at me, her face soft with gratitude.

"I know," Grace said, humoring me as she unbuckled her seatbelt. "I'm going to be careful. Everything is going to be fine. I think you guys are forgetting that I'm an adult."

"Well, you're still *my* baby," Ella insisted. "No matter how old you are."

Grace laughed. "Okay, Mom. I've really got to get in there."

"*Fine.*" Ella smiled back at Grace who had already flung open the door. Ella's face fell as she turned to open her own door.

I reached over and gave her shoulder a squeeze before we both got out of the SUV. I helped Grace with her suitcase, and we made the trek inside the airport. We checked Grace's bag at the British Airways counter, and as we approached security, I caught a glimpse of Sam's mop of red hair waiting in a cluster of people. I saw the moment his eyes landed on Grace and watched as his face came to life.

"Hey, Grace," Sam's chipper British accent greeted as we approached. "Good to see you, Cash. And you look lovely as ever, Miss Ella."

Ella beamed. "Thank you."

The band and crew looked like they weren't awake yet as they mumbled their hellos and stifled yawns.

Grace turned to Ella. "We better get going so we can get through security and get to our gate."

Ella nodded and pulled her daughter into her arms. "I'm going to miss you so damn much, kid."

"I'm going to miss you too, Mom," Grace replied.

"I know you're going to be busy, but please don't forget to check in with me, alright?" Ella placed a kiss on top of Grace's head. "I don't care what time it is."

"I will," Grace said. "Promise."

Ella finally broke their grasp and turned her attention to Sam. "You're quite adorable, Sam, but if anything happens to my daughter on your tour, I'll kill you and make it look like an accident."

Sam chuckled but also looked slightly terrified. "She'll be safe with me, Miss Ella. Cash already threatened us all within an inch of our lives."

"And I meant every last word of it," I said, narrowing my eyes at Sam.

"Bye, Cash," Grace said, enveloping me in a hug.

"Be safe," I said softly, smoothing my hand over her hair.

Grace nodded. "Look after Mom for me, okay? She's going to be going crazy without me." She turned and grinned wildly at Ella who made a face.

"I don't know what you're talking about." Ella pulled

her daughter in for one more hug. "It's going to be nothing but wild parties here. Let freedom ring and whatever."

"I love you, Mom," Grace said, kissing her mother's cheek.

"I love you too, sweetheart." Ella reluctantly released Grace from her grasp as Sam offered to carry the bag slung over her shoulder.

"I'm supposed to be assisting you." Grace laughed. "Not the other way around."

Sam grinned down at her. "Wouldn't be much of a gentleman if I let you just lug that thing 'round the airport, would I?"

Grace relinquished her duffle to Sam before tossing one last smile over her shoulder at Ella and me. I placed a comforting arm around Ella's shoulder, and we watched as Grace disappeared into the crowd.

I wondered if this was what it felt like to send your kid off to college. I felt a mixture of sadness and pride, and I couldn't begin to imagine what Ella was feeling.

Finally, I heard Ella take a deep breath before turning to look at me. "I guess we should get out of here. I need to get to the bakery soon. Katie knows I'll be late, but I don't want to keep her waiting long."

"Alright," I said with a nod as we took one last look at the space Grace had occupied. "Let's go."

———

"I sure am going to miss that girl," I said as I turned the key in the ignition.

Without warning, Ella burst into tears.

"Ella…" I said her name softly and reached across the

console to fold her in my arms. "It's going to be okay. It's just for the summer. She'll be back in no time."

"But this is how it starts." She sobbed into my shoulder. "First it's the summer, and next thing you know she's moving out and moving on. She'll be getting married and starting a life of her own."

"That's true," I said softly. "But you've raised her well, Ella, and no matter where life takes her, she's still going to be your daughter."

Ella pulled away, shaking her head. "It won't be the same. She'll have a husband and kids of her own one day, and I'll be alone. Who's going to eat pizza and watch *Gossip Girl* with me now? I can't eat a whole pepperoni pizza by myself. Well... I *can*, but my cholesterol says I can't."

"That pesky cholesterol." I chuckled and reached for her hand.

She looked at me through tear-stained lashes. "I'm really glad you came with us today."

My heart swelled. "Me too, but I have to admit that seeing Grace off wasn't the only reason I dropped by today."

"Duh," Ella joked. "I had your phone."

"That also wasn't the reason," I said, threading my fingers through hers. "I haven't stopped thinking about you. I couldn't wait to see you again."

The teasing facade fell from her face. "Really?"

I nodded, but before I could say anything else, Ella's phone pinged with a notification, and her brow furrowed as she looked down at it. "Dammit. That's Katie. She said the contractor left a message that he's coming an hour early. We're starting the renovations at the bakery this week."

"We better get you back home so you can get to work."

I put the car in reverse and set off in the direction of

Ella's house, and we settled into a thick silence. It wasn't one of those comfortable silences either. It was the kind of silence akin to the concentration of chess players. Ella looked out the window while I tried to steal glances of her every time I turned or changed lanes. The entire time I'd known Ella, she'd always had plenty to say. She was usually the brightest and loudest woman in the room, which only made her silence that much more deafening.

By the time we reached her house, beads of sweat had formed along my hairline from the sheer effort it took not to reach across the seat and kiss her. As I parked the car, all I could think about was how much I wanted to walk her to her door and repeat every single moment from our night together when Ella's voice broke the silence.

"I really like you, Cash," she blurted, "and I'd be lying if I said I haven't always had a little crush on you." Relief bloomed in my chest. "The other night was... fucking amazing. But that's why it can't happen again."

"What?" It felt like all of the air got sucked out of the car. The night we'd spent together *had* been amazing, which was exactly why it needed to happen again.

"Cash, you're Grace's boss. You're essentially Liv''s boss." She raked her hands through her hair. "But more than that, we're kind of stuck together no matter what. We're all part of this kind of extended family because of Jax and Liv. Could you imagine what would happen if this ended badly?"

"Yes, but—"

"We'd still have to see each other all the time."

"Don't you think—"

"Our friends would feel like they have to choose sides, and that would make everything awkward."

"Ella, would you let me say something?"

"I can't." She shook her head emphatically. "Because you're going to say something to try to change my mind, and I like you enough that I just might listen. But it's a bad idea." She seemed to be saying it more to herself than to me.

"I don't think it is."

"Cash..." Her eyes met mine, and there was heat in her gaze, but it was mixed with sadness. "If we got together and it didn't work out, Grace would be devastated. She's lost so much already, and she adores you. Having you in her life has been good for her. I never want that to stop, and I never want her to be in a position where she may feel she has to make a choice."

I raked my teeth over my bottom lip, considering what she said. I understood the loss Grace experienced—I knew it intimately. Ella and I were like two sides of the same coin, and I wouldn't hurt her or Grace for anything in the world. Perhaps I should have backed down, but something pushed me forward. A force I couldn't quite pinpoint was whispering in my ear, 'fight for her.'

"I would never want that either," I assured her. "Look, Grace is gone for the summer, and Liv and Jax have their hands full with the kids. Why don't we just spend some more time together? We have the whole summer to explore what this is before we have to worry about the rest of it."

"I don't know."

"Ella, if you can sit here and tell me that what happened the other night wasn't... that you didn't feel something—I'll walk away right now. We can pretend it never happened. If not, I think we owe it to ourselves to see what this is. We don't have to put any labels on it. We can even take it back a few steps and just keep getting to know each other." It would be hard as hell to feel something that good and walk away, but I'd do it if I thought that's what she really wanted.

She rubbed a strand of her golden hair between her fingers, appearing to mull over what I'd said. "Can I take a little time to think it over? These last few days have been a lot, and I can't pretend that I'm not a wreck over Grace being gone. And the person I would normally lean on has her hands full with two new kids I haven't even met yet."

"I understand that. Take all the time you need."

A soft smile spread across her face. "I better get going so I can get ready for work."

I nodded, and she reached for the door handle to get out of the car, but I grabbed her hand. "Hey, Ella?"

"Yeah?"

"You can lean on me if you need to."

She squeezed my hand and opened her mouth as though she were going to say something, but no words came. Instead, she nodded once before bounding up the walk and disappearing behind the front door.

NINE

Ella

THE CONTRACTOR, AN OLDER GENTLEMAN WHO CALLED himself 'Big Earl' and smelled like sawdust and tobacco, was already waiting for me by the time I made it to work a little after ten a.m. We met out front so Katie and I could assist any customers who came in.

The small boutique next door had relocated a few months before. We'd been itching to expand the bakery to a coffee shop with a small dining room, but we needed more space to do it, so we quickly contacted the owner of the building and started planning the expansion.

Big Earl was showing us the finalized blueprints of what our new coffee bar and dine-in area would look like and giving us a rundown of what to expect for the next three months. Aside from the noise aspect, we'd be running business as usual while the build-out took place.

"I'm estimating we'll be ready to install the new cases and bar in about three weeks, but I'll give you girls plenty of notice." Big Earl flashed us a toothy grin as he outlined the rest of the renovation plans with Katie and me, but my mind kept traveling back to Cash and everything he'd said.

He was right. We did have the whole summer ahead of us to explore this connection and what it meant. But that's exactly what worried me. What would happen at the end of the summer? Even if this *was* just some fling, how would we ever really go back to normal? *Well, Ella, don't you think you already screwed the pooch on that when you slept with him?*

I hated to admit it, but I had a point.

"Ella?" The sound of Katie's voice snapped me to attention to find her and Big Earl staring at me.

"You look overwhelmed." *Oh, Big Earl. You have no idea.* He gave me a sympathetic look. "I know any kind of expansion is a big deal. You're probably a little uneasy about making such a big change, but sometimes the right path isn't the easiest one. That's what my Mama always told me."

"She sounds like a wise woman." Why did it feel like Big Earl was talking directly to my soul about things that had nothing to do with countertops or paint swatches?

"Don't you worry, darlin'. Big Earl has everything under control. I'll have everything right as rain in no time." He gave me a reassuring pat on the back.

Will you, Big Earl? Because right now I'm looking at you but all I see is Cash... the slight wave of his hair, his hazel eyes and strong arms, his firm chest, his hard di—

"Right." I shook my head, trying to remove the thoughts threatening to take over my entire life. "That's great. Thanks, Big Earl."

"No problem, sweetheart," Big Earl said. "I'm going to get out of your hair, but the crew and I will be back at the end of the week to get started."

I nodded. "Sounds good."

"Thanks, Big Earl," Katie called after him, and he tossed a wave over his shoulder before shoving his way out the door of the bakery. Katie turned her attention to me, narrowing her eyes. "Are you alright?"

"I guess I'm just out of sorts with Grace leaving this morning." That was at least *partially* true.

"I know it's going to be weird without her, but she'll be back before you know it." Katie moved behind the counter, and I followed her, watching as she straightened up the pastry cases. "Have you talked to Liv?"

"Not really," I said. "I've been giving her some time. I figured they probably needed a couple of days to get the kids settled in."

"Yeah, that's why I haven't called either," Katie admitted. "How did your wedding date go? I feel like I didn't see you guys together after Jax and Liv left."

"That's because he left." I busied myself by wiping down the countertops. "He was more interested in his phone than he was in me, *and* he gets up early *on purpose* to do things like go hiking. It was clearly not meant to be."

"I'm sorry, girl." Katie frowned. "I wish I'd been there for you. I was so tired I asked Dallas if he'd mind taking me home."

I grinned. "And I'm sure he gladly obliged." I was fairly certain the only people who didn't know that Dallas and Katie loved each other were Dallas and Katie.

"Anyway, what did you and Grace get into after the wedding?"

"Actually, Grace had a sleepover with her friend, and I..." My stomach did a cartwheel. "I, uh... I—"

Katie squeezed her eyes shut and braced herself against the counter before opening them again.

I placed a hand on her arm, and as I looked at her

more closely, I noticed dark circles under her eyes. "Are you okay, Katie Bug?"

"I've just been getting a little dizzy here and there, and I think I need to get my eyes checked. My vision has gotten so blurry lately."

"You're also overworked and stressed out," I added, feeling a twinge of guilt. "I know we just hired those two new girls as our B Team to help prep and cashier, but I think we need to seriously consider hiring you more help in the kitchen."

"You're right." Katie sighed. "I just dread having to train someone else. Those new girls are sweet as can be but slow as molasses. I feel like I'm working twice as hard because I constantly have to go behind them. I'm sorry, Ella. I'm not trying to complain. I guess I really am stressed out."

I squeezed her shoulder. "I know you are, and I'm sorry I've not been more proactive in getting more staff in here. I've been dragging my feet, probably because I've been a little in denial about all of the changes happening lately. But I have the whole summer to do nothing but focus on the business." *And think about how sexy Cash's forearms are. Who knew forearms could be so fucking hot?*

"You've had a lot going on," Katie said. "I know it's a lot of change, but sometimes change is good."

"You're right." But was a change that could potentially wreck our friend group still good? It certainly *felt* good but—

"So, what were you saying earlier? About what you did after the wedding?"

The doorbell dinged, and a customer walked in.

"Welcome to Livvie Cakes," I greeted. "What can I do for you today?"

Saved by the bell. I needed to talk to someone, but Katie was stressed enough without me dumping my problems on her. I'd have to sort this one out on my own.

When I walked through the door a little after eight that evening, I was met with an unflinching silence. I padded to the kitchen, turning the lights on as I went and tossed my purse and keys on the counter. My heart ached in the absence of Grace's voice greeting me, asking what we were having for dinner. We'd only spoken briefly after she'd landed, and I missed her already.

I walked to the cabinet and pulled down a wine glass, placing it under the spout of a box of merlot. I filled it nearly to the brim, grabbed my phone from my purse, and dialed Liv as I headed to the living room.

By the time I'd flicked on the television and sank onto the sofa, Liv answered.

"Hey, Ella," she answered, sounding exasperated.

"Hey, babe. I wanted to check in and see how the kids are doing." I propped my feet on the soft cube in front of me. "Also, I don't even know your kids names yet. Everything happened so fast, and we haven't gotten to talk."

Liv sighed. "I don't want to get my hopes up by calling them ours. I'm afraid it won't happen."

"They steal your heart fast, don't they?" I thought about the time I first held Grace in my arms, and my heart swelled.

There was a beat of silence on the other end of the phone. "They do. Their names are Chloe and Jonathan. Chloe is two and Jonathan is five."

I squealed. "How are they adjusting so far?"

Her voice dropped to a hushed tone. "Chloe took to me quickly, but she cries constantly and wants me to hold her every minute she's awake. The social worker said they think she's really struggling with fear of abandonment. She and Jonathan have been in three foster homes in two years. He's a sweet boy, but he doesn't understand yet how to process his emotions. The smallest thing sets him off and sends him into a screaming, crying fit."

I took a sip of my wine. "That's a lot of change for anyone, let alone children so young. Having you and Jax will be good for them."

"What if I'm not what's best for them?" Liv asked.

"Sweetheart, you have the most important thing they need, and that's love," I reminded her. "Everything else comes with time. I can't tell you how many times I felt like I wasn't going to be enough for Grace."

"Shit," she said. "I completely forgot to call Grace this morning. How are you holding up?"

"I'm—"

I heard the shrill sound of a baby crying on the other end of the phone. "Dammit. That's the monitor. Chloe just woke up. I'm sorry, Ella. Can I call you back?"

"Sure thing. I love—"

Before I could finish my sentence, the line went dead. I clutched the phone to my chest and took a long drink of wine. With a heavy sigh, I rose to my feet and began to move through the house. The living room was small and cozy with a purple couch Grace, Liv, and I had found at a yard sale five years ago. One wall was covered in a bright, floral wallpaper. We called it an accent wall, but the truth was that after covering the one wall, Grace and I had thrown the rest of that shit in the trash. Wallpaper really should come with a warning label—may cause you to question all your life choices.

I lingered in the hallway and took in the lifetime of pictures that decorated the corridor in colorful collages of frames Grace and I had put together over the years. There were pictures from birthdays and Christmases past, trips we'd taken over the years with Liv, and a school photo of Grace for every grade from kindergarten through her senior year.

My favorite photo was at the center of them all. It was from Grace's fourth birthday party. Craig and I held Grace between us—the center of our universe. You'd never know from our smiles that we'd barely made the mortgage that month or that my parents had paid for the birthday cake in front of us. We didn't have a lot, but we had each other.

Until we didn't.

My gaze shifted down the hall toward the door to Grace's bedroom. I could still see Craig carrying her atop his broad shoulders and hear their laughter echo off the walls.

But that's all they were now… echoes.

I gulped down a swallow of wine and the lump that had formed in my throat. It was quiet—too quiet, and my world that had at one time felt so loud and full of life had suddenly fallen silent.

I'd been spoiled by having Grace here while she attended college. For so long, I'd been prolonging the inevitable, but one night alone and I was already losing my shit.

But I was nothing if not a woman of action.

I unlocked my phone screen, found the contact I was looking for, and hit send. The call connected, and the voice on the other end answered.

"Hey... It's Ella," I said tentatively. "I hope it's not weird that I'm calling you out of the blue like this, but I was thinking about something we talked about the other night, and I... I was wondering if I could get your help."

"ARE YOU SURE ABOUT THIS?" DEREK ASKED, RAISING HIS voice so that I could hear him over the sounds of enthusiastic barking. We were standing amidst all of the adoptable dogs at Nashville Humane Society. I'd ducked out of work a little early so I could make it in time to meet Derek before they closed. "Maybe you should start with a goldfish first."

"Fish are creepy looking with their beady little eyes and old-man mouths." I scrunched up my nose. "Besides, a goldfish isn't going to be happy to see me or want to cuddle on the couch. No... I can't go home to an empty house again. Last night was torture."

And it was. I'd fallen asleep on the couch to the sound of *Gossip Girl* on the television with my phone clutched in my hand because I couldn't stand how quiet the house was.

"This one has potential. His name is Sarge." Derek pointed to a large grey dog with pointy ears and a narrow snout. "He looks friendly."

I nodded. "He does, but I think that might be a little too much dog for me. I like to cuddle, but I also need my space, and I foresee that dog being a couch hog." My gaze traveled to a tiny chihuahua who appeared to be sleeping the day away. According to the tag on the cage her name was Buttercup. "What about this one? She's cute."

At that moment, Buttercup's eyes flew open, and she launched into a barking tirade that startled me so much that I yelped.

Derek covered his ears, shielding himself from the shrill sound. "That's a no from me." He quickly moved past the little yap muffin and stopped a couple of cages down. "Look at this cute little guy."

I joined him in front of a small grey and white scruffy dog. His hair was unkempt, and his ears were floppy. He was too big to fit into a purse, but small enough to snuggle. His tail whirled around so fast I thought he might take flight from excitement.

"Hey there, cutie." I knelt on the floor and reached my fingers through the cage. "What's your name?" The pup let out a soft whine and licked my fingers, his tail moving even faster.

I heard Derek chuckle from above my head. "You'll never believe this. His name is Cash."

I jumped to my feet and looked at the name tag on the cage. *Well that's... weird.* Yet somehow it also felt like a sign.

"That has to be a sign, right?" Derek asked as though he were reading my mind. I watched as he flagged down the staff member that had been assisting us. "Excuse me. Can we visit with this guy?"

"Sure you can," the young man said. He grabbed a leash off a hook by the door and joined us, opening the cage. He latched the floppy dog to the lead, and the pup ran straight for me. "He sure seems to like you."

I cupped his soft face in my hands and scratched behind his ears. "The feeling is entirely mutual."

The attendant guided us to a visitation room at the end of a long hallway. "You guys take your time. I'll be back to check on you shortly." He closed the door, leaving Derek and I alone with our new furry friend. We sank to the floor, and the pup ran circles between us, stopping to give us kisses every few steps.

"This might be the cutest dog I've ever seen," Derek said as Cash the dog made a running leap for me, landing his paws on my chest and his slobbery tongue on my face.

I exploded with giggles. "You're getting awfully fresh there, buddy. At least buy me dinner first."

Derek laughed. "You can't leave without this dog, Ella. I think he's picked you."

"I think I pick him too." I smiled. "But we already have one Cash around here, so I think we need a new name."

"You could call him Johnny or JC?"

I cocked my head and squinted at the fluff nugget. "I don't think those really suit him. Look at him—he's a real ladies man." The little dog whined in approval and nudged my hand so I would give him more love. "See? He's already got me wrapped around his little pinky paw."

"You've got a point." Derek rubbed his fingers along his chin. "We need a name that says charming but cute. A name with personality."

"Bradley," I said. "Bradley Cooper."

Derek choked on a laugh. "It definitely has a ring to it."

"Doesn't it? Besides, now I'll get to say 'I have to go home to Bradley Cooper,' 'Bradley Cooper and I are going to the park,' and my personal favorite, 'I didn't sleep a wink last night because Bradley Cooper was hogging the bed.' Isn't that right, Bradley Cooper?" He gave an excited bark and bounced over to Derek.

Derek scratched his fingers down Bradley Cooper's back, much to his approval. "What will Grace think?"

"She'll be over the moon." I grinned. "She'll probably also think I've lost my mind. I can't even keep a cactus alive."

"You've kept a whole person alive. I think you'll be okay."

My phone pinged with a notification, and I plucked it from my purse to see a text from Grace.

Grace: busy first day, but i love england already!!! i may never come back. ;)

Grace: jk mom. sorry i didn't call today, but things are nuts. talk tomorrow? love you!!!!!

I smiled down at my phone and sent her several pink heart emojis.

Ella: I'll drag your ass back here myself if I have to. Love you too. Talk tomorrow.

"That was Grace." I slid my phone back in my purse. "She's loving England so far."

"She's a lucky girl," Derek said.

I nodded. "Yeah, this is such a great opportunity for her. I miss her like crazy, but I'm glad she's happy."

"She's lucky because she has a mom like you. Anyone can see she's your whole world."

I shrugged. "That's just what parents do."

"Not all parents." Derek's smile faltered. "My relationship with my parents is… complicated."

"I'm so sorry."

"I always wished I had that Diane Keaton mom, you know?" He shook his head. "It's silly, but every time I see Diane Keaton play a mom in a movie, she's the perfect mother. Sometimes she's a little overbearing or overly involved, but she's always on her kids' side. She's the parent that's always proud of her kids, no matter what they do. I didn't think moms like that existed in real life until I met you."

I suddenly had the urge to reach out and hug him. "You don't think your parents are proud of you?"

The pained expression that flickered across his face was

all the answer I needed. In all the time I'd known Derek, I'd never seen him look so sad.

"That's not important." The corners of his mouth tugged into a smile. "What's important is how excited Grace is going to be when she finds out Bradley Cooper is at home waiting for her."

"Can I ask you something?" I blurted. Maybe it was the fact that Derek had confessed something so personal, or maybe it was simply that I was bursting at the seams to talk to someone that made me want to confide in him.

He nodded. "Of course."

"Have you ever felt like you've spent so much time building your life around other people that you forgot to build one for yourself?" I asked the question I hadn't been able to fully articulate till now.

Derek sucked in a deep breath through his teeth. "You have no idea."

"After my husband died, I devoted my life to Grace and Liv." I rubbed my hands down Bradley Cooper's back. "Now that they're both doing their own things, I've realized how much of my life revolved around them. As sad as it is, I think I liked it that way because as long as I was focused on their lives, I didn't have to think about what was missing in mine. Now I've had a taste of what I think I've been missing, and it's *all* I can think about."

He raised his brow at me. "And what's that?"

"I've met someone—more like I've *known* someone, but I'm just now seeing what we could be. " I pressed my lips together. "But he's kind of a big part of the lives of everyone I know, and if it didn't work ou—"

"It's Cash, isn't it?" Derek cut me off.

"So much for a guessing game."

"It's not hard to guess," he admitted. "You guys have

good chemistry together, and I'm pretty sure he's kinda had a thing for you for a while now."

"You think so?"

"He's never said it out right, but it's more in the things he doesn't say." He ran his fingers through his beachy blond hair. "It's in the way his eyes light up when you come into the room and how he always finds a way to be near you when we're all together."

He had me there. After Liv and Jax got together, we'd started a tradition of Sunday dinners when everyone was in town. I couldn't think of a single Sunday dinner we'd had where Cash hadn't sat beside me.

"You've really noticed all of that?" I asked, and Bradley Cooper touched his cold nose to my arm.

He nodded. "I may be the quiet one in the group, but that means I see everything."

I shook my head. "So, you see my predicament. You see why this is a bad idea."

"I don't think that's true at all," Derek said. "Why do you think it's a bad idea?"

"He's Grace and Liv's boss," I began. "Our friend group is more like a family. What if we get together and it ends badly?"

He shrugged. "But what if it doesn't? And right now, don't you kind of have a golden opportunity to figure it out while nobody knows what's going on? I know, but I won't say anything. Grace is out of the country, and Liv is a little preoccupied. You're getting a free trial before you have to pay the full price."

I laughed. "What if it's too expensive?"

"You have time to figure that out, but you'll never know the cost if you don't bother to look at the price tag."

"Were you a financial analyst in a past life?" I teased.

"Fair enough. Thanks for letting me get that off my chest. I've been going crazy not having anyone to talk to about all of this."

"Anytime. I'm glad you asked me to come with you today." Bradley Cooper sneezed and flopped at Derek's side.

"I mean, you *are* a dog whisperer. I kinda had to." I laughed. "And Derek... I know I'm only like ten years older than you, but I'd be honored to be your Diane Keaton."

He chuckled softly. "Well, Diane, what do you say we break Bradley Cooper out of this joint?"

Bradley Cooper raised his head and whined his agreement.

I nodded and rose to my feet, which caused the dog to jump in circles. "Alright, Bradley Cooper, are you ready to go home?"

TEN

Cash

IT HAD BEEN EXACTLY ELEVEN DAYS SINCE I TALKED TO Ella. Not that I was counting every minute.

I'd checked my phone constantly since the morning I'd dropped her off in front of her house after we took Grace to the airport. I pressed the button on the side of my phone, illuminating the screen just in case I'd somehow missed her text the twenty other times I'd looked at my phone that day. When I saw I still had no new messages, I placed the phone face down on the mahogany desk in my office at Carrie On Records.

The office was painfully quiet without Grace's music and her off-key singing that I adored. She'd been sending me text and email updates here and there about what was happening on tour, but it wasn't the same as having her energy bouncing off the walls like a rubber ball. Our team was small and worked from home most days, coming in only for meetings. Grace and I were the only ones that were there consistently. I considered calling a meeting just to have other people around.

The clock on the wall ticked a loud reminder of the time that was passing—all of it without so much as a word from Ella. I'd even considered asking Grace how her mom was doing but didn't want to raise any suspicion asking such a random question. Sure, I'd asked about her many times before, but that was before—before I'd known what it was like to want her this much, and it also wasn't via text. It was a lot easier to slip something like that into a casual conversation than ask in some work-related email. What if I somehow gave something away that clued Grace into what happened between her mom and me? I knew she didn't want Grace to know, and I respected that.

I didn't want to pressure Ella, but I couldn't stop thinking about her. When she'd said she needed time, I thought she meant a couple of days. I had no idea I'd be on day eleven without so much as a text from her. I wanted to respect her wishes, but this was killing me.

Yes, I missed her, but it was more than that. I knew this was a tough time for her with Liv being so preoccupied and Grace being gone. Would it be too soon for me to just check on her? Maybe see if I could take her some dinner? I sighed and raked my hands down my face, attempting to push the thoughts from my mind as I shifted my focus back to the laptop in front of me.

An email notification sounded, and I had to read the message five times because my mind continued to drift back to Ella. After tapping out what I hoped was a sensible reply to the email, I slammed my laptop shut with a dissatisfied snap.

I was reaching for my phone again when it started to ring. My heart lurched, and I lunged for it, sending the overpriced technology sailing to the floor. I dove under the desk, fumbling for the phone until I had it in front of me.

"Hey, Cash," Sam's British accent greeted me. "Everything alright, mate?"

"Yeah, sorry," I replied. "I should be asking you that. What time is it there? It's got to be nearing midnight."

"Yeah, I just got back to the hotel, but I wanted to touch base with you."

"Is everything okay there? Has Grace settled in with the crew?"

"Grace is... well, she's phenomenal," Sam said. "Everyone adores her."

"Don't get too comfortable," I teased. "She still has a job waiting for her here, and she's going back to school in the fall."

"I know, I know. I would never encourage her to step away from her goals, no matter how much I love having her around." He cleared his throat. "But that's actually not why I called. I'm having a bit of an issue. It's not related to anyone else. It's me."

"Oh?" Sam wasn't one to complain or stress over much. He wasn't a needy client, so I knew whatever was going on had to be pretty serious for him to tell me. "What's going on?"

"I've been feeling unwell. Truth be told, I wasn't feeling great before we began the tour, but I just thought I was a little run down," he began, and I noticed a hoarseness in his voice. "But it's gotten worse now that I'm performing each night. I feel like I've got this lump in my throat, and my voice doesn't sound quite right. Tonight was the worst it's been so far. I felt like I couldn't control my pitch."

"Sounds like we need to get you to a doctor," I said, opening my laptop and searching through my contacts. "What part of England are you guys in tomorrow?"

"Bristol," Sam answered. "I've got a bit of press

tomorrow morning, but I have some free time in the afternoon."

"I'm going to talk to Grace and have her cancel your upcoming press. You need to rest your voice while we figure out what's going on. Do you need me to cancel any shows?"

"No," he insisted. "I'm sure I'm just run down. Maybe I'm fighting off an infection or something."

"Okay, but if that changes—"

"I couldn't possibly cancel shows and let down my fans."

"Listen, Sam, I know your fans are important to you. But this is your health we're talking about, and that's got to take precedent here." I found the contacts I was searching for and opened up a new message window. "I'm going to send emails to a couple of my contacts over there and find someone who can get to you first thing in the morning. There's a great doctor that came and saw Luca after he hurt his shoulder while we were on tour in the UK. I'm going to reach out to him and see if he knows a specialist that could make a house call for you."

"Thanks, Cash." Sam's voice cracked. "I appreciate you."

"I need you to promise me something," I said. "If at any point it's too much, I want you to tell Grace immediately. I'm going to give her all the info she needs to handle canceling any of the shows on your roster, should she need to. We've got to keep you healthy, alright? We can reschedule a tour. We can have a hundred tours, but there's only one Sam Corbyn."

"Promise," he agreed. "I'll tell her straight away if I don't think I can continue my duties."

"I should get off here and shoot a text to Grace. In fact,

if you just got back to the hotel, I may be able to call and fill her in now."

"Um, actually, Grace is with me." Sam coughed. "We ordered a bite to eat and we're going to hang out for a few minutes."

I wasn't sure whether to grin or give him a lecture. "Is that so?"

"A couple of the guys on the crew are joining us," he added quickly.

"Right," I said. "Well, then, do you mind putting Grace on?"

"Sure thing," he replied, and I heard the sound of muffled voices for a moment before Grace's voice came over the phone.

"Hey, Cash!" I could practically hear Grace's smile. "So, Sam caught you up to speed?"

"He did," I said. "I'm copying you on a couple of emails, and I'm going to send you some info on what to do if we need to cancel any tour dates in a hurry. I know this is a little different than what you're used to doing. Are you still feeling comfortable with everything? Do you need anything?"

"I'm fine, *Dad*," she teased, and my heart lurched. "I'm doing great. Really. It's a lot of work, but it's what I signed up for."

I chuckled. "Alright, but if you need anything—"

"Call you right away." She finished my sentence for me. "I know. I promise I will, but I've got it handled. Like Olivia Pope."

"I don't know who that is, but I'm assuming this Pope lady has her ducks in a row."

"*Olivia Pope*," Grace emphasized every syllable. "From *Scandal*."

"Still don't know."

"Ugh. You know, for someone who works with celebrities you sure don't know who many celebrities are." She feigned disgust. "Anyway, how are things there?"

"It's awfully quiet without you here," I admitted. "The boys are keeping a low profile right now while Jax and Liv get settled with the kids, you and Sam are gone, and most everyone else is on tour or in-studio sessions. I've had a couple of meetings, but it's been quiet. I miss you, kiddo."

"I miss you too," she said.

The words formed on my lips before I could stop them. "How's your mom been holding up?"

"Oh, she's all but forgotten about me." She giggled. "Bradley Cooper has been keeping her busy."

I choked on my own spit. "What?"

"Seriously, she's obsessed," she continued, "but with that face, who could blame her? Everything is Bradley this, Bradley that. I swear, I get ten new pictures a day. He seems to be keeping her on her toes."

Her words came at me like paintballs, splattering across my chest, leaving behind welts and bruises. All this time, I'd imagined her grief-stricken, elbow-deep in a pint of Jeni's ice cream, crying over missing her daughter and best friend. But no, she'd been elbow-deep in—

"Bradley is basically her whole world now." Grace laughed. "Who would have thought?"

I coughed, my entire body seeming to reject the idea that Ella had already found someone else. My heart couldn't take it.

"You alright over there, Cash?"

I cleared my throat. "Uh-huh. Allergies," I lied. "So, where did your mom me—"

"Hey, Cash? Sam is getting another call. I'm going to

have to let you go, but I'll keep you posted on everything over here. Don't worry. I've got everything under control. Talk soon," she said, and the line went dead.

I scrubbed my face with one hand and held my phone in the other, staring at it. Who the hell was this Bradley guy? His name sounded familiar, but I couldn't place him. How had Ella had time to meet this dude anyway? It had only been *eleven days*.

I didn't know whether I was hurt or impressed.

Hurt. Definitely hurt.

But I had to hear it for myself. I had to hear it from her.

I found Ella's name in my phone and hit send.

"Hello?" Ella answered on the third ring. "Hold on!" Her voice sounded tight, like a rubber band about to snap. She disappeared for a couple of moments, and I could hear a rumbling in the background and the distinct sound of Ella muttering strings of expletives. "I'm sorry—who's there?"

Sadness nipped at my heart. I knew she had my number saved, but it was like she had no idea who I was. "It's Cash. I just wanted to call and see how things were going." *And to hear about this Bradley asshole. And why I haven't heard from you. And to hear your voice because I miss you.*

"Shit," she said. "I'm sorry, Cash. I was so distracted that I didn't even see the name when I swiped to answer the phone." She genuinely sounded distraught. "Well… things are… not great at the moment," Ella replied. "I'm sorry I haven't called recently. I was actually going to call you tonight, but I'm kind of in the middle of an issue."

My chest twisted. Had Bradley broken up with her? I was ready to fight this jerk for hurting her. *You can't hate the guy for being with her and for breaking up with her, Cash. Pick a struggle.* I pressed the base of my palm to my forehead.

"Oh? Is everything alright?" I asked.

I heard her heave a sigh on the other end of the phone. "Actually, I'm kind of a mess at the moment. I hate to ask this, but could you—"

"I'll be right there," I said, answering the question before she'd even asked.

"Thank you, Cash," her voice sounded small, defeated even.

"I'm always here for you, Ella." It was true. No matter what she decided, I cared too much about her to step aside. This Bradley character would just have to deal with it. Even if she was with this guy, I wasn't going to let her go without a fight. "I'll be right there."

Put your dukes up, Bradley. May the best man win.

ELEVEN

Ella

I REALLY HAD INTENDED TO CALL CASH EVEN BEFORE THAT moment. But every time I picked up the phone, my hands turned clammy, and my stomach started doing this weird swishy thing. So, I threw myself into Bradley Cooper and adjusting to our new life together. Which also turned out to be necessary seeing how he was an actual terror—a terror with separation anxiety.

We were in the middle of renovations at the bakery and starting the interview process again, but I had to leave work every few hours to take him for potty breaks and to see what fresh hell awaited me. I felt awful leaving Katie while I went to check on Bradley even for just a few minutes, but she loved seeing pictures of the furball and hearing stories about his art of destruction. Though I suspected she really just wanted to keep my mind off of missing Liv and Grace.

Liv didn't even know about Bradley yet. I'd barely spoken to her except for a couple of quick texts and frazzled conversations where one of the kids was inevitably screaming in the background. I'd told Grace all about her new furry brother, but left out that he'd turned our home into a fucking biohazard.

In the ten days I'd had him, he'd peed *everywhere*, murdered the mini blinds in the living room, used my espadrilles as a chew toy, and pooped on my favorite rug. And this wasn't just any poop. It was like someone had lit a stick of dynamite up Bradley Cooper's ass. It reminded me of when Grace was a little over a year old and she'd gotten a stomach virus. She had a poop explosion while we waited at the pharmacy—one of those where you wonder how it's possible to shit so hard it goes all the way up your back.

I'd thrown out the rug along with my pride when I finally called Derek and begged him to come take Bradley Cooper for a walk while I attempted to remove the smell of dog shit.

The destruction had culminated in me having a break-down on this particular afternoon when I'd come home to discover that Bradley Cooper had thrown up on my favorite quilt. I'd thrown it in the wash, and the next thing I knew the small room had been overtaken by bubbles.

I glanced over to the laundry room door where Bradley Cooper eyed me with concern, probably wondering why I'd collapsed in a heap of tears amidst a growing sea of bubbles. He might be a terror, but he was mine.

"You're never going to leave me, are you?" I sniffled.

His tail whipped around like a propeller as he ran to me, licking the tears off my face. He yipped over the sound of the washer that continued to churn and vomit bubbles.

I rolled my eyes, annoyed with myself for crying over a fucking washing machine. The damn thing had held on through thousands of loads of laundry over the course of nineteen years.

I felt like I was losing so much already, and the universe had to go and take my fucking washing machine too?

Grace had been telling me for the past three years to get a new one. But it wasn't that easy. It wasn't *just* a washing machine.

The doorbell chimed, and Bradley Cooper barked once to inform me. "Stay," I told him as I pulled myself from the floor and trudged to the front door.

I swung the door open to find Cash standing there looking like he walked out of a Men's Warehouse ad. He was impossibly handsome in his dress pants and lavender button down with the sleeves rolled up. His forearms seemed to have become my own personal aphrodisiac.

"Hey." I gulped down the fire that had ignited at the core of my belly. "Thanks for coming."

Cash nodded. "Of course."

He stepped over the threshold, and I closed the door behind us. My mind flickered to the night we'd stumbled through that very door, unable to keep our hands off each other.

"Is everything okay?" Cash asked.

Before I could answer, Bradley Cooper bolted toward us, barking and covered in fluffy, white bubbles, leaving a trail of foam behind him.

"What the——" Cash startled as the shaggy terrier jumped on his leg, his helicopter tail spinning out of control. He crouched on his knees, laughing as the pup smothered his face in kisses. "Since when do you have a dog?"

"Since the day after Grace left. I couldn't take being in this house alone," I said. "Meet Bradley Cooper."

"*This* is... I mean, you named your dog Bradley Cooper?" Cash asked.

I shrugged. "Yeah. Why?"

He cleared his throat. "It's just… it's a unique name for a dog. But I like it. Suits him." He turned his attention to Bradley Cooper who was still licking his face. "Isn't that right, Bradley? Who's the best boy?" Cash's voice had turned to molasses as he spoke to the dog. He scratched behind his ears and accepted the puppy kisses graciously. Bradley Cooper was so excited he peed a little bit. *Me too, buddy. Me too.*

There was something about a man who was good with dogs and babies that was undeniably sexy. Thank God there weren't any babies in the vicinity for Cash to snuggle because my ovaries might have put him in a chokehold and held him hostage.

Finally, Cash rose to his feet and touched my shoulder. "It's good to see you."

"It's good to see you too." I averted my gaze to keep from throwing myself into his warm, strong arms.

His eyes crinkled with concern. "So, what's going on? You look like you've been crying."

"It's the washing machine," I said. "I think it's dead."

He chuckled. "Okay, let me take a look."

"I don't know what happened. I did what I always do," I explained as I led him to the laundry room. "But *this* happened."

We came to a stop just inside the room that looked like it was covered in snow. Thick bubbles continued to foam from the top of the agitated Maytag, creating a waterfall of soap.

Cash's eyes widened. "Oh, wow."

Bradley Cooper dove into the white fluff, nipping at the air.

I sighed. "I tried to turn the damn thing off, but it just

keeps going. I don't know what to do. It's too heavy for me to move to unplug it."

"Do you have any tools?" Cash grinned. "I'm going to need a wrench."

"Uh… yeah." I pointed to the top shelf where I kept Craig's old tools. They remained up there because they were basically useless in my hands.

He nodded and moved to retrieve the worn and dusty tool bag, his muscular arm extending above his head. After digging around the bag for a moment, he withdrew what I assumed was the tool he needed and sprinted from the room with Bradley Cooper yipping in his wake.

I followed him and watched out the window as he jogged outside near the street. He opened what looked like some sort of secret portal made of cement. Within seconds, the house fell silent. The washing machine had finally turned off. I was both relieved and crushed. It had taken its last breath without me.

He crossed the yard and came back inside, and I followed him back to the laundry room. I watched as he pulled the machine away from the wall with what looked like very little effort. He unplugged it and flashed me a satisfied smile as my eyes welled with tears.

"Hey," he said softly, moving toward me as Bradley Cooper danced at our feet. "It's just some bubbles. Don't worry. I'll help you clean it up."

"It's not that." I shook my head. "It's stupid. I'm crying over a fucking washing machine. Craig and I got this damn thing the night before I had Grace. The one that came with the house had died that morning, and I was panicked because I'd waited till the last minute to wash her newborn clothes. I had a meltdown right here." I pointed to the spot in front of the washer. "Because if I couldn't even wash my baby's clothes, how could I take care of her? I just knew I was going to be a terrible mom. Craig, being the saint he was, took me to Sears ten minutes before they closed. He bought this Maytag brand new and paid his buddy a hundred bucks to help him take it out of there that night just so I could wash Grace's baby clothes."

Cash gave me a wistful smile as he reached out and squeezed my arm.

"I ate pizza while he hooked these things up, and then he stayed up all night with me, making sure all of Grace's clothes were washed." The memory was vivid in my mind —the way he held me when I was just a pregnant heap on the floor. He laughed gently because, sure, he had a lot of doubts in the world. But my ability to be a good mother was never one of them. He never once doubted me or us.

"Well, the good news is that Maytag is gonna live to wash many more of Grace's clothes," Cash murmured. "Who knows—it could outlive both of us."

"What?" I sniffled. "But I thought—"

"It's just the inlet pressure valve."

"I'm going to pretend I know what that means."

He laughed. "A trip to the hardware store and I'll have your washing machine working again."

"Are you serious?" I asked, and he nodded. I threw my arms around him and felt tears of relief slip down my face. "Thank you, thank you, thank you."

He folded me in his arms. "What do you say we mop this up, and then we'll go to Home Depot and get the valve we need. Maybe pick up some dinner while we're out?"

"I'd like that," I said, but something was eating at me. If I was having a meltdown over a fucking washing machine because of the memories it held with my dead husband, was I *really* ready to date?

———

"HIS NAME WAS CASH? SERIOUSLY?" CASH ASKED incredulously as I swallowed the last bite of my orange chicken. We'd cleaned up the laundry room, gone to Home Depot, and picked up Chinese takeout on the way back. "That *was* a sign. But I like Bradley Cooper. A good name for a good boy. Right, Bradley?" Bradley Cooper huffed. "How'd you come up with it?"

I choked on a laugh. "You know who Bradley Cooper is, right? The super famous, *super hot* actor? "

Cash rubbed his hand along his jaw that was peppered with the perfect five o'clock shadow.

"The Hangover? Silver Linings Playbook?" I pressed my lips together, and he gave me a blank stare. *"A Star Is Born?"*

A look of recognition flashed across his face. "Oh yeah! I know that one. That 'Shallow' song was good."

I shook my head and grinned. "We've got to work on your pop culture knowledge. You work with famous people, for crying out loud. You never know when Bradley Cooper will call, and if he does, I better be the first person you tell."

Bradley Cooper whined and settled near our feet at the bright, coral kitchen table.

"Deal." He stood and grabbed my empty container, piling it on top of his, and tossed them in the trash bin near the back door. "Now, let's go fix this washing machine." He extended his hand to me and pulled me to my feet.

His hand was warm when he laced his fingers through mine. Bradley Cooper trailed behind us as Cash guided me back to the laundry room. Once inside, he released my hand and reached for the tool bag we'd left on the floor by the washer.

"You're a man of many talents, Cash," I said, leaning

against the door frame. "You can sing, you can dance, *and* you can rescue a damsel who's in distress over a washing machine. What can't you do?"

He smiled at me over his shoulder as he set to work on the washer, screwdriver in hand. "Identify any celebrity in a lineup."

"Accurate." I craned my neck slightly to get a better view of his forearms at work. His muscles flexed and tightened, and I could see the outline of his bicep with each twist of the screwdriver. "Thank you for doing this, by the way. Not just for being here and fixing it, but for not thinking I was a weirdo for being upset over a stupid washing machine."

His eyes found mine. "It's not weird at all. I get it. I think we often take for granted how many memories live inside everyday things. For me, it was this red tea kettle Carrie used. I never had a taste for tea, but she loved it. She had an entire drawer devoted to these exotics teas. Smelled like a damn jar of potpuri. Every night, she made a cup of tea before bed. The sound of that kettle whistling was like nails on a chalkboard to me. But I'd kill to hear it again."

"You never boil water in it, you know, just to hear it?"

He shook his head. "I keep the kettle on the stove. Even though Carrie never lived in this house, having that beat-up old kettle on the stove somehow makes it feel more like home."

"Was it hard? Leaving the home you shared together?" I asked.

He chewed his lip thoughtfully. "Yes and no. Yes because everywhere I looked, I saw her there."

"And no?"

"Because everywhere I looked, I saw her there."

It felt like a hand had closed tight around my heart. "I

still see Craig here too. Honestly, I've thought about moving dozens of times. I hate keeping up the yard, and when Grace does decide to break my heart and permanently leave the nest, this will be more house than I really need. But I don't think I'll ever be able to bring myself to move. This house is one of the few things Grace has left of her dad. I want her to always have this to come back to."

Cash gave me an empathetic smile. "It's important to have things or places or even people that we can visit when we need to be reminded of those we lost. I'm still close to my in-laws. My dad died in a car accident when I was seven, and my mom... well, she never really bounced back from that. She started drinking, and at first, she hid it well. But by the time I turned thirteen, I was coming home from school and cooking dinner for us both. I had to wake her up so she could get to work on time. By the time I went to college, she couldn't hold down a job for more than six months at a time. My junior year of college she got diagnosed with cirrhosis of the liver. She passed a year after I graduated."

"I'm so sorry, Cash," I said. "Did you have any other family?"

"No siblings and my aunt and uncle really washed their hands of my mom, and by default, me. My grandparents passed when I was little. So, when Carrie and I got married, her family kind of took me in."

"That's really sweet. What are they like?"

He grinned. "Her dad, Richard, is a high school principal, and her mom, Delilah is actually a romance novelist. Or she was. She's retired now."

"No way! Wait... romance novelist... Delilah..." My eyes widened. "Is your mother-in-law Delilah Davis?"

"That's her. Do you read her stuff?"

"I definitely read a few of her books growing up, but that's because my mom loves—um, loved her." I could picture my mom curled up on the couch with one of her treasured romance novels, worn and dog-eared. "She doesn't really read anymore. She has Alzheimer's."

Cash's forehead wrinkled with concern. "Damn, Ella. I'm sorry. She… she's got to be so young, though, right?"

I nodded. "It was early onset."

"And your dad?"

"He passed eight years ago. Heart attack." I gave him a wistful smile. "I'm an only child too, so it's just Mom, Grace, and me. And now Bradley Cooper, of course."

"I can't imagine how hard that's been for you."

I shrugged. "It has been. But it was harder back when dad was alive when I had to watch him go through this as her husband. When you take vows and say that whole 'for better or worse' thing, you hope that worse won't ever come. You hope that your 'worse' will have a little mercy on you. For my dad, worse was reminding my mom of who he was when she forgot. Until even worse came and he had to remind her of who *she* was when she forgot."

He placed the screwdriver on top of the closed washer and crossed the room until he was standing in front of me. Bradley Cooper looked up at us from his spot on the floor, and Cash placed a hand on my arm.

"I was always in awe of what he did. He never once lost his patience. He never complained about the hand they'd been dealt." I looked down at my feet, twisting the sole of my shoe into the checkered tile. "One day, I asked him how he did it all without falling apart. He said on the good days it was like he had his wife back and no time had passed. On the bad days, he said he got to spend hours just reliving their lives together and reminiscing about the woman he fell in love with. He told me it was a small price to pay for the love of a lifetime."

"I would have to agree with him," Cash said softly. "Getting to hold the hand of someone you love when it feels like the world is falling apart is… well, it's a privilege."

"It is." I swallowed hard as I looked up into his warm face. I paused a moment, unsure of the question I was about to ask or why I was asking it. "Would you want to do it again? Even knowing what you know now?"

He cocked his head to the side as though he were thinking, and sadness flickered in his hazel eyes. "After Carrie passed, the idea of falling in love again felt about as likely as getting struck by lightning twice. I didn't believe it was possible. But lately…" His words trailed off, but he held me tight within his gaze.

It was like every bit of moisture left my mouth all at once. I wanted to speak, to say something, *anything*, but it seemed that my words had dried up too. The space between us dissipated as his hand found my cheek, and the smoothness of his thumb stroked my skin.

I wanted to kiss him, though I was also hyperaware of the fact that this man had witnessed me have a breakdown over an appliance and everything it meant to me. But it didn't scare him off or weird him out. He'd understood, and that made him even sexier, which was no easy task considering how fucking amazing his forearms were.

"Lately?" I prodded him to finish his sentence.

"Lately I feel like I have something to believe in." He pressed his forehead to mine, and the warm of his breath sent electricity through my veins. "Ella, I know you said you needed some time to think things over, and I want to respect your wishes. But I really want to kiss you right now. Is that okay?"

I nodded, and his lips touched mine, soft as a whisper.

I wanted to launch myself at him like a spider monkey. I wanted to wrap my legs around his waist, tangle my hands in his hair, and let him carry me to my bedroom. But I kept both feet planted firmly on the ground.

Maybe it was because I wasn't ready for whatever this thing with Cash was, or maybe it was because I had something worth believing in too.

All I knew was that if I was going to jump in with both feet, I wanted to be sure.

TWELVE

Cash

I WOKE TO WHAT FELT LIKE AN ICE CUBE ON MY ARM followed by a soft whine. When I rolled over, I nearly fell off the couch and directly onto Bradley Cooper who was watching me expectantly through eyelashes that looked like they belonged on a muppet. I blinked a few times and registered that I was in Ella's living room. A colorful throw blanket I hadn't seen before was tucked around me, and Ella was nowhere to be seen. She must have woken in the night and gone to her bed, but not before covering me up and turning the television off.

The night before started to replay in my mind, hazy like the morning sun. After we had dinner and I'd finished repairing the washing machine, Ella made some popcorn, and we started a Bradley Cooper movie marathon. She was insistent upon educating me on all things pop culture, and she felt that Bradley Cooper was where we needed to start. We'd laughed our way through *The Hangover* and kissed through *Silver Linings Playbook*. By the time we started the one where his friend gave him a pill that made him a genius, Ella had snuggled into my chest, and soon we fell asleep.

Something felt different between us. When we'd kissed in the laundry room, it was as though some invisible barrier had been removed. It felt like Ella might be open to seeing what we could be. The first night we were together felt like an explosion, but it seemed that initial fire had become a slow and steady blaze.

Bradley Cooper pulled me from my thoughts with a dissatisfied huff as he touched his nose to my arm again.

I reached out and ruffled the wiry hair atop his head before grabbing my phone from the end table. The screen illuminated to show that it was a little after seven a.m. "You need to go out, Bradley Cooper?"

He gave one quick, sharp bark. I never had a dog of my own before, but I took that bark to mean he needed to go out.

"Okay, okay," I whispered. "I'll take you. Let your mom sleep." I tossed the blanket off of me, and Bradley bolted through the house, paws clicking against the hardwood. I shoved my phone in my pocket and moved quietly behind him until I found him in the kitchen waiting at the back door.

He scratched his paw against the wood.

"Alright, buddy." I opened the door, and he darted out into the grass. I watched from the back porch as he did his business before bounding back to me. "Good boy."

We went back inside, and the scruffy pup immediately ran to his empty food bowl and gave an annoyed snort.

"You're ready for some breakfast, huh, bud?" I glanced around the cozy kitchen in search of the dog's kibble. I moved quietly to a narrow door on the other side of the refrigerator that I assumed was the pantry and opened it.

"Jackpot." A clear container sat on the floor inside the pantry, and I could see before I even removed the top that it was filled nearly to the brim with dog food.

Bradley Cooper turned in a circle and whined as I popped open the plastic lid.

"Hang on a second, buddy," I said, taking the scoop from the container and filling it. The dog's paws skittered happily against the floor as I carried the food across the room and dumped it in his bowl. He lapped it up eagerly, sending bits of kibble flying across the floor. "Now, to make some breakfast for your mom."

With Bradley Cooper occupied, I scanned the kitchen counter for the coffeemaker and set to work locating the filters and coffee grounds. Once I got the coffee brewing, I opened the stainless steel fridge and spotted some eggs and turkey bacon. I pulled my phone from my pocket and found my favorite Frank Sinatra playlist, setting it to play softly as I located the skillets and removed them from the cabinets, careful not to make much noise. While the bacon was frying and the eggs were cooking, I retrieved some wheat bread from the pantry and popped a couple of pieces in the toaster.

I was humming along to "I've Got You Under My Skin" when the coffee finished percolating. I pulled a couple of oversized mugs from the cabinet above the coffeemaker. One said 'BUT FIRST COFFEE' and the other said 'THERE'S PROBABLY WINE IN HERE.' Chuckling, I poured coffee into both. I breathed in the smell of hazelnut and maple as I brought one of the mugs to my lips and took a sip.

Bradley Cooper finished his breakfast, licking up every morsel he spilled onto the floor before watching me locate the plates and silverware. His big brown eyes widened as I transferred the food to the plates.

"Don't look at me like I didn't just feed you," I said with a laugh. He watched as I retrieved the half and half from the fridge and poured it into Ella's mug. "Your mom said she likes her coffee with more cream than coffee." The dog's ears perked as though I'd told him a secret. I examined the liquid in the cup that had gone from black to the color of a vanilla milkshake. "That should do it. What do you think, Bradley Cooper?" He cocked his head to the side and let out a soft yelp. "I'll take that as your approval."

"What's all this?" Ella's voice came from the entryway to the kitchen, still raspy with sleep. She wore a matching sleep set with an avocado print and the words 'GUAC IS EXTRA AND SO AM I' in big letters across the front. Even with her hair messy and a pillow indentation across her forehead, she made my heart skip a beat.

I glanced at the clock that read seven twenty-eight a.m. "Well, I was about to bring you breakfast in bed, but I know you don't like it before seven thirty. Coffee?" I extended her mug of nearly white coffee toward her.

"God yes." She padded across the kitchen in her fuzzy pink slippers and grabbed the mug, taking a long swig. Her head leaned back, and she closed her eyes as she let out a satisfied breath. "Thank you."

"You're welcome," I said as she smiled at me. "Good morning." I reached for her hand and slowly intertwined our fingers, unable to keep my mind from thinking about all of the hills and valleys of her body that my hands wanted to explore.

She nestled herself into my arms, still maintaining a firm grip on her coffee mug. "You remembered how I like my coffee."

"Did I put enough cream in there?"

"It's perfect. I could get used to this." Ella sighed. "A Saturday off and breakfast that doesn't resemble cold pizza or a hot pocket."

I chuckled and kissed her forehead gently. "Come on. Let's eat before it gets cold."

"I just need to feed Bradley Cooper and let him out real quick."

"Already done," I said. "Don't let that cute face fool you. He had his breakfast before I even started on ours."

The dog huffed and plopped onto the floor as though he were annoyed that I'd just ratted him out.

We took our breakfast and coffee to the table and ate quietly under close surveillance from Bradley Cooper. Ella's fluffy-slippered foot gently rubbed my leg. It was the kind of gesture that would make you think we did this every day and that we'd be doing it every day after. It both comforted and scared the shit out of me that being with Ella felt so easy.

The sound of the song "Baby Got Back" blared from down the hall, piercing through the silence.

Ella's eyes lit up. "That's Liv. I'm gonna grab that."

"Of course," I said as she sprinted from the room.

I could hear Ella's voice as it floated back towards me. "Hey, Mom of The Year! How's it... what? Liv, I can't understand you. You've got to calm down." Ella reappeared in the entryway, her brow furrowed. "Where's Jax? Is Brady there? Are you and the kids safe? Sweetheart, I can't understand what you're saying. Someone got in the house? *Something?* The cat did what? Is she okay?" Ella's voice was shrill with alarm, and before I knew it, I was on my feet and in front of her. "It's going to be okay, Liv. I'll come to you. Hello? Liv? Liv, are you there?" She pulled the phone away from her ear and looked over at me with terror in her eyes. "I've got to go. Something's wrong with Liv."

My stomach twisted with worry. "I'll go with you." I jogged to the living room to put my shoes on.

"I need pants," Ella shouted and ran from the room, emerging only a moment later wearing jeans and her pajama shirt. She nearly toppled over as she quickly stuffed her feet into a pair of leopard printed slides.

"What's going on?" I asked.

She shook her head. "All I could make out was that she and the kids were hiding in a closet. She was hysterical, and her phone died. Jax is gone, and I don't think she can reach him. I'm going to try." She quickly tapped across her screen and put the phone back to her ear as we ran to my Range Rover parked out front. After a few seconds, she dropped the phone back to her side. "No answer."

I sucked in a deep breath, fear gnawing at my insides as I put the car in drive. Liv was Ella's best friend, but she was also like a sister to me. "I'll get us there as fast as I can."

Other than Ella's frantic attempts to reach Jax, we made the drive in a worried silence. She grabbed my hand at some point during the drive that felt like an hour despite the fact that I was driving like I belonged on the track at NASCAR. Every couple of minutes Ella gave my hand a squeeze.

When we finally made it to Liv's about twenty-five minutes later, Ella launched herself from the car before I'd even fully put it in park. "Liv! I'm coming, Liv!'

I cut the engine and jumped out, sprinting to catch up with Ella who had already pushed her key into the lock of Liv's front door and shoved her way inside.

"Ella, please. Let me go in there first." I caught up to

her and gripped her arm. "There could be an intruder or—"

"Liv!" Ella screeched. "Where are you?" She looked around the expansive living room and ran to the fireplace where she snatched a fire poker. She held it with two hands as though it were a baseball bat as she tore up the stairs with me on her heels.

"Ella," I whispered loudly. "Stop." I held a finger to my lips, as a rustling sound came from further down the hall. Before I could step ahead of her, Ella had already begun to creep slowly toward the noise. She gripped the fire poker, holding it closer to her chest. I was right behind her when a door flung open at the end of the hall. Ella screamed, and I jumped in front of her.

"Stand down," I boomed, and the sound of a wailing baby filled the air.

"Cash? Is that you?" I heard Liv's voice before she peeked her tear-streaked face around the door.

I pulled the door the rest of the way open to reveal Liv holding a crying toddler. A small boy who appeared to be about four or five was hiding behind her legs, trembling.

"Liv!" Ella pushed past me and ran to Liv's side, pulling her and the screaming baby into her arms. "Are you okay?"

"I'm sorry," Liv choked out. "I freaked out. Jax and Brady went to pick up the furniture we had made for the kids' rooms. We found this couple that custom makes furniture, but they're over an hour away. He wanted to get an early start while they were still asleep, but they woke up no sooner than he pulled out of the driveway. And then—"

Mama, Liv's ornery rescue cat, bolted past us toward the end of the hall with something in her mouth.

Liv startled, which caused the baby to shriek even louder. "Mama," she hissed at the cat who paid her no attention. "Mama brought a mouse in the playroom. I was in there with the kids, and I screamed and, well, it's been about like this since it happened."

Ella scrunched her nose. "A dead mouse?"

The little boy behind her started to cry, and Liv instinctively reached to comfort him.

"It's *very* much alive. I freaked out, and that made the kids freak out because things are a little..." Liv trailed off and gulped.

"Oh shit." Ella said and then seemed to remember there were young ears among us. "I mean, snickerdoodles. Oh snickerdoodles."

"It's going to be okay," I assured her. "We'll get it out of here. The room is down here?" I pointed in the direction Mama had scampered off to.

Liv nodded. "Thank you. I'm so sorry. I panicked."

"It's okay, babe." Ella squeezed her friend's arm. "Take the kiddos downstairs, and we'll figure out how to get it out of here."

"See?" Liv's voice was soft as she spoke to the kids. "My friends Ella and Cash have come to help. Everything is going to be alright." She gathered the distressed children and started down the hall. "Let's go get some juice."

I raised my brow at Ella, a grin tugging at the corners of my mouth. "You ready for this?"

"If I can take on a Chad, I can handle a measly mouse in my sleep." She flicked her golden hair over her shoulder and went in search of Mama and the mouse.

We reached the end of the hall and on the right was the playroom, that was still very much a work in progress. Mama was in the middle of the floor with the mouse in her mouth. It gave off a high-pitched screech to let us know it was, in fact, still alive and well. I closed the door behind us, and without warning, Mama released the mouse and swatted it with her paw.

The mouse was flung across the room, and Mama watched for a second before raising her back leg up to clean herself.

Ella rolled her eyes. "Seriously, Mama?"

A box of blocks to my left caught my eye, and I ripped the top from it, scattering the blocks on the floor. I held on to the box and advanced in the direction the mouse had scurried off to.

"Maybe I can corner it and trap it in here," I said. "Guard the door so we can keep it from getting out into the rest of the house."

"I can play goalie." She clapped her hands together. "Mickey, your ass is grass."

I spotted the tiny grey blob as it scuttled across the floor. Every time I got close, it managed to weave its way under a piece of furniture.

"This is not going well," I said as I waited for the mouse to pop out from beneath the toy chest.

Ella grabbed for one of the blocks I'd scattered and sent it sailing toward the chest which was enough to get Mama interested again. She began to paw under the chest, and another screech sounded through the room as it ran past my feet. I pounced on it and slammed the box on the floor, narrowly missing it. The shock, however, was enough to send the mouse fleeing in Ella's direction.

"Shit, shit, shit!" Ella shrieked before lunging at the floor with her hand poised like one of those claws inside an overpriced arcade game. "I got it! Oh shit. I got it!" She cupped her hands together to contain the tiny rodent. "Now what the fuck do I do with it?"

"Shit," I exclaimed, running to her and opening the

door. She screeched and darted down the hall with the mouse in her hands and me close behind.

"So help me, if you shit in my hand, Mickey, I will burn down the entire *Mickey Mouse Clubhouse*," Ella bellowed as we bolted down the stairs. She ran past Liv and the kids who were still crying and flung herself through the front door. I watched from the front steps as she ran several feet out into the grass and sent Mickey sailing through the air.

THIRTEEN

Ella

I WATCHED AS THE LITTLE GREY MOUSE RAN FOR HIS LIFE, and then I looked at my hands, suddenly remembering that the germ-covered rodent had been there only seconds before. "Ew, ew, ew, ew!"

Cash's laughter roared as I sprinted back toward the house. I ran past him, Liv, and the kids, and I didn't stop until I reached the kitchen sink where I proceeded to wash my hands until they resembled the color of a lobster.

"I... can't believe... you did that," Cash spat out as his shoulders shook. By then, Liv had dissolved into a fit of giggles, the baby had settled, and the little boy was miming my mouse-throwing curveball with a fruit snacks wrapper, cracking himself up.

I laughed. "I could have a lucrative future in organic pest control if this whole bakery thing doesn't pan out."

"I'll make sure to call if we get another mouse," Liv said before raising her brow at me. "Or spider crickets."

I shook my head. "Oh hell no. Never again. I still have stress dreams about those things."

Liv's smile stretched across her face.

"Spider crickets?" Cash asked.

The little boy's interest was piqued. "Did they jump really, really high?"

"They sure did." Liv nodded. "They're crickets that look like spiders, but they jump just like regular crickets."

"But instead of jumping away from you, they jump *at* you." I used my hand to mimic a spider jumping onto Cash's shoulder, and the little boy scrunched his nose.

Cash shuddered.

"So, imagine you're in the shower and you see a spider on the wall, but when you go to smush it, it jumps at your face." I emphasized the last part as though I were telling a scary story.

"Ew!" The boy half shrieked, half giggled.

"And Ella here basically made a Hazmat suit out of a bikini, plastic wrap, and a snorkel mask, and she went in there with bug spray and one of those bug bombs." Liv gripped my arm as we both erupted with laughter from the memory.

"It was so bad we had to rent a hotel room for three days," I recalled.

"The real question is, do you have any pictures of the Hazmat suit?" Cash's eyes flickered over to mine.

I cleared my throat. "Thankfully, the only pictures that exist are in Liv's mind."

Liv beamed. "But the memories will last a lifetime."

"Livvie, can I have more juice?" The boy tugged at the hem of Liv's shirt.

"Of course," she answered, moving to the fridge with the baby still balanced on her hip. She pulled out a juice box and placed it in the child's waiting hands before directing her attention back to Cash and me. "You guys want anything?"

Cash shook his head.

"I'm good," I replied.

"Let's take your sister in the living room, and you guys can watch some *Paw Patrol*," Liv said, and the little boy squealed with excitement.

We followed Liv into the living room and settled on the plush sofa as she turned on the television for the kids, placing the toddler on a blanket beside her brother. Both children fell quiet as the cartoon began playing on the screen. The living room that had once looked like it could be featured in a magazine spread was now scattered with toys and sippy cups. My stomach flip flopped at the realization that this place that had once felt so familiar to me now looked like it belonged to someone else entirely.

"That will give us a solid thirty minutes." Liv sat in the oversized blue wingback chair with a relieved sigh. "Seriously, thank you so much for coming. I don't know what I would have done without you guys."

"Of course, babe," I said. "Cash was doing some serious *Fast and the Furious* driving on the way over here. Just call him Vin Diesel."

"Who's that?" Cash asked.

"Wait." Liv's brows knitted together. "Didn't I call Ella? How did I get both of you?"

Shit. Damn. Fuck. "The stars must have aligned so that we could both be here. The washer overflowed, and Cash came to help me. Bradley Cooper and I were in a state of despair."

Liv narrowed her eyes at me, and it took everything in me not to squirm beneath her questioning gaze.

"I'd called Ella to check on her because I knew she was probably missing Grace," Cash explained.

"Right," I said, "and the washer was vomiting bubbles, and I was having a bit of a meltdown."

"So, I came over to help," Cash added with a smile that I think was supposed to be reassuring, but looked more like a child that got caught with his hand in the cookie jar.

Liv looked from me to Cash, then back to me. "Bradley Cooper? Like *the actor*?"

"Oh." I laughed nervously. "I haven't gotten a chance to tell you yet. Well, you see, it's a funny story. I got a dog."

Liv's mouth fell open. "A dog. *You* got a dog. When?"

"A little over a week ago," I replied, shifting in my seat, suddenly feeling very hot.

Liv blinked slowly and pressed her lips together.

I slid my hands beneath my thighs to keep from fidgeting as I launched into the story. "I was just feeling really lonely with Grace gone, and the house was too damn quiet, so I called Derek to go with me to the shelter an—"

"You asked Derek to go with you?" Liv's face fell, her mouth turned down into a soft frown.

"I mean, you've had your hands full, and it wasn't that big of a big deal," I said with the wave of my hand. "It was a spur of the moment thing."

Liv chewed her lip a moment and nodded.

I cleared my throat, desperate to cut through the silence that permeated the air. I dug my phone out of my pocket and found a picture where Bradley Cooper looked at the camera with his mouth open in what looked like a smile. "This is him."

"Wow." Liv nodded. A small smile spread across her mouth, but it didn't quite reach her eyes. "Well, he sure is a cutie. So, his name is Bradley Cooper?"

"Actually, his name was Cash." I felt Cash's eyes on me, but I kept my focus on Liv. "But we couldn't have two of those around here. I mean, how weird would that have been?" An awkward laugh bubbled out of my throat. "I would have been like, 'Cash, don't pee on the rug. Cash, quit humping my leg.' That would have been, uh..." I swallowed and nearly choked on my own spit. "Anyway, I thought Bradley Cooper was a good name because then I could be like, 'Oh, sorry, I can't tonight. I have to get home to Bradley Cooper.'"

Cash's face twitched with amusement as he leaned forward so that his elbows rested on his knees. His hands were clasped together so tight that his knuckles turned white. "Yeah, if you said you had to get home to Cash, that could get confusing."

Way to play it cool, Cash. I chewed on the inside of my cheek. "Exactly. So confusing. But he's the cutest dog. You're going to love him. He's so sweet, and he loves long walks and eating my shoes. Anyway, enough about my status as a dog mom. Tell us about the kids."

Liv's eyes rested on me for a moment before she started to speak. "It's weird how your life can change in the blink of an eye. With one decision, you can be living what feels like a completely different life. For so long, I thought the possibility of being a mom was behind me, but now, with Chloe and Jonathan... It's like living in a dream I never truly let myself believe was possible."

"Chloe and Jonathan." Cash repeated their names, beaming with pride.

Liv shook her head, pressing her palm to her face. "I'm so sorry, Cash. I just realized we hadn't even told you their names yet. I've been kind of a mess."

"You don't have anything to apologize for," Cash assured her. "You've got a lot going on."

"How are they adjusting?" I asked. "How are you and Jax doing?"

"They've had a hard go of it, but they're so resilient. I think they're happy here. I hope they are." Liv's eyes moved to where Chloe and Jonathan giggled in front of the television. "Jax is a natural. He was meant to be a dad. But I... I don't know. I worry I'm doing something wrong. What if I'm not a good mom?"

"Honey, I still feel that way, and Grace is nineteen." I reached over and squeezed her knee. "I promise. All parents feel like this. None of us know what we're doing."

"It's more than that." She sighed. "I feel myself holding back."

"How so?" Cash furrowed his brow.

"A lot can happen in this situation." Liv shrugged. "Just because we have them now doesn't mean we'll get to keep them. The closer I get to them, the more it will hurt if we lose them. It's this endless cycle that keeps me up at night. What if their birth mom comes back in the picture? Am I a horrible person if there's part of me that hopes she doesn't?"

"Honey, no." I shook my head. "That doesn't make you horrible."

"It makes you human," Cash added gently.

"You care about these kids," I said. "You want what's best for them, and honestly, I can't imagine what it feels like with that constant fear hanging over your head. But what I do know is you'll never regret giving them all of you. Even if you only get to give them all of you for a short time, you're going to be as much of a gift to them as they are to you."

My own words echoed through my mind as I looked over at Cash whose eyes rested on me. Before I could consider what that meant, my thoughts were interrupted by the sound of Chloe's cries.

"Hey now," Liv cooed as she rushed to pick up the toddler. "Oh, I think someone needs a diaper change. Sorry, guys. I'll just be a minute."

"Actually, we should probably head out," I said. "I need to go check on things over at the bakery, and uh, Cash still has to drop me off at my house."

"Right." Cash nodded. "We should probably go then."

Chloe wailed as Jonathan sang along to a song that played on the cartoon.

"You go take care of that sweet baby. We'll let ourselves out, and I'll lock the door behind me." Cash and I rose to our feet, and I pulled Liv into a brief hug while Chloe squalled.

"Thank you both for coming." Liv said, kissing me on the cheek. "Seriously, you guys are lifesavers."

"Anytime." Cash squeezed her shoulder.

"Tell Mama to stop being a little b-i-t-c-h." I grinned as I spelled out the word.

"Jonathan, come take a potty break while I change your sister." Liv grabbed the remote, bringing the show to a freeze frame. She held out her hand to the boy. "I paused the show, and you can finish it in a minute. Say bye to Ella and Cash."

Jonathan reluctantly took her hand. "Bye Ella. Bye Cash."

"Bye, buddy." Cash waved at him.

"Love y'all," Liv said over her shoulder as she steered the little boy from the room with Chloe howling in her arms. "Thanks again."

"Love you too," I said as she disappeared from the room.

I turned to Cash who shoved his hands in his pockets. "Ready?"

He followed me out the front door, and I locked it behind us. "That was a close one, huh?"

Cash nodded, but didn't say anything else as we started down the walk. When we got to the car, Cash placed his hand on the passenger door handle. "You know, you were right back there."

"About what?"

"What you said to Liv." He tucked a piece of hair behind my ear. "About how even if you're afraid of losing someone, you'll never regret giving them all of you."

I opened my mouth to say something, but no words came out. Instead, I kissed his cheek as he unlocked the door for me. As we made the drive back to my house, I laced my fingers through his and wondered if maybe, just maybe, I was right.

FOURTEEN

Cash

"Thanks again for going with me." Ella squeezed my hand as we pulled to a stop in front of her house. "And for saving my washing machine. And for breakfast. You're kind of my own personal hero. Like Captain America but with *way* more useful skills."

I chuckled. "And what skills do I have that could possibly be better than Captain America's?"

She unbuckled her seat belt without removing her hand from mine. "I mean, I don't think Captain America is doing things like replacing inlet valves or making breakfast."

"Because he's too busy saving innocent people from the bad guys." I unbuckled as well and opened my door as she started fishing her keys out of her bag. "That's a pretty epic life skill."

"That's fair," she replied, "but I'd rather eat. If the bad guys come for me, I already know I'm going to die. I probably had it coming anyway. Just let them kill me, but let me eat first."

I laughed as I rounded the SUV and opened the door

for her. "So, the way to your heart is through your stomach?"

"Absolutely. Especially now that Liv's all husbanded up and Grace is out of the country. Who do you think has fed me all these years?"

"You don't ever cook?" I asked as we meandered up the walkway.

She shook her head. "The kitchen is mostly just for show. My signature dishes include lightly charred pizza rolls and anything UberEats delivers." Ella grinned at me as we came to a stop at her front door. "So…"

"So," I repeated, a smile spreading across my lips as I shoved my hands in my pockets. "It almost feels like I'm dropping you off after a date."

She pressed her lips together and tucked a piece of hair behind her ear. "There *was* a shared meal, and that whole mouse thing was as good as any movie I've ever been to. It was practically dinner and a show."

I raised my brow at her. "Not quite, but I'd like to change that. Will you let me take you to dinner?"

She laughed softly and beamed at me, which was enough to make my knees feel like they'd been turned to goo. "I love that you just asked me if I'd *let* you, as though it's an honor to be in my presence."

"It is," I said simply.

Her eyes sparkled and settled on me as she appeared to consider my question. Finally, she nodded. "I'd like that. When?"

"Tomorrow night? Tonight? Right now?"

"It's not even ten a.m."

"It's five o'clock somewhere."

"Even five o'clock is too early for dinner," she quipped.

"Unless, of course, you're eighty and going for the senior special at Captain D's."

"I'd eat dinner with you anytime, anywhere. Even at Captain D's."

"I'd low-key throw down some of that battered fish. And those hush puppies?"

I choked on a laugh.

"Tonight would be great," she said.

"I'll pick you up at four thirty so we can make our five p.m. reservation at Captain D's," I joked.

"Listen, don't threaten me with a good time."

"How's six thirty?"

"Perfect," she replied. "Should I pack some wet naps for all the fish grease?"

"I'm thinking of something a little nicer since it's our first date and all."

Her eyes widened. "Our first date. Wow. This is... this is happening."

"As long as you're comfortable with it. I don't want you to do anything you don't want to do."

"No, no," she said quickly. "I do. Want to, I mean. I'm just... weirdly nervous. Even though it's not like you haven't already seen me naked. Not that you're going to see me naked tonight. That's not what I meant. Not that I wouldn't want you to see me naked, because then I'd also get to see you naked, but—"

"Ella—"

"Actually, I'm going to stop talking, and I'll see you tonight."

I grinned. "Okay."

With that, she squeezed my arm before shoving her key in the lock and disappearing inside.

I BLEW OUT A BREATH AS I APPRAISED MY REFLECTION IN THE full length mirror of my bedroom for the hundredth time. Ella wasn't the only one who was nervous about our date. I'd changed shirts at least half a dozen times, and I was so excited that I'd managed to get ready almost a full hour early.

"You act like you've never been on a date before," I said to my face in the mirror. "It's just a date."

Even as the words left my mouth, I knew they weren't true. This was my first since I'd lost Carrie, and it wasn't just any date. It's not like I got back out there and had a practice run before going out with someone I really cared about. No, instead I'd done a swan dive off into the deep end of the pool without knowing if I still knew how to swim.

All I knew was how good it felt to be around Ella and how much she made me laugh. Being with her was… easy. Exhilarating. Comfortable. For so long I'd been drowning in grief, but Ella was like coming up for that first gulp of fresh air after being sucked beneath the currents.

My phone rang from where it was plugged in on the nightstand, pulling me from my thoughts. I crossed the room to grab it and smiled when I saw the name that flashed across the screen.

"Delilah," I answered. "How are you?"

"Cash, it's so good to hear your voice," my mother-in-law said. Her voice had that slight echo that told me I was on speaker.

"How are you, son?" my father-in-law asked before I could say anything else.

"Richard's here," Delilah informed me.

"What's the weather like there, son? It's hotter than a billy goat's ass in a pepper patch here," he said.

"*Richard*," Delilah scolded him.

"What?" he asked. "It's the truth."

I laughed as I listened to them bicker for a moment. My chest tightened when I realized how much I missed them. It had been a little over six months since I'd been able to visit, and in that moment, I felt every single day.

"Anyway, as you can see, some things never change." Delilah chuckled. "But how are you, dear?"

"I'm good," I replied. "Work has been busy, but it always is. Even with Midnight in Dallas off the road, there's always plenty to do. One of my artists is on tour over in England right now."

"It's that Sam fellow, isn't it?" she asked.

"That's the one," I said.

"Ah, yes. Didn't that lovely young girl who works with you go? Grace?" I could practically hear Delilah's smile through the phone.

"She did," I answered. "How did you know?"

"Grace told me. Anytime I call you at the office, I always talk to Grace. She's just the sweetest thing. I can tell she really loves working for you."

I cleared my throat. "I love having her. The office is too quiet without her."

"I know you must miss her," Delilah said. "But enough about work, how are *you*? Are you doing okay?"

"I always tell Delilah that if you weren't doing well that you'd call us, but she doesn't listen to me," Richard piped in.

"Let him answer the question, Richard," Delilah hissed.

I coughed to stifle a laugh. "Actually... I'm doing really well."

"You sound better than you have in months," Delilah said. "Happy, even."

Richard's voice sounded farther away this time. "I've told you, he's a good egg, that Cash. Always got his shit together. Isn't that what I always say, Delilah?"

"*Richard,*" Delilah fussed. "Anyway, Cash, you've been on our minds. You always are. You know we love you like a son."

"He knows that, Delilah." Richard's voice was muffled by a repetitious *thock, thock, thock* sound.

"Richard, must you do that right now?" Delilah asked incredulously.

"The Millers will be here for dinner in half an hour," Richard replied. "This salad isn't going to put itself together, woman."

I covered the mouthpiece of the phone and snickered. "You two go get ready for your dinner. We can catch up later."

"I told you we should have called tomorrow when we had more time," Richard said.

"I know what you said, Richard." Delilah sounded both amused and exasperated. "But something just told me I needed to talk to him today."

"Delilah got one of her *feelings* again today." Richard's voice had come back close again. "I need to go fire up the grill, so I'm going to leave you to Delilah. You take care now, son. We'll talk soon. Come see us when you can."

"Will do, Richard," I said.

A few seconds later it was so quiet I thought that perhaps Delilah had accidentally hung up.

"I swear that man drives me up a wall sometimes." Delilah laughed. "But I sure do love him. And I love you, and we miss you."

"I miss you both too." My throat tightened. "I promise I'll get down to see you soon."

"Don't you worry about that. You come whenever you're able." She was quiet for a moment, before she finally spoke. "I know Richard thinks I'm crazy, and maybe that's true. But you know how I am. I get those feelings sometimes. It's like a little birdie in my ear that gives me messages that don't always make sense."

I knew those feelings well. She always seemed to know about things before they happened, like when I came to ask for their permission to propose to Carrie. She answered the question before I even asked. When I'd made the choice to start Carrie On Records, she called because something told her to call and congratulate me, though she wasn't sure why.

"You know Carrie wanted nothing more than for you to be happy, right?" Delilah finally said. "Even if she couldn't be here to see it, all she wanted was for you to be happy."

My eyes stung, and my throat felt thick. "I know."

There was silence on the other end, and for a moment I thought she already knew about Ella somehow. "You really do sound good, Cash. Whatever you're doing, keep doing it."

I took a deep breath. "I will. I promise I will."

Though Delilah always seemed connected to the world on a totally different plane of existence, I wasn't sure if I believed it was possible for me to receive messages from the universe or the Great Beyond. And maybe Delilah's call wasn't a message. Maybe it was just a coincidence.

But it sure felt like a sign that I was on the right path.

FIFTEEN

Ella

"AND THEN THE GOAT *SHIT* ON ME," I EXPLAINED, RELIVING the Nightmare on Goat Street that was Liv's bachelorette party. We'd just been seated at Moto Cucina, a gorgeous Italian restaurant over on McGavock Street and were waiting for our server. "They literally gave me a shirt that said that."

Cash laughed. "And are you going to wear it?"

"Obviously," I said, glancing over the menu in an effort to stop salivating over how hot Cash looked in his charcoal-grey suit jacket. "I need everyone to know just how inconvenienced I was."

"You're not the least bit bitter," he teased.

"I still have stress dreams about that goat, Cash." I glanced up from my menu with a smirk, smoothing my hands over my little black dress. "I've been scarred for life."

He chuckled, surveying his menu while I scanned the room. It was dimly lit by soft globe lights that extended from the ceiling, and the walnut bar and seating gave the place a warm, cozy feel. On either side of us sat couples sharing bottles of wine, deep in conversation, seemingly oblivious to the world around them. My eyes were drawn back to Cash who was somehow even more gorgeous in the glow of the flickering votive that sat at the center of the table.

"This place is nice," I commented, tearing my gaze away from him and placing it firmly on the menu. "What's good here?"

"I've actually never been," he said. "I've wanted to come here for a while now but haven't had a good enough reason till now."

I felt my cheeks burn as a petite woman with her dark hair pulled in a bun stopped beside us placing two glasses of water on the table.

"Hey there," she greeted. "Welcome to Moto. I'm Kelsey, and I'll be your server this evening," she said before launching into a list of their specials, each sounding more delectable than the last. "Can I get you started with something to drink? A cocktail perhaps? I'd be happy to bring you our wine list."

"What sounds good to you?" Cash looked at me, taking a sip of water.

"You know, I'm normally a vodka tonic girl, but I'm really feeling a Moscow Mule tonight," I answered. "Two limes."

Cash coughed and a funny, almost shocked, expression came over him.

"And a diet coke," I added as Cash began to choke on his water. "Are you okay?"

"Fine." He cleared his throat, waving off my concern, but he still had a deer in headlights look about him. "I'm fine, really. I'll have a whiskey neat and an unsweet tea."

"You've got it," Kelsey said. "I'll give you two a few

minutes to look over the menu, and I'll be back with those drinks."

"Thank you." I turned to Cash as he took a huge gulp of water. "Are you sure you're okay?"

"I'm good," he replied, but his face didn't look *good*. In fact, he looked like he'd seen a ghost.

I narrowed my eyes at him.

"Really, I'm fine." He averted his gaze and looked at the menu.

"Uh-huh. Then why are you being weird all of a sudden?" I asked.

"I'm not being weird." He kept his eyes glued to the menu as though it were going to somehow save him.

"You're being weird, and it all started when I ordered my drinks." I leaned closer. "Cash Montgomery, are you judging me for my drink choices? Are you a cocktail snob?"

He shook his head. "No, not at all. That's not it. I promise."

"Spit it out."

"It's not a big deal."

I crossed my arms over my chest. "I'm really not going to let this go, so you should probably just get it over with and tell me."

He sighed and chewed his lip thoughtfully. "What you ordered... that was Carrie's exact drink order. Down to the two limes and the diet coke."

I winced. *Way to go, Ella.* "Oh... I'm sorry. I shouldn't have pressed the issue. I—"

"No, it's not a bad thing at all," he assured me. "If anything, it's exactly the opposite."

I furrowed my brow. "How so?"

"Before I left tonight, Delilah, my mother-in-law, called," he said. "She's kind of known for getting these *feel-*

ings. Premonitions, sort of. Almost like messages from the universe, the Great Beyond—however you want to look at it."

"Is your mother-in-law the *Ghost Whisperer?*" I asked in a vague attempt to lighten the mood.

He chuckled. "Not quite. But she said something was telling her to call me today, and she wanted me to know that Carrie wanted me to be happy."

"And are you?" The question escaped my mouth before I could even consider the weight of it. "I didn't mean with me, of course, and you don't have to answer that if you don't want to."

"I'm the happiest I've been in quite some time." He reached across the table and took my hand in his, sliding his thumb over my fingers. "And I have you to thank for that."

Warmth bloomed in my chest, and I squeezed his hand. "Cash..."

"This may sound crazy, but between what Delilah said to me and you ordering Carrie's favorite drinks, it just feels a lot like a sign from her that I'm right where I'm supposed to be." His eyes crinkled at the corners when he smiled at me, and even seated, I felt my knees go all wobbly like a giraffe on roller skates.

"I love that you still have that bond with your in-laws," I said, and I meant it. "Craig's family was never in his life, but I've gotten to see him in Grace every single day."

He nodded. "I'm grateful to them. For loving me and for the ways they help me remember her. Like how on the first Saturday of every month, Delilah and Richard send me this toasted praline coffee and a box of macaroons from a little mom and pop store in Charleston because they were Carrie's favorite. I loved them too because it was something we always shared together. We looked forward to that package every month. Our tradition was that we'd do the Sunday crossword puzzle and have a pot of that coffee while we enjoyed the macaroons."

I didn't know Delilah and Richard, but I loved them already. "And they still send it to you?"

"Every single month." He placed his elbow on the table and propped his chin on his hand. "But the other thing I love about them is that they've always given me room to live how I need to in order to move on. Like that first year after Carrie died, I spent Thanksgiving with you guys at Liv's because the thought of being at her family's home for the holiday without her was just too much. They weren't upset. There were never any hard feelings or guilt trips. They've helped keep Carrie's memory alive, but they've also helped remind me to keep living."

"They sound like amazing people, Cash."

"They are," he said. "One day I want you to mee—"

He was interrupted by the sound of my phone singing "Girls Just Want To Have Fun" from my purse that hung on the back of the chair.

"Sorry. That's Grace." I grabbed my purse, fiddling with the zipper. "Do you mind if I take this? I haven't been able to talk to her in a couple of days."

"Of course not," he replied as my hand finally landed on the phone.

I swiped across the screen and brought it to my ear. "Hey, honey. Are you okay?"

"Yeah, I'm fine. We're just now getting to the hotel. The meet and greet ran late after the show. Things have been insane, but I missed you, so I wanted to call you before I crashed."

"I miss you too." I glanced up at Cash with my hand clutched to my chest. "Be careful at those meet and greets.

Last time we went to one of those your Aunt Liv found herself a husband."

"*Mom.*" Her voice was raspy with fatigue but she giggled.

"I'm just saying. I don't want you bringing home any English boys because I'm saving up all our shows on the DVR to watch when you get home. So, unless he wants to watch *Grey's Anatomy* and *Shark Tank*, he stays in England." A loud group of friends walked by and were seated directly behind me.

"Where are you?" Grace asked. "It's so loud."

"Umm, I'm picking up some dinner." *I mean, it's not a total lie.* "Italian."

"It makes me sad to think about you eating dinner alone every night," she said.

I wondered how she would feel knowing that not only was I not alone, but I was also having dinner with her boss. "What is Bradley Cooper? Chopped liver?"

"Bradley Cooper is cute, but he doesn't count." She sighed into the phone. "Listen, I need to get off here because I still need to call Cash before I head to bed."

My eyes widened, and I swallowed hard. "You need to call Cash?"

Cash raised his eyebrows, his face awash with confusion.

"Yeah, I need to update him about Sam's throat," she replied. "I haven't had a chance to fill you in, but Sam has been having some issues with his voice."

I seemed to be having some trouble with mine too because when I spoke again, my voice was a squeak. "That's awful."

"Yeah," she said. "I gotta call Cash and tell him it unfortunately seems to be getting worse." She chuckled to herself. "When I talk to him I'm going to tell him he should have dinner with you one night so you don't have to eat alone."

This time it was me who nearly choked.

"Are you okay, Mom?" she asked.

"Uhh, yeah." I coughed. "Just the, you know… the pollen."

"Okay." She was so tired she was clearly unfazed by the fact that I don't even have allergies. "I'll give you a call in a couple days, and of course, I'll text you. I'm going to go call Cash real quick because I'm exhausted."

"Alright, honey," I said. "I love you. Get some rest."

"Love you too," she replied, and the line went dead. A half a second later, Cash's phone was ringing.

"What do I do?" Panicked, he fumbled for his phone inside his jacket pocket.

"You have to answer it. Just be cool." I took a swig from my water and prayed my cocktail would come soon.

Cash took a deep breath before answering her call. "Hey, Grace. How's it going?" He was quiet for a few beats. "Oh yeah, I'm out to dinner." More quiet. "No, not a date." I was afraid he would choke on his own spit again. "Uh, a client dinner… yeah."

Out of the corner of my eye, I could see our server making her way over to us, but she was stopped by another patron asking a question.

"Okay, I'll touch base with the doctor tomorrow," he said. "You're doing a great job taking care of everything." A few more seconds of silence. "You want me to have dinner with your mom, huh? I'll have to check my schedule and make that happen. I hate to think of her being lonely." The shit-eating grin that spread across his face was amplified by the soft flicker of the candle. "You think she'd be up for that? Okay, then. I'll see what I can do. Alright. Good night, Grace."

"Well, that was a close one," I said as Kelsey appeared with our drinks.

"Here you go." She placed them on the table. "Are you guys ready, or do you need another minute?"

"I think we need another minute." I picked up my drink and tossed back half of it. "And maybe another one of these?"

"Coming right up," she said before disappearing again.

"So..." Cash took a sip of his whiskey. "Your daughter thinks I need to have dinner with you. She's concerned you're lonely. Are you lonely?"

I shook my head and smiled, downing the rest of my drink. "Not even a little bit."

"THOSE BAKING LESSONS WITH LIV AND KATIE REALLY DID pay off, huh?" I asked Dallas who moved around the kitchen of the bakery with an ease that shocked the hell out of me. "I am, as the kids say, *shooketh.*"

"Do the kids still say that?" Dallas quipped, sticking his tongue out at me.

"I have to admit, I wasn't sure you could pull it off." Derek looked over his shoulder from where he stood at the sink, washing the heap of dishes we'd managed to dirty up.

"Oh yee of little faith," Dallas said with a grin, handing me a tray of freshly decorated Strawberry Fields cupcakes to place in the display cases out front.

"I've got a batch of Lemon Blackberry ready to be decorated, Dal." Cash maneuvered around Dallas like an expert sous chef and placed the perfectly risen confections on the island. "The Dark Chocolate has three minutes left in the oven, and I'm about to whip up the Raspberry frosting now."

I placed a hand on my hip, balancing the tray of cupcakes in the other. "And you, Cash Montgomery, are full of surprises."

Cash's eyes found mine, and he gave me a subtle wink. "You have no idea."

Derek turned and caught my eye, raising his eyebrows, but Dallas thankfully remained oblivious. He was deep in concentration working a piping bag over some Wedding Belle cupcakes, his tattooed arms flexing with each swirl.

I didn't know what I'd done to piss off the universe, but over the course of two weeks, everything that could go wrong at work, did. Renovations got behind when Big Earl and his crew all managed to get the flu within days of each other, which in and of itself wouldn't have been the end of the world, but Katie managed to catch it too. That left me and the B team girls at the bakery to run things, and Katie wasn't exaggerating when she said they were slow as molasses. Of course, this was when all of Nashville seemed to collectively decide they needed a cupcake.

The girls and I managed to hang on by a thread for six days, but on the seventh day, the two girls had gone out together and gotten completely hammered. They'd left me with six drunken butt-dial voicemails and zero help. I'm a resourceful woman, but I'd watched enough *Hell's Kitchen* to know I was what Chef Gordon Ramsey would refer to as an 'idiot sandwich' when it came to all things baking.

"Seriously, I can't thank you enough. I have no idea what I would have done without you guys. You saved my ass and kept me from having to close the store and lose money." I shook my head in awe of the crack team that had assembled to help me at a moment's notice. "You're like the Avengers if the Avengers were on *The Great British Baking Show*."

I called Cash that morning in the midst of a meltdown, and in true Captain America fashion, he'd swooped in to save the day, bringing Derek and Dallas for reinforcements. Between the four of us, we managed to keep Livvie Cakes going. I ran the front of the store while Dallas and Cash baked and decorated the cupcakes. Derek handled the dishes and periodically went to check on Bradley Cooper for me. We only broke down and cried three times in the week Katie had been gone. And by we, I mean me.

"Well, they're definitely not as pretty as what Top Chef Katie does," Dallas said, "but they taste damn good if I say so myself." He popped one of the fluffy white cupcakes in his mouth and moaned. "That's it. I'm quitting the band and going to culinary school."

"Do you like baking, or is it the eating that you really want to do?" Derek teased.

"Both," he said through a mouthful of buttercream as he crossed over to the sink to wash his hands.

"Can you imagine what I could have charged if I'd told people that one half of Midnight in Dallas was here baking cupcakes?" I asked. "Too bad Luca was in Kentucky."

Dallas snorted. "It's not like he would have done anything to help anyway. He's too busy brooding to actually do anything productive." He winced, seemingly surprised by his own bitter words. To be fair, in all the time I'd known Dallas, I'd never heard him say a bad word about anybody. "Sorry... Luca and I... we've been butting heads a little recently. Nothing to worry about."

Cash flashed him a look of concern.

"I'm just being sensitive." Dallas waved him off. "I'm

fine." The timer dinged, and he effectively changed the subject by pulling the Dark Chocolate cupcakes out of the oven. "Know what else is fine? These cupcakes. Look at these beauties. I'm going to run some soup by Katie's place later, and I was thinking I might take her one. Think she'd be up for it?"

Derek chuckled. "In other words, you want Katie's stamp of approval on your hard work?"

"*No,*" Dallas said defensively. "Okay, maybe."

"I think she'd love that," I assured him. "She texted earlier this afternoon and said she was feeling better. She wanted to come in and get a head start on tomorrow's stock, but I insisted she wait. Because of you guys, we had it all under control. Hopefully tomorrow she'll be feeling even better. Especially since it's just going to be us again for a while until we can hire some new people."

"I could always come help tomorrow too," Dallas suggested. "You know, in case she's still not feeling 100%."

I smiled and silently hoped that one day Dallas and Katie would find their way to each other because this was almost too painful to watch.

Derek gave me a pointed look as though he knew exactly what I was thinking and that I should really practice what I preached. I knew he was the observant one, but I much preferred it when his observations weren't aimed at me.

I cleared my throat. "I'm going to put these in the case and close up out front."

"We're almost finished," Dallas said. As I turned to head through the door to the front, I noticed him placing two cupcakes in a box, setting it off to the side.

About thirty minutes later, Cash brought up the remaining cupcakes and placed them in the display case.

"Dal and Derek are cleaning up. Here's the last of them. They don't look half bad, if I do say so myself. "

"Captain America to the rescue again," I said as he slipped his arms around me. I allowed myself to sink into the comfort of his embrace, inhaling notes of mint and musk in his cologne.

"You still up for ordering in some dinner?" he asked, his breath warm on my neck.

"Absolutely," I answered. "There's nothing I want more than to be curled up on the couch with you and Bradley Cooper."

"I hope we're still talking about the dog," he joked.

I smirked. "Either would be fine, really." My phone rang from the back pocket of my jeans, and I reluctantly withdrew myself from Cash's arms to extract it. My face creased with worry when I saw where the call was coming from. "It's my mom's nursing home. They rarely call unless there's something wrong." Cash's brow furrowed as I answered the phone. "Hello?"

"Ella, it's Nicole." Her voice sounded tense.

My stomach twisted. "Is everything okay?"

"It's your mom…" Nicole began. "She's lucid. More lucid than I've seen her in a long time. I have no way of knowing how long it'll last, but I thought you'd want to know." My mouth hung open, and I must have stayed that way for a moment because I heard Nicole's voice again. "Ella? Are you there?"

"Yes," I said. "Sorry. I'm just… I'll be right there."

SIXTEEN

Cash

"YOU'VE GOT TO BE KIDDING ME," ELLA SHOUTED, slamming the door to her SUV and then kicking it for good measure. "My fucking car won't start."

"It's okay," I assured her. "I can take you. Come on."

"Are you sure you don't mind?" Ella asked as I steered her toward the passenger side of my Range Rover that was parked behind the bakery.

"I won't go in," I said. "I can wait for you in the car."

Ella sighed and pressed her palms to her forehead. "You already helped me so much at work. You didn't sign up for all of this."

I placed my hands on her shoulders. "Ella, I'm signing up for anything that has to do with being there for you... if you'll let me. Let me help you."

She chewed her lip for a moment before nodding. "Okay."

I opened the door for her, and once she was safely inside, I sprinted to the driver's side. We drove in silence other than Ella's directions to the nursing home. I reached over and threaded my fingers through hers, giving her hand a squeeze.

When we arrived fifteen minutes later, I pulled up to the door. "I'll park right over there." I pointed to a spot near the front shaded by a dogwood tree. I started to pull my hand out of hers, but she tightened her grip.

She took a deep breath before looking over at me. "Would you... come up with me? Look, I know this is a bit unconventional and probably crazy soon. But with my mom, I never know when or even *if* she'll be lucid again. And regardless of what happens between us, you're someone special to me, and you're special to Grace. My mom would want to meet you, and I *want* her to meet you. If it's too much too soon, I understand. I'll—"

"I'd love to meet your mom." I brought her fingers to my lips and kissed them. I quickly parked the car, and we started toward the building. Once inside, the lady behind the front desk waved to Ella as I followed her through the lobby. There was a cozy sitting area with big, poofy couches, but even the extravagant flower arrangement on the coffee table couldn't cover up the scent of rubbing alcohol and cafeteria food.

Ella tapped in a code on a keypad to the side of the elevator, and the doors popped open. "I don't mean to brag, but I'm kind of a VIP here," she joked.

I grinned. "You've got the special door code and everything."

"Actually, the elevators are password protected to avoid any of the patients sneaking out." Once inside, she hit the button for the third floor, and the doors closed. The elevator gave a loud groan before lurching upward, and Ella reached for my hand.

We could hear the sound of metal grinding as the

elevator screeched to a halt, releasing us on the third floor. She turned right, and we walked down a long hallway beyond the nurse's station and didn't stop until we reached room 3012. She exhaled sharply before knocking softly on the door and turning the handle.

"Hey, Mama," Ella called out as we entered the room. A thin figure with white hair that grazed her shoulders looked up at us from her blue armchair. "Nicole called, and I got here as quick as I could." The woman had eyes like Ella's that lit up when her daughter reached down to kiss the top of her head.

"Hello, dear." She reached for Ella's hands, holding them.

"It's so good to see you, Mama. I have so much to tell you. Grace is in London working, and she's doing great. I got a dog," Ella said, talking ninety miles a minute. "His name is Bradley Cooper, and one day I'll see if Nicole can help me sneak him in to see you." She looked over at me, motioning me closer with her head. "And I have someone I want you to meet. Mama, this is Cash Montgomery. He's Grace's boss, and he's someone very special to us both. Cash, this is my mama, Betty."

"Hi, Betty." I extended my hand to her, enclosing her small hand in mine. "It's a pleasure to meet you."

Betty beamed up at me. "You have such kind eyes."

"Thank you, ma'am," I said. "It looks like your daughter and granddaughter got their pretty blue eyes from you."

She nodded and smiled, but her eyes searched my face. "Such kind eyes. Where did you two say you were from? Are you friends with the nurse, or are you from the church?"

It felt as though all the air had been sucked from the room.

Ella's chin quivered, but she forced a smile. "No, Mama." Her voice was small and soft.

The door opened, and a petite woman in purple scrubs came rushing to Ella's side. "I'm sorry. I got paged and was on my way back to call you, but they said they already saw you walk by the nurse's station."

"It's okay, Nicole," Ella said. "Really. It's not your fault. How long ago?"

Nicole reached out and touched Ella's arm. "About ten minutes ago."

Ella nodded as tears streamed down her face.

"I know, honey." Nicole pulled Ella into a hug. "But you need to know the first thing she did was ask for you. She asked if I'd seen you and Grace, and she wanted to know that you were both okay."

She pressed her lips together and nodded again. "I should... we should go," Ella said, stepping back toward me. "I don't want to upset her, and I can't..." She trailed off, shaking her head.

"Are you going to be okay? Is your friend here driving you home?" Nicole's gaze shifted to me, and I nodded.

"Don't cry." Betty looked up at Ella, her eyes filled with concern. "There's plenty more fish in the sea. You're too pretty to be crying over some boy."

"Thanks, Nicole." Ella's voice cracked, and she reached for my hand. "I'll see you soon, Mama."

Betty nodded once, and we turned to leave.

By the time we reached the door, I heard Betty's hushed voice. "Why was that girl so sad? The one who was with the man with the kind eyes. She looked so sad."

I prayed Ella hadn't heard it. But when I closed the

door behind me, she flung herself into my arms and dissolved into tears.

"I REALLY AM SORRY I MELTED DOWN ON YOU. *AGAIN*." ELLA sank back into the sofa. After we'd gone back to the bakery and jumped off Ella's car, we'd ordered dinner from her place. The remnants of the pizza we'd eaten were on the coffee table alongside two glasses of wine that had been largely untouched. Bradley Cooper was curled up in a blue leopard print dog bed, thoroughly dissatisfied that he didn't get to partake in our pizza party. "You've seen me break down far too many times already. I'm not always such a mess... I don't think? Fuck. Maybe I am."

I tucked a piece of her golden hair behind her ear. "You are not a mess."

She tilted her head. "Need I remind you that I broke down because I was waxing nostalgic over a washing machine?"

"That's one of the most beautiful things about you, Ella," I said. "The little things... they mean something to you. Because you understand that the little things are really the big things. You weren't just crying over a washing machine. You were crying over what it represented." I wrapped my arm around her, pulling her into me. I felt her relax as she leaned into my chest. "And I can't imagine how it felt to see your mom tonight, thinking you were going to get to really talk to her. You have every reason to be sad."

Ella sighed. "I think what hurts the most is not knowing if I've talked to her for the last time. Because she's here, but she's not really *here*. Sometimes it's almost as though someone else is occupying my mother's body. She's standing right there in front of me, but she's completely unreachable. Those moments of lucidity keep getting farther and farther apart. And eventually, she'll have her last one. She'll remember me for the last time."

"I'm so sorry." The weight of her words hung heavy around us, permeating my chest. "I know watching someone you love battle a terminal illness is... unbearable."

"When Craig died, it was sudden. He was in an accident on his way home from work. A college kid ran a stoplight and crashed into the driver's side going fifteen miles over the speed limit. It happened so fast. There was no slow decline. We didn't spend weeks or months preparing to live without each other. One minute he was here, and the next he was gone." She gazed ahead, lost in thought, and I kissed the side of her head. "Have you ever seen the movie *My Girl?*"

"I think I saw that when I was growing up. The one with the kid from *Home Alone?*"

She nodded. "At the end, McCauley Culkin's character dies when he gets stung by hundreds of bees. That was my mom's favorite movie when I was a kid. We used to have girls' nights where we'd watch movies and make ice cream sundaes. Every time it was her turn to pick the movie at Blockbuster, that was the one she'd choose. I watched it again a couple of years ago for the first time in ages, and those bees made me think about what it feels like to lose someone."

"How so?"

"You get stung by a bee, and it fucking sucks, right? Even when it stops hurting, you always remember what the sting felt like. That's what it was like to lose Craig. But losing someone slowly is different. It feels like hundreds of bee stings. Just when you think it can't get worse, there's another bee and another and another, until you can't breathe. It's death by a thousand cuts, and you're just waiting for that final blow to give you some relief."

I swallowed hard, thinking about the last weeks of Carrie's life. Though mentally she was still present with me, her every waking moment was spent in pain. I never imagined that I'd be asking God to take the one person I'd give anything for, but I did. In Carrie's last days, I realized I'd rather suffer every second of the rest of my life than for her to endure another moment. "It's an agony I can't begin to describe."

"Shit. I'm an insensitive asshole. Of course you know how all of this feels. I'm preaching to the choir." She cleared her throat. "Damn, I really took us to the dark side. I'm sorry for being such a killjoy tonight."

"Ella." I pulled back slightly so that I could look into her eyes that were still red from crying. "Stop apologizing. I want to know every part of you. Even your dark side."

She placed her hands on the sides of my neck, drawing me closer until our foreheads touched.

I took her beautiful face in my hands, grazing my thumb along her bottom lip before kissing her softly. We melted into each other, two white flags surrendering to any hesitation that had been lingering.

When she finally broke our kiss, there was a burn in her gaze that set me on fire from the inside. "Will you stay with me tonight?"

SEVENTEEN

Ella

"ARE YOU SURE?" CASH ASKED TENTATIVELY. "I KNOW YOU wanted to take things slow, and I respect that."

I nodded and gripped the collar of his shirt, pulling him close until my lips met his. "I was just scared. So many things in my world were changing, and this was another change. But you've made me realize that sometimes change is good." I kissed him again. "Really, really good." I stood and pulled him to his feet, my heart already pounding in my ears. "Come with me."

When we started toward the hall, Bradley Cooper whined and raised his head to look at me.

"You stay here, buddy," I told him. I scanned the room for his favorite bone made out of allegedly indestructible material and gave it to him. He happily received it, gnawing away at the toy. I turned to Cash, took his hands in mine, and guided him toward my bedroom, slowing only to kiss him every few steps. We crossed the threshold into my room that was lit only by the soft glow of the bedside lamp. "That bone will buy us at least ten minutes."

He chuckled softly and took my face in his hands, tenderly tilting my face up to his. "Then we may need a few more of those." His lips barely brushed mine, but I felt the electricity prickle from the top of my neck to the base of my spine.

My breath caught in my throat as his eyes lingered on mine, and I realized I was actually nervous. "Why's that?"

"Because I plan on taking my time with you." His voice was low and seductive, causing a warm ache to spread deep into my core. He slid his hands beneath my T-shirt, his fingers brushing softer than silk across my skin. "I want to know what makes you feel good."

My eyes closed as his hands made their tantalizing journey up my sides, along my rib cage. His thumbs lightly caressed my breasts over the satin of my bra causing my nipples to perk. "This feels pretty great." A nervous laugh bubbled up from my chest. It was hard to think straight or form words with him touching me like that or with the warmth of his breath next to my ear.

His hands moved down my back, and then he grabbed the hem of my shirt, tugging it gently over my head. I let out a shallow breath and mentally kicked myself for not having a few more sips of that wine with dinner to calm my nerves. It wasn't like the man hadn't seen me naked before. But this time was different, wasn't it?

In the weeks since we'd had sex, Cash had seen me stripped down in a way that only one other man had ever seen me. Sex was one thing. I didn't mind him seeing my cellulite or the beginnings of the varicose veins on my legs. I was confident in the softness of my body even if it didn't look quite like it did twenty years ago, and I knew I had a temple worthy of worshipping.

But this wasn't *just* sex. Since the first time we'd slept together, Cash had seen me completely unguarded and vulnerable, and I felt things for him that extended well beyond how good the touch of his hands made me feel. I was used to being the caregiver, but he made me feel cared for. He made me feel safe, and he had a way of looking at me like I was the most beautiful creature he'd ever laid his eyes on.

"No body Tupperware this time," he teased as he traced the outline of my pale, pink bra with his fingers, sending shivers across my shoulders.

"No body Tupperware," I confirmed. "And not to brag, but my bra even matches my thong."

The flames in his eyes flickered brighter at the mention of my underwear, and I felt my cheeks blush.

Though I hadn't planned exactly when this night would happen, I'd made sure my underwear game had been strong ever since that first night. Just in case.

His eyes bore into mine as I undid the buttons of his shirt one by one, revealing his firm chest covered in a spray of whiskey-colored hair that disappeared below his belt. "I love the way your hands feel on me." He groaned with pleasure as I rubbed along the V shaped lines that beckoned me southward.

His eyes were dilated, changing them from their usual hazel to pools of dark chocolate. I pushed the shirt down his biceps until it hit the floor, running my fingers over the curves of his arms for longer than necessary. The way he watched me undress him made my heart race and caused beads of sweat to form on the back of my neck.

"Is it weird that I'm a little nervous?" I asked, smoothing my quivering hands up his chest.

He shook his head. "I'm a little nervous too." He pressed a kiss to my forehead. "We don't have to do anything you're not ready for."

Sweet Jesus, this man melts me. And I knew he meant it. He'd wait for me for as long as I wanted, but waiting was not on my agenda. "I promise it's not that," I assured him. "I'm ready. *Really* ready. It's just..."

"It feels different this time, doesn't it?" he asked, as though he could read my mind.

I nodded. Hearing him say my thoughts out loud was both validating and terrifying. It was as though we'd been playing poker, but he'd been looking at my cards over my shoulder the entire time.

He slipped his arms around my waist, pulled me closer, and leaned his head against mine. "Ella, I..." He trailed off and pressed his lips together as though he were sealing his words inside.

My mouth went dry. "You what?"

"I want you to know how much this means to me," he whispered. "How much *you* mean to me." Thousands of goosebumps erupted over my skin, igniting the yearning clawing up from deep in my belly.

I cupped his face in my hands, my eyes locked on his. "Show me."

He paused for a beat, holding my gaze. "I can do that." He scooped me up with his hands under my butt, lifting me onto the bed so that he hovered over me.

His lips crashed into mine, and I kissed him hungrily.

"I need these gone," I said as I fumbled with his belt buckle.

With his help, I was able to get his belt undone and his pants off so that only his black boxer briefs remained, the cotton fabric straining hard against his bulge.

"I hope you don't mind if I savor this view a little longer." He leaned back and appraised me, running his hands down my denim-clad thighs. I wanted to savor what it felt like to be wanted by Cash Montgomery. But I also wanted to do that while we wore a few less clothes.

"The view beneath these jeans is a lot better," I promised, unfastening my jeans and shoving them down my hips.

His tongue flicked across his lips as he gingerly slid my jeans down, pulling my legs out one by one. He took one of my legs in his hand and blazed a trail of kisses from my ankle all the way up my thigh.

"God, you're so sexy, Ella." His fingers toyed with the strap of my thong and lightly grazed my folds, causing me to whimper, the ache at my center reaching a fever pitch.

"I need you inside me." I grabbed onto the waistband of his boxer briefs and slid them down until his hardness sprang free. I took him in my hand, smoothing my palm over his length. "I need to feel you."

He moaned and reached his hands around me, unhooking my bra and tossing it to the floor. My hands twisted in his hair as he placed open-mouthed kisses down my neck, all the way down my breasts, coming to a stop at the edge of my thong. "Not yet."

"Please," I murmured as he exhaled a hot breath over my center, and I bucked against him.

His tongue teased the sensitive skin along the outline of my thong before sliding it off, leaving me completely naked. He took me in for a moment, his eyes fixed on mine.

"You make me feel things I haven't felt in a long damn time," he said, kissing the inside of my thigh. "I want you to feel things too." He began teasing me with his tongue with featherlight pressure before licking me from opening to clit.

"Fuck," I cried out, arching into his mouth. My body writhed and wriggled beneath his steady motions as his thumb added pressure to my clit, pushing me close to the edge.

"Ella, you are a goddess," Cash whispered, drawing away from me. Before I could cry out in protest, he was buried deep inside me, thrusting slowly so that I could feel every inch of him. I clenched around him as his eyes peered into mine. "You make me feel like I'm falling."

Wait. What?! Did he mean falling like falling from this glorious high we were on, or like, *falling?* Falling in love or like 'oh shit, I'm falling off a fucking cliff'? As I looked into his eyes, I knew it didn't matter. I clawed at his neck, my hands tangling in his hair, relishing in how good it felt to be in his arms. Wherever Cash Montgomery was falling, I was going with him.

"Cash... I..." I tried to form the words to say how he made me feel, but before any words could form, his mouth covered mine, and I was lost in him. His tongue searched my mouth as though he could somehow extract my emotions one by one. I wrapped my legs around his waist drawing him closer and deeper into me.

"You feel so good." He gripped the sheets by my head, his biceps and forearms flexing with every movement, which I was quickly coming to realize was my own personal Achilles heel. I never knew that forearm veins could be so sexy. With every thrust, he picked up speed, and I tightened my body around him until my orgasm ripped through me.

I cried out his name, and my limbs trembled as I tumbled over the edge.

"Christ. My name on your lips is the sexiest thing I've ever heard." His breathing became ragged as he pulsed into me, sending delicious aftershocks coursing through my muscles that were already gooey and dreamy like melted caramel. His hands glided over my skin, and his thrusts came faster and harder until he finally let go, his body shuddering around me.

I kissed his shoulder as he sagged against me, and we laid there breathless for a moment, our bodies entwined.

"That was…" he trailed off as he looked into my eyes, seemingly at a loss for words.

Perfect? Fucking amazing? I haven't felt like that since… Of course, I didn't say any of that out loud. I couldn't tell Cash that I was falling in love with him. Not yet. Instead, I nodded and said, "Yeah. It was."

Just then I heard a yelp coming from the side of the bed, followed by a sharp bark. Together, we peered over the edge of the bed to see Bradley Cooper looking up at us, his tail wagging furiously. He let out another yip, his front paws giving an excited little bounce.

"Bradley Cooper," I exclaimed. "You furry little pervert. How long have you been standing there?"

The dog whined in response.

"So, he likes more than one type of bone, huh?" Cash joked, and we collapsed into a heap of laughter as Bradley Cooper took a flying leap onto the bed.

"I'm not excited about any of these resumes." Katie sighed and slapped the meager stack on the counter at the bakery late the next afternoon. It was Saturday near closing time, and I was itching to get out of there to see Cash. He'd looked so peaceful when I left early that morning that I hadn't wanted to wake him. Instead, I'd left a note telling him I'd see him after work. But he'd been texting me all day, sending me pictures of his and Bradley Cooper's 'boys' day' along with a few suggestive messages that hinted at what he may want to do to me later.

"We'll run another ad," I said. "Maybe we can get a new crop of candidates."

"We'll need to start looking for baristas soon too," she reminded me.

"Maybe I could learn how to do it," I suggested. My phone pinged with a text, and I picked it up, unable to stop myself from smiling at the picture of Cash and Bradley Cooper at the dog park. "You know, just until we can hire someone."

"I love you, Ella," she said, "but that's a third-degree burn waiting to happen. Need I remind you of the torch incident when Liv tried to teach you how to make creme brûlée?"

I stuck my tongue out at her from over my phone. "You and Liv are always reminding me about that."

"Okay, what gives?" Katie asked. "You've checked your phone at least a hundred times in the last thirty minutes. You've been weird and squirmy all day."

"I'm not squirmy."

"Weird, squirmy, and also very smiley," she added.

"I'm always smiley," I pouted. "I'm a freaking ray of sunshine."

She narrowed her eyes at me, and I placed my phone screen-side down on the counter.

"What?" I asked defensively. "I am."

"I've known you long enough to know something's up," Katie insisted.

Something was *definitely* up, but I wasn't quite ready to tell everyone I was in love with Cash Montgomery. I still wasn't sure how our friends, and most importantly, my daughter, would take the news. Hell, I wasn't entirely sure how *I* was taking the news. All I knew was my insides got all warm and squishy just thinking about him. And it wasn't like I was going to *not* tell everyone. I just needed to wait until the right moment.

"I guess I'm still giddy over Bradley Cooper," I lied. "I mean, have you seen him?" To further prove my mistruth, I picked up my phone and showed her one of the dozens of pictures I'd saved on it.

"Uh huh," she said. "He's very cute, but nobody gets that lusty look over a dog. Unless you're a Pomeranian or something."

Shit. I chewed my lip. I suppose I had been looking a little lusty. The pictures Cash had been sending me were works of art. I always knew guys got hotter when they held a dog—that was just science. But when that guy also happened to be holding *your* dog? That was *peak* hotness.

Katie chuckled and shook her head.

"I'm so glad you're feeling well enough to be up my ass," I teased.

She laughed. "I'm always well enough for that."

"Does this mean you'll be coming to Sunday dinner tomorrow?" I asked.

She nodded. "Cash hosted last time, so it's at Derek's place this time, right?"

"Yep," I answered. "He and Dallas are sharing the cooking responsibilities since they live in the same building. Besides, I think Dallas looks for every opportunity to impress you with his chef skills."

Katie chose to ignore that last remark. "Do you think Liv will bring the kids? I can't wait to meet them."

Sadness tugged at my gut. I had barely talked to Liv since the mouse incident other than a few random texts that were always pretty brief. "I don't know. I think they've got their hands full."

"You've at least told Liv what's got you all twitterpated, right?" Katie pinned me with her all-knowing eyes, but I didn't answer. I swear the woman was a damn psychic. "Is everything okay with you two?"

I shrugged. "Things have been a little different, you know? I know she's got a lot on her, and I don't want to bother her."

She raised her eyebrows and crossed her arms. "Bother her with things like your life and feelings? Ella, she loves you. Liv will always make time for you. She's your family."

"Oh, I know." I waved her off. "But it's nothing serious."

Even as I said the words, I knew they weren't true, and from the discerning stare Katie gave me, I was pretty sure she knew it too.

"I better get out of here," I said, changing the subject. "Bradley Cooper will be needing a pee break."

"So, I assume the house training must be going well?" she asked.

"Eh, it's a little better," I answered. "But he still can't seem to go more than five hours without a potty break. We're still working on it."

Katie's mouth curved into an amused grin. "Well, that's interesting."

My forehead creased with confusion. "Why?"

"You usually go home around lunch to let him out, but you've been here for eight and a half hours straight." She smiled and started toward the door to the kitchen. "I'll see you tomorrow."

Shit, shit, shit. I hadn't even thought about the difference in my routine that day.

I was going to have to come clean about my relationship with Cash, and I was going to have to do it soon.

EIGHTEEN

Cash

"For fuck's sake, Luca!" I heard Dallas before I saw him. "What were you thinking?"

I'd just arrived at Derek's apartment for Sunday dinner. Ella had driven herself, leaving a little early to visit her mom before dinner. She insisted we drive separately until we'd told everyone our news. I knew she wanted to tell Grace first, and I respected that.

After knocking on the door with no response, I turned the handle to find it already unlocked.

"What's your fucking problem?" Luca's voice yelled as I closed the door behind me and walked through the foyer and into the living room. I looked around and noticed a young woman in a pink dress that barely covered her backside standing outside on the balcony smoking a cigarette. *What the...*

"You, Luca." Dallas was getting louder and louder as I headed toward the kitchen. "You are my fucking problem."

"Hey, guys." I cautiously rounded the corner to see Dallas and Luca facing each other with their arms crossed and Derek leaned against the island with his head in his hands. "What seems to be the problem?"

"Him," Luca and Dallas said in unison, each pointing at the other.

"Whatever, Luca." Dallas snarled. "I'm so sick of your shit. Why don't we tell Cash what your dumb ass did?"

"Does it have anything to do with the young lady smoking on the balcony?" I asked.

"This idiot brought a stranger to Sunday dinner." Dallas ran his fingers through his hair. "And they both showed up drunk out of their damn minds."

Luca shrugged. "Hey, at least I was early this time."

"Liv and Jax are bringing their kids here to meet all of us for the first time." Derek was struggling to keep his voice even. "You can't bring just anyone to these dinners."

"Who's to say Mandy couldn't be 'family?'" Luca held up his fingers in air quotes.

"Brandi." Derek threw his hands up in frustration. "Her name is Brandi. She only said it five times when you got here. Brandi with an i." He mimicked a squeaky voice. "How do I know her name, and you don't?"

Luca smirked and took a swig straight from a half-empty bottle of Jack Daniels. "I don't exactly need to know her name for what we're doing, if you know what I mean."

"Okay, that's enough." I held up my hand. "Derek is right. You can't be bringing people you don't even know, especially not tonight. This is a big deal. Also, what if this girl is some crazed fan? Now she knows where Derek lives."

"Trust me. She's already too drunk to remember. She thinks I'm a Backstreet Boy." Derek pressed his lips together to suppress a laugh. "And she's certain she saw Dallas at one of those male stripper shows in Vegas."

"The Thunder From Down Under, mate." Dallas said in a terrible Australian accent.

That was enough to break the tension and have us all laughing.

I chuckled and gave a resigned sigh. Nobody was going to sour the good mood I was in. I'd had a perfect weekend with Ella, and I wasn't about to let that get ruined by drunk Luca. We'd deal with it. "This can't happen again, Luca. These dinners are for family only."

Luca brought the bottle of liquor to his lips, but I intercepted it before he could take another sip.

"Don't even think about it." I crossed the short distance to the sink, draining the amber liquid. "I think you should drink some water, eat something, and sober up."

Derek moved to the pantry and pulled out a bag of pretzels, pushing them in Luca's direction.

Luca rolled his eyes like a petulant child.

"The lasagna will be ready in ten," Dallas said, setting to work chopping vegetables for a salad.

"And you owe everyone an apology." I raised my brows at Luca.

"You're such a fucking dad, Cash." Luca took a handful of pretzels and popped them in his mouth. "I'm sorry I invited Mandy."

"Brandi," Derek corrected. "With an i."

"And?" Dallas asked.

Luca shrugged. "And what?"

"And sorry I got drunk before we even had dinner and for being a dick?" Dallas continued. "Should I go on?"

Luca huffed. "I'm going to go find Mandy."

Derek held up a finger. "Brandi."

"With an i," Dallas added. "And she needs to leave before the kids get here."

"Whatever." Luca flipped us off and slinked out of the kitchen.

"Do you need help with anything, Dal?" I asked.

"Nope. Not unless you can talk some sense into that asshole," he answered. "You guys go hang out. The table is already set."

Derek and I made our way to the living room where a very gorgeous but confused Ella stood talking to our new guest.

"I'm Brandi." Her voice was so high-pitched it was almost bird-like. "With an i." She stuck her hand out. "What's your name?"

"I'm Ella," she answered as Luca looped his arm around Brandi.

"You're *so* pretty, Ella." She beamed at Ella who wore an off the shoulder floral sundress before turning her attention to Luca. "Babe, where were you? What'd you do with the booze?"

"It appears we've been cut off," Luca said, giving me a pointed look.

"By who?" It took Brandi a few extra seconds to follow Luca's gaze over to me and Derek. She zeroed in on me, deep in concentration, before letting out a shriek. Or maybe it was a dog whistle. "Oh my God! You're one of the other Backstreet Boys! The old one!"

Ella choked on a laugh.

I raised a brow at her before extending my hand to Brandi. "Cash Montgomery."

Brandi pushed past my hand and threw her arms around me. "I can't believe it! My mama would be so proud. She used to listen to the Backstreet Boys all the time when I was little. Lucas better watch out. The old one's always been my favorite."

"I think you mean Luca," I said.

"Right." She winked up at me and mimed a tiger scratch. "Rawr."

Ella cocked her head to the side and pursed her lips.

I cleared my throat and flashed angry eyes at Luca who pulled Brandi back under his arm.

There was a knock on the door, and Derek opened it to reveal Katie holding a homemade pie.

"Hey, Katie." Derek freed her hands of the pie and gave her a hug. "How are you feeling?"

"So much better," she answered. "Thanks for filling in for me."

"Hi, Katie," Brandi said, immediately honing in on the new addition to our group. "I'm Brandi. With an i."

"Hi." Katie took Brandi's outstretched hand, uncertainty veiling her face.

"Hey." Dallas suddenly appeared at our sides. "Jax just called and said they'll be a little late and that we should start without them. Everything's about to come out of the oven."

"I'll help you." Katie smiled as she and Derek followed Dallas back toward the kitchen.

"You think Justin Timberlake will be here?" Brandi asked Luca as he steered her away from Ella and me.

I turned to make sure the coast was clear before pulling Ella into my arms. "Hi."

She pressed a kiss to my lips. "I thought I was going to have to kick drunk Barbie in the shins."

"I've seen ass-kicking Ella before. She is not to be trifled with." I touched my nose to hers.

"That girl's not really staying for dinner is she?" Ella asked. "She seems perfectly nice, but this is not a good night for new guests. Liv and Jax are probably nervous enough as it is."

I released a dissatisfied sigh. "I know. I'm hoping Luca will do the right thing and ask her to leave."

She snorted. "Luca? Do the right thing? You must be joking."

I tucked a piece of hair behind her ear, trying to put Luca out of my mind. "God, I can't wait to get back to your house. This dress is gorgeous on you."

"It'll be even more gorgeous off of me," she teased.

"I can't wait until we don't have to keep us a secret anymore."

"Soon," she said. "I promise. I just need to tell Grace first, and I haven't quite figured out how to do that yet."

"You guys coming?" Luca's voice asked, causing us to startle and jump apart. "Am I interrupting something?"

"Cash was um… helping me with my necklace," Ella improvised, instinctively reaching for the small chain around her neck.

"Yes," I added. "It was caught in her… uh…"

"Hair," Ella finished for me. "It was caught in my hair."

Luca's forehead creased as he narrowed his eyes at us, and I just knew we'd been busted.

"Right," he said finally. "I was just fixing Mandy's neck-lace earlier too. Dinner's on the table."

"Luca, wait a second." I paused, choosing my words carefully. "I think you should ask Brandi to leave before the kids get here." I attempted to reason with him, hoping I'd have a better shot without the other guys around. "We need to do what we can to make them comfortable."

Luca appeared to consider what I was saying for a moment, and I thought I might have gotten through to him. Finally, he let out a roaring belch. "No." With that, he turned and started back toward the kitchen.

"So," Ella muttered. "Guess she's staying."

I slipped my hand in hers and took a deep breath. *Here goes nothing.*

"SORRY WE'RE LATE," LIV SAID AS SHE AND JAX ENTERED the dining room where the rest of us sat at a large oak table. Chloe was wide-eyed and resting atop Liv's hip while Jonathan zoomed in with two toy cars in his hands. "We went ahead and fed the kids first because they're still working on getting comfortable with more foods. Then, the little one here had a messy diaper right before we walked out the door. She's been a grump today." She kissed the top of her head. "The cutest grump."

"We've missed y'all." Ella rose from her seat to hug Liv and Jax and to ruffle Chloe's hair.

"We've missed you guys too," Jax said, hoisting a large pink diaper bag off his shoulder and placing it on the floor.

"I hate that Antoni couldn't make it," Liv said, "but he texted and said he sends his love. He's meeting Nate's family this weekend."

"You guys look great." Katie beamed.

"Parenthood suits you," I agreed, and I meant it. It filled me with pride to finally see Jax have his happy ending. Jax didn't have much in the way of a family before the band, and I knew how much it meant for him to find Liv and start a family of his own. Ella returned to her seat next to me, and I couldn't help but wonder if we'd get our own happy ending.

"Look at that baby," Brandi cooed from beside Luca. "My ovaries are exploding. Lucas, I want one of those."

Luca pretended he didn't hear her.

Liv was startled as she noticed Brandi for the first time. "Oh, um, hi. I don't believe we've met. I'm Liv, and this is my husband Jax."

"I'm Brandi." She waved.

"With an i," the rest of us said, joining her.

Brandi giggled. "That's right."

"She's Luca's… guest," I explained.

Jax shot Luca an annoyed glare. "I see Luca hasn't changed a bit. Still does whatever he wants."

"And whoever," Luca fired back. If Brandi heard him, she didn't let on.

"How you doing, Mama Cupcake?" Dallas asked Liv as he stood, leaning in to kiss her cheek. Chloe eyed him curiously.

Liv sucked in a deep breath. "Good. We're finally getting into a routine, I think. This is Chloe, and that little ball of energy is Jonathan."

"Hi!" Jonathan yelled, continuing to run around.

"I'm going to go heat up your food," Dallas said, disappearing into the kitchen.

Derek ambled over to Liv and gave her a one-armed embrace. He hid behind Liv's shoulder, playing peek-a-boo with Chloe. Within a couple of moments, she was giggling and waving.

"Wow, I didn't know Uncle Derek was a baby whisperer," Liv said. "She hasn't smiled all day."

"Why don't you let me hold her while you two eat?" Derek asked, reaching out his hands to Chloe. "Want to come hang out with Uncle Derek?"

Chloe smiled shyly at him before looking up at Liv for

her approval. "You can go sit with him if you want." Finally, she leaned into his hands, allowing him to extract her from Liv's grasp.

I chuckled. "You might need Uncle Derek to babysit so you guys can have a date night."

Dallas returned with two plates of lasagna. "Nobody is babysitting without Uncle Dallas."

"And Auntie Katie," Katie chimed in.

"I'll hang out with them when they're teenagers," Luca said from beside me. "Teach them how to sneak out without getting caught."

I elbowed him. "Luca." As everyone settled back in their seats, I let my eyes wander to take in each of the faces around me. My gaze settled on Ella, and I thought about how blessed I was. For this second chance to have a family, for Ella, for everyone gathered at that table. Even Luca. Maybe not Brandi, though I was sure she was a nice girl.

"Remind me to never leave our kids alone around you," Jax said pointedly to Luca.

"Every family has a crazy uncle," Ella said. "Guess Luca is ours."

"Where's the ladies room?" Brandi chirped.

"Down the hall and to the left," Derek answered.

"Really, Luca?" Jax asked once she was out of earshot. "Why tonight of all nights?"

"What?" He feigned innocence. "What's wrong with Mandy?"

"Brandi," the rest of us shot back.

Luca rolled his eyes. "Whatever."

I let out an exasperated sigh. "How do you still not remember her name?"

Ella shrugged. "You know, they really might be made for each other. She can't remember his name either."

Luca snorted as Ella's phone rang from her purse, and she quickly extracted it from her bag,

"It's Grace," she exclaimed, swiping across the screen. "Hey, honey! You're on speaker."

Grace was greeted by a cacophony of voices.

"There was no way I was going to miss Sunday dinner," Grace said. "I miss you guys."

"We miss you too," Liv called out.

"Aunt Livvie," Grace cried. "How are you? I can't wait to meet Chloe and Jonathan."

Jonathan's eyes lit up. "That's me."

"That's right, buddy." Jax nodded. "That's your Aunt Grace."

"We're doing good," Liv replied. "I think we're all starting to adjust."

"And Liv is a great mom," Jax added, giving Liv's shoulder a squeeze.

"Of course she is," Grace said. "We all knew she would be."

"We can't wait for you to see the bakery. It already looks so different," Katie chimed in. "We've got about a month of renovations left, but it's starting to come together."

Grace squealed. "I can't wait."

"How's England?" Dallas asked.

Grace sighed. "I'm exhausted, but it's been so much fun. The weather here kind of sucks, though. It rains so much."

"How much longer are you gone for?" Derek asked.

"Well, actually, it's funny you should ask." Grace paused for a moment. "We were supposed to be gone until the first of September, but Sam has been having some trouble with his voice. I haven't even gotten to tell Cash this part yet because it just happened. Sam saw a specialist this morning, and it turns out he has nodes."

"He has *what?*" Ella asked incredulously.

Luca snickered. "Sam has nudes."

Grace laughed. "Nodes—nodules on his vocal cords. The doctor has put him on strict vocal rest effective immediately."

"How's Sam taking it?" I asked. I knew how much it must hurt him to have to cancel shows.

"He's pretty bummed," Grace said. "He feels like he's really letting down the fans."

"We can always reschedule the tour. The fans will understand," I assured her. "But Sam and his health come first."

"That's what I keep telling him," Grace said.

"Wait." Ella squinted. "Does this mean what I think it means?"

"Yep," Grace answered. "We're coming home early. Our flight gets in at four p.m. tomorrow."

Ella's eyes widened, and though I knew she was ecstatic Grace was coming home, I also saw a look of panic in her eyes.

"Do you need us... I mean, one of us, to pick you up from the airport tomorrow?" I questioned.

"Nope," she said. "We've already got a car scheduled to pick us up."

"If you'll excuse me, I need to go drain the main vein," Luca announced, rising from the table to a simultaneous groan from everyone else.

"Was that Luca? What did he say?" Grace asked. "I think my phone cut out."

"He said he misses you and to travel safe," I said quickly.

Everyone laughed, and Chloe clapped her hands in Derek's lap.

"I miss you guys so much," Grace said. "This has been amazing, but I can't wait to be home again."

"We've got to celebrate," Ella suggested. "We'll go to dinner if you're not too tired when you get in."

Grace gasped. "Yes! Please. And can we go to Frothy Monkey? I've missed their coffee."

"Of course," Ella replied.

"Okay, I better get going." Grace sighed into the phone. "I still have to pack and try to get some sleep before we have to leave for the airport."

"We love you, Grace," Ella said, and we all sang our chorus of goodbyes before Ella hung up the phone. She must have felt my gaze on her because when her eyes finally met mine, a nervous smile flickered across her face.

NINETEEN

Ella

"The flu? You poor thing," Liv said to Katie before taking the last bite of her lasagna.

Katie took a sip of wine. "And then those girls we hired got drunk and no-showed, leaving poor Ella to fend for herself."

Liv gasped. "Ella, I'm so sorry."

Dallas spoke up before I could say anything. "It all worked out, though. You and Katie taught me well. Between me, Derek, and Cash, we had everything under control."

Liv's forehead creased. "You guys baked the cupcakes?"

"Yep." Dallas beamed. "We did a pretty good job too."

"Ella, why didn't you call me?" The hurt in Liv's voice was unmistakable. "I would have come to help."

Katie's eyes met mine, and she mouthed the word 'sorry' to me.

"Babe, I know you would have," I said quickly. "You've had so much going on. I didn't want to bother you."

She chewed her lip thoughtfully for a moment, and the

room fell silent apart from Jonathan's car noises as he flitted about the room.

I opened my mouth to speak again, but was interrupted by the sounds of moans and breathy screams floating down the hallway. My eyes gaped open, and Katie stifled a laugh. Luca might have been the worst, but he did have impeccable timing.

"Is that…" Cash paused. "Is that what I *think* it is?"

Dallas hid his face in his hands, and Jax seethed.

Derek shook his head in disgust. "I'm going to have to move now."

Jonathan covered his face with his hands. "It sounds like that lady is hurt." He ran into Liv's arms.

"No, buddy," Jax reassured him. "Uncle Luca and the lady are just playing a game. You know how sometimes when we all have tickle fights, we get a little loud?"

Jonathan appeared to consider this. "Yeah."

Liv forced a smile. "That's all they're doing. They're just playing."

Satisfied with this answer, Jonathan pried himself from Liv's embrace and went back to playing on the floor with his cars as Luca and Brandi with an i's screams escalated.

It took everything in me not to storm to the bathroom and drag Luca out by his ears, but I knew we had to play it cool so as not to draw even more attention to them and upset the kids.

The noise was enough to cause Chloe to fret, so Derek took her back to Liv and sprinted down the hall, beating on the bathroom door. "Knock it off, you two!"

"So." Cash cleared his throat as Derek returned to the table. "Any thoughts on when Midnight in Dallas may want to get back in the studio?"

"I'm ready." Dallas leaned back in his chair and crossed

his arms. "I've been working on some new beats I think you guys are going to like. I've been dying to get back in the studio."

Jax nodded. "We should start doing some writing. I'd like to take the rest of August off with the kids, but we could start writing the first week of September. Maybe get some studio time in October?"

Derek spoke up. "Actually, I have some stuff already scheduled this fall."

"What?" Dallas asked incredulously.

"Well, you know how much I love photography. I finally decided I wanted to learn more about it." Derek shifted uncomfortably in his chair as all eyes focused on him. "I'm going to be spending some time with Antoni's uncle in New York. He was a photographer for *Vogue* for like fifty years. He's agreed to take me under his wing and teach me some stuff."

"Antoni's told me about his uncle before," Cash said. "That'll be great for you."

"Seriously?" Dallas huffed out a breath. "Why didn't you tell me about this?"

"I didn't know for sure that it was going to work out until a couple of days ago," Derek explained. "I just bought my plane ticket this morning."

"How long are you going to be gone?" Dallas fired back.

"All of September and October and most of November," Derek answered. "I'll come back the week before Thanksgiving."

Dallas looked like he'd been slapped. "Are you kidding me right now?"

The screams down the hall returned, and Brandi with an i was sounding more like a wounded seagull.

Chloe whimpered, and Liv attempted to console her by rubbing her back, shooting laser beams of death down the hall with her eyes.

"Dal, hold up a second. Let's—" Jax tried to speak but Dallas cut him off.

"No," Dallas said flatly. "Photography is your hobby. The band is your *job*, and this band doesn't work without *all* of us."

Derek flinched, and the mama bear in me wanted to hug him and tell Dallas to calm the fuck down.

Cash kept his tone even. "I don't think it would hurt for you guys to wait a little longer."

"People are going to forget about us." Dallas pinched the bridge of his nose. "I am all for everyone having their own thing. I support Jax and Liv having their own thing, having a family. I support Luca doing... whatever it is Luca does, and I support Derek having a hobby, but we all agreed to make this band a priority."

Cash pressed his lips together, appearing to choose his words carefully. "Dallas, don't you think you're being a little harsh?"

Dallas shook his head. "Not even a little."

"It's okay. Dallas is right. I made a commitment to the band. I'll cancel my trip." Derek gave a resigned shrug, quickly surrendering to Dallas. "Maybe I can go in the spring."

"Sure," Dallas said. "If the band isn't doing shows by then, absolutely."

Cash flashed Dallas a warning glance. "I'm sure we can find a time you can go, Derek."

Derek opened his mouth to speak, but closed it just as Chloe's whimpers turned into a full-blown cry that only amplified the tension in the room.

Katie cleared her throat. "I need to get going. I've got to be downtown in thirty minutes, and I always worry I won't be able to find parking."

Dallas frowned. "Where are you going?"

"I have a date," Katie said as she rose from her seat. "We're meeting at The Stillery."

Dallas looked like he'd been slapped for the second time that evening.

"That's great!" Liv beamed at Katie. "I can't wait to hear all about him."

"This is just our first date," Katie said as she made her way around the room, passing out goodbye hugs.

"Where did you meet him?" Dallas's tone had a bite to it.

"Bumble," she answered as the screeches from the bathroom finally came to an end.

"I didn't know you were on Bumble," I said.

She arched an eyebrow at me as a reminder that she wasn't the only one at this table with a secret. *Fair enough.*

"Um, I guess tell Luca and his girlfriend I said bye," Katie mumbled. "Bye, Jonathan. I'll see you soon."

Chloe whined as Katie patted her on the back before waving at us and letting herself out.

Luca and Brandi reappeared, joining the table as though we hadn't all heard them doing a live performance of the entire Kama Sutra. Liv shot eye-daggers at Luca from across the table.

Brandi combed her fingers through her platinum blonde hair and tugged at the hem of her dress. Meanwhile, Luca gave zero fucks that he looked like he'd just been, well, fucked.

Luca took a swig from the glass of water in front of him on the table as all eyes settled on him. "What?"

Cash shook his head disapprovingly. "Really, Luca?"

Luca rolled his eyes. "Don't act all superior like you haven't been taking Ella to Bonetown."

All of the oxygen left my body, the room, the entire fucking planet. *Luca has to die.*

Dallas's eyes brightened, and Jax broke into a big grin.

"What?" It was Liv's turn to look like she'd been slapped. "Ella, is this true? Are you and Cash together?"

This was not how I wanted things to go down. I'd wanted to tell Grace and Liv privately before we told anyone else. I opened my mouth, but no words came out.

Cash pressed his lips together and looked to me to answer, but the words were lodged in my throat like a damn chicken bone.

Finally, Liv turned her accusatory eyes on Cash. "Is this true?"

"Um..." Cash looked to me again for help, but there was no help to be found. This ship was going down. *Mayday! Mayday!* "Yes. Ella and I are dating."

"Oh." Liv blinked slowly as though her brain had been overloaded by this new information and she was rebooting. "How long has this been going on?"

"Well, we actually went out after your wedding, but we just recently decided we were ready to see where this could go." Cash reached for my hand under the table, or at least I think he did. I wasn't entirely sure because my soul had left my body.

"And I knew it the whole time," Derek said proudly, driving the last stake through Liv's heart.

Chloe clearly read the room because she let out a squall so loud it caused her to turn beet-red. Jonathan, who was concerned about the five alarm siren going off inside his sister, came running, tripping over his own feet. He, too, started to wail right there on the floor, and I wanted to join him.

Jax scooped him up, speaking to him in a soft, soothing voice.

Tears welled in Liv's eyes as she stood so she could rock Chloe.

Derek noticed and immediately glanced over at me. "Shit. I'm so sorry."

I finally found my voice. "Please don't be mad. I was going to tell you. I haven't even told Grace yet."

"This has been going on since the wedding? That means you guys were together when you came over…" Liv's voice was sharp over the sound of the baby crying. "And you didn't tell me?"

I immediately came to my feet, pleading with her. "I know Cash is your manager and Grace's boss. I should have consulted both of you first. Please don't be upset."

Tears spilled down Liv's cheeks. "You think *that's* why I'm upset? I'm not mad, Ella. I'm happy for you both. I'm just… I'm hurt. All night I've heard about things going on in your life and at the bakery that other people knew, but I didn't know anything about any of it. I feel like I'm hearing about someone I don't even know. Now that I'm starting a family of my own, you're treating me like we haven't been each other's family all these years. I have stood beside you during every phase of your life. Why can't you do the same for me?"

My hands flew to my chest as though they could somehow shield me from the tidal wave of her words, but nothing could have stopped them from pulling me under.

"Come on, Jax," Liv said finally, brushing past me. "Let's get the kids home." She turned and addressed the room, her eyes settling on everyone but me. "Sorry, everyone. Thanks for dinner."

Jax gave me an empathetic smile and squeezed my shoulder as he said his goodbyes and trailed after Liv.

Tears stung my eyes as Cash made his way to me. "I'm sorry, Ella. I did not mean for this to happen."

"Oof," Brandi squawked. "That was awkward."

My sadness gave way to anger as I remembered why this happened in the first place. I was so angry, in fact, that before I could stop myself, I snatched a glass of water from the table and threw it in Luca's face.

"YOU THREW WATER IN LUCA'S FACE?" KATIE ASKED WIDE-eyed late the following afternoon. "I can't say he hasn't had that coming for a while. I just didn't think it would be coming from you."

"Funny," I said, though I didn't laugh. "That's exactly what he said when I finally apologized to him." Things were slow at the bakery, and I seized my opportunity to tell Katie about the events from the night before and get her advice before I needed to leave to get home for Grace.

She pressed her palms to the sides of her face, shaking her head. "I still can't believe Cash blurted it out like that."

"What else was he supposed to do, though? I'd forgotten how to use words, and he panicked," I explained. "I'm not upset with him. I'm upset with myself. I should have been the one to tell Liv." I rubbed the back of my neck. "She's so upset with me, Katie Bug. She won't return my calls."

"You've got to give her some time." Katie squeezed my arm. "This is a lot to process."

197

"But to just not talk to me?" I asked. "To not even give me a chance to explain?"

She sighed and leaned against the front counter. "Look, if it had been my best friend Jo withholding something like this from me, I'd be pretty upset too. I'd get over it, but it would take a second."

I felt a fresh batch of tears cooking behind my eyes.

"I know this has been hard on you," Katie said gently. "It's been a lot of change all at once, but you have to remember that you're not the only one things are changing for. Liv got married and was immediately thrown into this whole instant family. Even if it was everything she ever wanted, it's still an adjustment. There were bound to be some growing pains."

"I know." I pressed my palms to my forehead, trying to relieve some of the pressure that had been building in my head since the day before. "I thought I was being sensitive to that by not bothering her with stuff."

"Ella, by not bothering her with anything you kind of cut her off from everything she's ever known at a time that's full of nothing but new and uncertain things."

Shit. I'm a selfish asshole. I sighed. "I never thought about it like that. I guess... I don't know. I felt like she had this whole new family, and she didn't need me anymore."

Katie chuckled softly. "Do you realize how silly that sounds? Not *need* you? She loves you. She's the Meredith to your Cristina, the Monica to your Rachel. You're each other's person." She gave me a sympathetic smile. "Jo and I are a lot like you and Liv. She's been my best friend since the sixth grade. When Jo finally moved to Chicago for her big-girl broadcasting job, it was a hard time for us. It was this weird adjustment period because her priorities in life shifted. It was hard for me for a while because everything in her life was new and exciting. Meanwhile, everything in my life was exactly the same, but I was doing life without her. It felt like there was a wedge in our friendship there for a while."

"How did you guys get past it?" I asked.

Katie shrugged. "It took time for us to adapt. It meant we both had to adjust our expectations a little. Her job is pretty demanding, and she doesn't take much in the way of vacation, so I'm the one who usually travels to see her. But she stays up way past her bedtime every Wednesday night just to talk to me. No, we don't get to see each other nearly as much as we would like, and we don't get to have marathon phone conversations all the time, but if Jo called me and needed me, I'd be there in a heartbeat. No question. You and Liv will find the balance that works for you too, but it will take time."

I swiped at my cheeks with the back of my palm. "Do you think she'll forgive me?"

"Ella, sweetheart." Katie pulled me into a hug. "Of course she will. You guys are just trying to find your footing. This is going to be nothing but a minor bump in a long road together for you two. I promise. Liv will come around. Especially once she hears what you did to Luca. That was legendary."

I laughed through my tears. "Thank you for being here for me. Not just now but literally all the time. I don't know what I would do without you."

"Of course, girl. I'm always here for you." She touched my shoulder. "Look, I love you. Dry those eyes. You need to get out of here to go see Grace. Has she landed yet?"

I nodded. "She texted me a few minutes ago. Shit. I didn't even ask you about your date." My phone rang from my back pocket.

"Eh, nothing exciting to report, I'm afraid," Katie said. "I'm going to go finish up. You get that."

"Thank you," I said again, fumbling for my phone. An unknown number flashed across the screen. I almost shoved the phone back in my pocket, but thought better of it. Grace should be on her way by now—what if she lost her phone? "Hello?"

"Is this Ella Claiborne?" an unfamiliar female voice asked.

"Yes," I said. "Who's this?"

"My name is Dr. Haversham. I'm calling from Vanderbilt hospital about your daughter Grace."

My blood turned to ice, and I felt a buzzing in my ear, almost as though I was holding one end of an electrical current. "Grace... Where's Grace? Is she okay?"

"Ms. Claiborne, I'm afraid your daughter's been in an accident."

"What?" My own voice sounded disembodied, like it didn't belong to me. I felt like I'd been shoved out of an airplane without a parachute.

I was falling, and the only thing waiting for me when I landed was pain.

TWENTY

Cash

"Hey, you," I answered the phone as I climbed into my car after work. "Did Grace make it in?"

My question was answered with the sound of indecipherable shrieking and crying.

Panic clawed its way up from the pit of my stomach. "Ella, baby, are you hurt? Where are you?"

There was more wailing, and I plugged my other ear with my finger, trying to work out the words between her cries.

"Sweetheart, I can't understand you." I tried to keep calm, but fear was beating on the walls of my chest. "Try to take a breath, and tell me where you are."

I heard her draw in a shallow breath. "It's Grace," she choked out. "She's been in an accident. She's at Vanderbilt hospital."

I'd only felt this kind of fear once in my life—the day I'd sat next to my wife in a colorless room and heard the word 'cancer.'

"Ella, are you driving?" I asked. I couldn't make out

everything she said, but I did hear her say Katie's name. "Katie is driving you?"

"Yes," she sobbed.

"Okay," I said, struggling to keep my composure. "I love you, Ella. Everything's going to be okay. I promise. I'm on my way."

I ended the call and turned on my hazard lights, peeling out of the parking lot. I swallowed hard, remembering the last time I'd made that promise. *Everything's going to be okay.*

Tears blurred my vision when I remembered how that had turned out. The world around me moved in fast forward, but I felt like I was crawling through quicksand. The pit in my stomach grew wider and wider, threatening to swallow me whole.

I sped into the parking lot of the hospital, barely remembering how I got there. I saw Katie standing outside the entry to the emergency room talking frantically into her phone. I parked the car and sprinted toward her. "Where is she?"

She dropped her phone to her side. "Come on." She led me inside the hospital, weaving down a corridor to the right. "Liv is on her way now. I just talked with her."

Katie walked right toward a red-headed nurse wearing grey scrubs who appeared to recognize her. "Is this the girl's father?"

Father? "What?" I asked, and Katie quickly pulled me into a hug.

"Do it now, ask for forgiveness later," Katie whispered. "Ella needs you. I'll be in the waiting room."

"Follow me, sir." The nurse guided me to the end of the hall, opening the last door on the left to reveal Grace in a hospital bed hooked up to all kinds of wires and monitors that beeped ominously. "She's on a light sedative and some pain medicine right now, so she might not wake up right away. I'll be back in a minute."

The sight of Grace with a large bandage over the right side of her cheek, her arm in a cast, and stains of blood on her skin was enough to make me want to fall to my knees. Her eyes were closed. She appeared to be resting peacefully.

I knew I had to appear strong for Ella who rose to her feet, throwing herself in my arms the second she saw me. Her body heaved and shook in my arms. I blinked back tears of my own as I rubbed her back and whispered comforting words I didn't entirely believe. I didn't exactly have a good track record in places like this.

It smelled like despair and disinfectants—the kind that lingered within you and burned your lungs long after you'd left the room. When Ella finally pulled back to look at me, her eyes were red, and her face was tear-stained.

"She has a couple of broken ribs, and her arm is broken. The doctor said it was a clean break and won't need surgery." Ella sniffled. "They sedated her because she had a panic attack. She was so distraught she was pulling her IVs out. They want to watch her for a couple of hours, but they said they would likely discharge her soon." She looked back at Grace, a forlorn expression painting her face. "This is my worst nightmare, Cash. What if..."

She didn't finish the sentence, and she didn't have to. Because it was the same scenario that had played on repeat in my head since we'd hung up the phone.

"But it didn't," I said with more confidence than I felt. It didn't, but this was a jarring reminder that it always could. "She's going to be okay."

I slowly crossed the room to Grace and placed a hand on her shoulder. She looked weak and fragile, as I placed a gentle kiss on the side of her head that wasn't covered in gauze. I could smell the iron from the dried blood matted in her hair.

There was a soft knock on the door, and the nurse in the grey scrubs appeared again. "I'm sorry to interrupt," she said softly. "I was hoping I might be able to get your help with something. The young man your daughter came in with... we're having a hard time reaching his emergency contact. I was hoping you might have a lead on how I can reach his family."

My stomach plummeted, gravity pulling it to the floor. I'd been in such a daze that I'd left my phone in the car. "It's me. I'm his emergency contact. Cash Montgomery." Sam's parents hadn't been in the picture since he was a baby. He'd been raised by his grandmother, but she'd long since passed.

A troubled expression settled into the lines of the nurse's face, and though it was probably only seconds until she spoke, it felt as though the time had stretched into hours. "Mr. Montgomery, I need you to come with me."

I SHOVED MY WAY OUT OF THE EMERGENCY ROOM EXIT, loosening the grip my tie had around my neck. *How did this happen? How did I get here?* Only hours before I'd been looking forward to Grace being home, to her knowing about Ella and me. I knew it wouldn't all be easy, but I felt we had a shot at becoming our own family.

But seeing Grace in that hospital bed all banged up and bruised... then finding out about Sam...

The cool brick was the only thing tethering me to the

earth as I leaned against the side of the building and choked back a sob.

I sucked in a deep breath of the humid evening air and pleaded with the universe to let me go back to a few hours before—back when I thought that maybe happy endings were possible.

You have to keep it together, Cash. There's no room for doubt right now. Ella needs you.

"Cash!" I was wrenched from my thoughts by the sound of Liv's voice as she launched herself at me, wrapping me in her arms. "How is she?"

"She was resting when I was up there last," I said. "I got called out of the room to see about Sam."

Liv furrowed her brow. "How is he? Is Sam okay?"

I raked my hands through my hair and shook my head. "He's in surgery right now. His spleen ruptured, and they said he had a lot of internal bleeding."

Liv covered her mouth with her hands. "Oh my God."

"They're most concerned with getting the bleeding under control." I scrubbed my hand down my face. "They said when the other car ran the traffic light that it hit Sam's side of the vehicle head on."

"Poor Sam." Liv shook her head. "And Grace. I'm so thankful she's okay. How's Ella holding up?"

"As well as could be expected," I said. "She's shaken up."

She squeezed my arm. "And how are you?"

I paused for a moment, unsure how to answer her question because I felt like I was falling apart. "I'm okay. It's just hard not to think of how differently this could have ended up."

"But it didn't," she insisted. "That's what matters." Her eyes filled with tears. "I want you to know how sorry I am about how I acted last night. I'm so thankful Ella has you to lean on. And Grace too. They're lucky to have you in their lives."

I wanted to respond. To tell her that maybe I wasn't the man she thought I was. To confess how shattered I felt seeing Grace in such a helpless state. To attempt to assuage my guilt for not being strong enough to stand at Ella's side. Instead, I didn't say anything at all. There was no fight and no flight. I was merely frozen.

"You want to head back inside?" Liv asked finally.

"You go ahead," I said. "I, uh… I need to grab my phone out of the car."

"Okay." She gave me a sympathetic smile. "I'll see you in there."

As I watched her disappear inside the building, I wondered how lucky Ella and Grace really were when I was outside trying to console myself instead of being the man they could count on.

TWENTY-ONE

Ella

I WATCHED GRACE'S CHEST RISE AND FALL, THANKFUL FOR every breath she took. I knew we'd been lucky. Most kids didn't escape their youth without at least one broken bone or a hospital stay, though, I'd hoped somehow that Grace would. She'd been through enough pain. Didn't she deserve a pass? Didn't kids who lost a parent deserve to miss some of these other painful rites of passage?

"My sweet, sweet girl." I placed my hand over hers, gently rubbing her fingers with the pad of my thumb. I thought about all the times Craig and I had counted her little fingers and toes when she'd been born, when they were nothing more than tiny, wrinkly nubs.

Her fingers were long and elegant now. I knew she wasn't a kid anymore, but she would always be my baby. Salty tears dripped down my face and onto my lips. I wondered where Cash was and said a silent prayer that Sam would be okay. He was a sweet kid, and I had a feeling Grace cared about him more than she'd ever admitted to me. If anything happened to him...

No. I wouldn't even let myself think about it.

Broken bones could be healed with surgery or casts made of plaster, but broken hearts were different.

"Ella." I was so deep in thought I didn't even hear the door open.

As soon as I saw Liv I was on my feet throwing my arms around her, sinking into the comforting warmth of my best friend's embrace. "You're here."

"Where else would I be?" she asked, smoothing my hair with her hands. She rocked me back and forth as I cried. "It's going to be okay. Everything is going to be alright."

"I'm so sorry, Liv," I cried into her hair.

"I'm sorry too," she said softly in my ear. "I love you so much."

"Mama?" Grace's voice was gravelly and small.

I turned and closed the distance between us, folding her hand in mine. "Hey, honey. I'm right here. How are you feeling?"

She groaned. "Everything hurts."

"Hey, sweetie," Liv said, going to her other side and squeezing her hand. "It sure is good to see you."

"Aunt Livvie." Grace gave a faint smile.

"Can I get you anything, baby?" I asked, desperate for anything I could do that could provide her some comfort or relief.

Grace shook her head.

"How about something to drink?" I asked. "Or some ice chips?"

"Some ice would be good," Grace answered.

"I'll go get it," Liv offered. "I'll give you two a minute." She patted Grace's leg and disappeared out the door.

Grace's lip quivered as she looked up at me, her blue eyes glistening with tears. "I need to see Sam. Is he okay?"

I gently wiped away her tears with the back of my hand. "Cash is checking on him right now, sweetheart."

She shook her head in disbelief. "It came out of nowhere."

"I'm so sorry, baby." I stroked her arm, attempting to soothe her. When she was a little girl she always used to ask for 'arm tickles.' "I know you're worried about Sam, sweetheart. Cash is finding out everything he can, but we need to keep you calm, okay?"

"Mama." She looked at me tentatively, her eyes still heavy from the medication. "I need to tell you something, and I need you to promise you won't be mad."

"Well, considering how pitiful you look in this hospital bed, it's going to take a lot to make me mad, so you're at an advantage," I joked. "What is it, sweetie?"

She took a deep breath. "Sam and I... we're kind of a thing."

"I can't say I'm surprised," I said.

She pressed her lips together, her tired eyes filled with trepidation. "We've been a thing for a while. Like since before Aunt Liv's wedding."

"Okay, *this* surprises me," I admitted.

She hesitated before speaking again. "Do you remember the night of Liv's wedding when I told you I was going to stay the night with Lexi and that Sam was going to take me?"

I narrowed my eyes. "Let me guess. There was no sleep-over with Lexi."

She sighed and shook her head.

"Grace, why didn't you feel like you could tell me about this?" I asked.

"I don't know," she said, her blinks slow and fluttery. "I

guess I thought you might think I was too young for a serious relationship."

"So, is it?" I questioned. "Serious, I mean?"

She nodded. "I love him, Mom."

I sat quietly for a moment, processing what she was telling me.

"You're upset with me, aren't you?" she asked.

"I'm not. I promise," I said. "I do wish you'd told me, though. I certainly have no room to judge anyone ever. You know I was your age when I met your father, right? Sometimes the heart wants what it wants. But, as your mother, I want to make sure you're being safe."

"We're not having sex yet, if that's what you mean," she added slowly.

I breathed a sigh of relief. "And as it happens, I can't be too upset because I have some news I haven't shared with you yet either, and I'm not really sure how you're going to take it."

She tilted her head to the side, wincing slightly.

"While you were gone, I…" I let out a sharp breath. "Cash and I started dating."

Her eyes widened, and then she broke into a smile which caused her to flinch. She instinctively reached for her bandaged cheek. "Are you serious? Mom, that's amazing."

"Do you remember that night you called and said something about how you were going to tell Cash he should have dinner with me?" I gritted my teeth together.

She squinted as she thought for a few seconds, her foggy brain not quite putting the pieces together. "Yeah…"

"We were actually together when you called that night," I confessed.

"Shut up," she said in disbelief, her voice slow and sleepy. "Oh my God, this makes me so happy."

"Really? You don't think it's weird since he's also kind of your boss?"

"It's not weird. It's *awesome*. I'm really happy for you, Mom." Her face fell a bit. "Do you think Sam is going to be okay?"

The truth was, I wasn't sure. I'd thought Cash would have returned already, and the longer he was gone, the more worried I became. "I think so. I hope so."

"Will you go see if you can find Cash?" she asked. "And maybe find out when I can get out of here so I can go see Sam?"

I squeezed her hand. "Of course. I'll be right back."

The hope in her eyes glowed so bright, and I said a silent prayer that I wouldn't have to deliver news that would turn that light to darkness.

ONCE GRACE WAS DISCHARGED WITH SOME PAIN MEDS AND A plan to follow up with the orthopedist, I insisted Liv get back to the kids. Cash was there for support, and we were all just sitting around waiting anyway.

I'd offered to take Grace home so she could at least clean up a little bit and get something to eat. I thought perhaps that could distract her while we waited for news on Sam, but she was immovable. She wouldn't leave the hospital until she knew he was okay, and I couldn't blame her. All we knew was that Sam was still in surgery. Every time someone came through the waiting room, our eyes shot up, hoping it was someone with any sort of news on his condition.

Katie had made sure we all had some dinner before she headed out, taking Grace's luggage with her and dropping it by my house. She offered to take Bradley Cooper for a walk and make sure he'd been fed. Dallas and even Luca had called to check on Grace and Sam, and Derek had shown up with some flowers and a 'Get Well Soon' teddy bear for Grace.

Cash was quiet, his mouth set in a firm, stoic line. I knew he was worried about Sam. We all were.

"I need some coffee. And not whatever that dirty caffeine water is over there." I pointed to the coffee carafe set up in the waiting room.

"I think there's a coffee cart around the main entrance," Derek said. "I only know that because I came in the wrong one."

"Anyone want anything?" I asked as I stood.

"I'm good," Cash whispered so as not to wake Grace who was sleeping against his shoulder. He turned, pressing a soft kiss to her head.

"I'll walk with you," Derek said, rising to his feet. "I should get going anyway."

I leaned down to give Cash a quick kiss on the lips. "I'll be right back."

"I'm so glad Grace is okay," Derek said as we walked. "I can't imagine how terrifying that was."

"I can't describe how terrifying it was." I crossed my arms to ward against the chill of the hospital. "Getting the call that she'd been in an accident was one of my greatest fears come to life."

"I hope Sam is alright," he said. "Keep me updated, will you?"

"Of course."

"Listen, Ella, I wanted to apologize," he began. "For making things worse last night. I just assumed Liv knew by now, but I should have kept my mouth shut."

"You have nothing to apologize for," I insisted. "I should have told Liv. That was on me."

He gave me an empathetic grin. "I still feel bad."

"You know who should feel bad? Luca. That's who should feel bad."

He chuckled. "Shockingly enough, I think he did."

"You think?" I asked.

"He asked me what I thought he should do to make it up to everyone for being such an asshole."

"Well, color me surprised." I placed my hand on my chest. "I hope he finally learned Brandi's name."

"Let's not give him too much credit," Derek said. "Luca is only capable of so much."

I laughed. "I knew as soon as I said it there was no chance."

We fell into a comfortable silence for a moment before he spoke again. "It's really good seeing you and Cash together."

"It feels really good being with him," I said. "He really showed up for me and Grace today."

Derek nodded. "As he should."

I wanted to ask Derek a question and get his insight. Once things had settled down, something Cash had said lingered in my mind, seeping into my thoughts. "Derek, can I ask you something?"

"Of course," he replied.

I chewed my lip thoughtfully for a moment. "When I called Cash earlier in a total panic, he said something that kind of stayed with me before we got off the phone."

His brow furrowed. "Oh?"

"He said he loved me, and I'm not sure how I should take that. I mean, it was an intense moment. I had just told him Grace had been in an accident. Emotions were high…"

Derek nodded. "And you're wondering if he meant it or if he said it in the heat of the moment?"

"Exactly," I answered.

A pensive expression came over his face as we stopped near the coffee cart in the main lobby of the hospital. "I think that those intense, scary moments are when we're our most vulnerable selves. So, to answer your question, yes, I believe he meant it."

Relief bloomed in my chest. "You really think so?"

"I do." He studied my face. "How do *you* feel about that?"

I sighed. *Relieved, ecstatic, completely petrified.* "I feel good. It felt good to have him here today. He brings a sense of stability to my life I haven't experienced since Craig, which is amazing, but…"

"Also kind of scary because of what that implies?" he asked.

I nodded. "I love him. And not just a little. A *lot.* And that is terrifying."

"It's never easy to be vulnerable, but I imagine it's even less easy after you've experienced a loss like the one you and Grace had." He placed a hand on my shoulder. "But I think you're both in good hands. He knows how precious this is because he's shared the same kind of loss."

"You may be the youngest in the band, but you're also the wisest." I grinned. "And for what it's worth, I think you should have kept your plans to go to New York and told Dallas to shove it. I love the guy, but it wasn't cool how he handled that."

"Over the years I've learned that sometimes it's just better to keep the peace." He gave me a wistful smile, and I couldn't help but wonder how many times he'd shoved down his own desires to keep the peace within the band. "Anyway, if you need anything, let me know. I'm happy to go by and check on Bradley Cooper for you if you and Grace need to be here with Sam over the next few days."

"I might take you up on that." I smiled. "You're a gem, Derek Knights, you know that?"

He winked. "I try."

"No you don't," I said. "And that's why I love you."

"Love you too." He hugged me. "Keep me posted."

"I will," I said as I got in line at the coffee cart and watched him disappear out the door, his words still dancing in my mind.

TWENTY-TWO

Cash

GRACE STIRRED AT MY SIDE, CAREFULLY LIFTING HER HEAD off my shoulder. She winced as she readjusted in her chair.

"How are you feeling?" I asked.

"Like complete crap," she answered. "Where'd Mom go?"

"She just went to grab a coffee," I said. "She'll be back in a minute."

Grace eased her head back on my shoulder and placed her hand that wasn't in the cast on my arm. "I'm glad you and Mom are together. Aside from finding out that Mom got Bradley Cooper, this is the best news I could have hoped for."

I feigned offense. "You mean I got beat out by the dog?"

"Well, I've wanted a puppy pretty much my entire life." She chuckled and flinched, clutching at her ribs. "Ouch. It hurts to laugh. Anyway, did you know that the nurse thought you were my father?"

Father. There was that word again. I'd panicked when I

saw Grace in the hospital bed, but with her tucked away safely by my side, I felt more steady. Like I could be the type of man that made a good father. I could be a man that didn't run out of the hospital gasping for air at the first sign of trouble... right?

I wanted to believe that, but the more the minutes ticked by without an update on Sam, I felt that sense of doubt building in my mind again.

"Katie told the nurse I was your dad so they'd let me back to see you," I explained.

She got quiet again, and for a moment, I thought she'd drifted back to sleep. "Is it weird for me to say that sometimes I wish you were? I love my dad, and I miss him. But is it so bad for me to wish I had a dad that was actually here?"

My heart caught in my throat.

"That's weird, isn't it?" she said. "I'm sorry. I'm still loopy, I guess."

I cleared my throat in an effort to mask the emotion that crept into my voice. "That's not weird, sweetheart."

"I don't remember a lot about my dad, but I remember the way he felt. He felt... safe, like he'd always protect me." She sighed softly. "You feel like that too. Like a dad."

I swallowed hard, afraid that if I tried to speak, I'd completely break down. After how scared I'd been, I didn't feel I deserved her words. Dads wouldn't buckle under pressure, would they?

No, they'd have stayed by her side the entire time. They'd have watched over the hospital staff to make sure they were giving her the best possible care. They wouldn't be a coward, like I'd been.

"Mr. Montgomery?" A voice tore me from my thoughts. I looked up to see a man about my age in a white lab coat staring down at me.

I nodded. "Yes, that's me."

"I'm Dr. Williams." He glanced at Grace who lifted her head from my shoulder. "May I have a word with you in private?"

I felt Grace's grip tighten around my arm as I stood to follow the doctor. "It's okay. I'll be right back."

He led me to a corridor outside the waiting room just as I saw Ella return to Grace's side.

"Is Sam okay?" I asked as we came to a stop.

"Mr. Montgomery, I removed Sam's spleen and was able to get his bleeding under control," the doctor said, "but we had a hard time controlling his blood pressure during the procedure, so he's still intubated. We're keeping him in the ICU to monitor him more closely, but I feel optimistic his condition will improve over the next few hours, and we'll be able to extubate him tomorrow. I expect he'll make a full recovery, and barring any complications, we should be able to discharge him in about a week."

Thank God. I felt my entire body sigh with relief. "That's great news!"

"It is." Dr. Williams didn't smile, his expression completely unreadable. "However, something else came up during surgery that I'm a little concerned about."

My stomach dropped. "Okay…"

"Sam has a mass on his pancreas. It measures about one point five centimeters, which isn't huge, but it's large enough to give me pause," he informed me. "I'm running a biopsy so we can confirm whether it's malignant or benign."

Malignant. My head felt like it was spinning. "Wait." I placed my hand on the wall in an attempt to ground myself. My heart was beating out of my chest. "Are you saying Sam could have… cancer?" *No, no, no, no. This can't be happening.*

"Let's not jump to conclusions," the doctor said. "We'll see what the lab results show and go from there."

"Right." My chest was tight as though I had a five hundred pound weight on top of me. "When will those come back?" The air suddenly seemed hot, causing me to feel dizzy.

"We should have them back within a couple of days."

I nodded. "Can we see him? I don't want him to be alone." I couldn't stand the thought of him being by himself in that room with nothing but the sounds of beeping monitors. He may not know if he was alone, but I would know.

"Of course," he answered. "A nurse will come get you and take you to his room."

My stomach churned. "Thank you," I said as he shook my hand and started off down the hall.

Cancer. The word on my tongue made me feel like I was being choked. I leaned against the wall and scrubbed my hands over my face. What if Sam had cancer? I thought about the sweet girl in the waiting room who was desperate for some good news about the guy she cared about and how much that one little word could wreck her. I thought about how that word had wrecked me too.

I looked up at the ceiling tiles with the angry fluorescent lights flickering. When I closed my eyes, all I could see was Carrie's face.

———

"I HATE THIS," ELLA WHISPERED, WRAPPING HER ARMS around my waist and leaning into me. "I hate that she's hurting, and there's nothing I can do to make it better."

We were standing outside of Sam's room in the ICU,

watching through the glass as Grace took a few moments with him. After I'd told her what the doctor said, she'd been dead set on not leaving his side. But once she realized I would be staying with him, she'd agreed to go home long enough to clean up and sleep for a few hours before coming back.

"I know." My mouth felt like all the moisture had been sucked out of it, yet my insides sloshed around like an abandoned life raft at sea. I felt powerless against God, the universe... life. The events over the previous twenty-four hours seemed to be flashing neon signs reminding me that at any moment, everything I love could be ripped out of my grasp. "I wish I could do something."

"You being here." She looked up at me, her eyes puffy and swollen. "That's something."

Except I wasn't there, was I? Physically maybe, but my mind was drowning.

I knew I loved Ella and Grace. I was certain of that. But along with that certainty came the realization that I couldn't bear the risk of losing them.

"Hey," Ella said, breaking through my thoughts. "You look like you're a million miles away. Are you okay?"

I forced a tight smile and nodded. "It's been a... trying day."

"I know," she replied. "But I believe that Sam is going to be okay. I truly do."

I shook my head. "How can you be sure?" Even if he turned out to be okay, the threat was always looming. It was always there. My life was always one diagnosis, one car accident, one phone call away from being over again. Could I handle that? Could I possibly lose Ella or Grace and survive it?

She sighed. "I can't, but what's the alternative? Worrying about it is only borrowing from tomorrow's problems. What matters is that Sam is important to Grace, and that makes him very important to me. So, no matter what it is, we'll deal with it. Sam has Grace and the two of us, and I know the others think a lot of him too. We'll make sure he has all the support he needs."

I opened my mouth to say something but closed it again, afraid I would give myself away for the coward I was.

"I should get her home," Ella said. "Are you sure you're okay to stay here tonight? I could get Katie to come stay with Grace and come back?"

"No, I'm fine." I kissed the top of her head, inhaling the fresh lemony scent of her hair. "You two go get some rest."

Her hand lingered on me, and I followed as she entered Sam's room. "Grace, we should get going."

Grace was at his side, holding his hand in hers, tears slipping down her cheeks. She was quiet for a few moments before finally nodding. She stood and made her way to me, nestling herself under my arm. "Take care of him," she murmured.

"I will," I promised.

Ella placed a soft kiss on my lips. "We'll see you in the morning."

"Let me know you made it home safe."

Ella nodded, placing her arm around Grace's shoulders. "I know Bradley Cooper's going to be ready to break out the welcome wagon for you," she said as she steered her from the room, leaving me alone with Sam.

I took the seat by the bed that had been occupied by Grace, resting my elbows on my knees and my head in my hands. "Sam, buddy, I'm here, okay? I don't know if you can hear me, but I'm right here."

The room was cold, the kind of cold that could cut you in half, which was fitting because I felt like I was being pulled in two different directions. Half of me longed to be with Ella—to be the type of man she and Grace could depend on. But the other half knew better. A happy ending like the one Jax and Liv had? They were rare and hard to come by.

They possessed a certain magic—the kind movies were made about that sparkled across the screen in technicolor. Any movie about my life would be made in black and white and shades of grey. And no matter how much I wished it to be different, it was very possible that when the credits rolled on my movie, a sad song would be playing as the screen faded into darkness.

I closed my eyes, the silence in the room punctuated by the rhythmic sound of the ventilator and the hums and beeps of the monitors Sam was hooked up to. It was a soundtrack that was both unnerving and hauntingly familiar. With my eyes closed, I remembered sitting in another sterile room much like the one I was in, waiting for Carrie to wake from surgery. It was the day we found out that what was supposed to be a new beginning was really the beginning of the end.

In my mind's eye, I saw myself at Carrie's bedside with her hand in mine. In the early days of her diagnosis, we'd talk about everything, and her light continued to shine despite her circumstances. But when her light started to dim, I watched as her hands that had once been warm and pink with life turned cold and ashen.

Tears pooled in my eyes as I opened them, and I placed my hand on top of Sam's. I said a silent prayer that he would come through this unscathed and that Grace would never have to know the heartbreak of watching the person she loved slowly disappear.

A gnawing feeling settled into my gut, buried deep inside like a parasite. What if this had all happened to show me that I couldn't survive another loss like Carrie's and that maybe I wasn't as ready to move on as I thought I was? What if I was never ready?

TWENTY-THREE

Ella

"You know, I'm a little offended that you've already stolen my dog," I joked as I sat beside Grace at the kitchen table. I handed her a glass of orange juice and her morning dose of meds. Bradley Cooper lifted his head to look at me only to flop it back down beside her foot.

"We had some lost time to make up for." She winced as she shifted in her seat, her cast looking bulky in comparison to the rest of her. "Any word from Cash?"

I shook my head. "I'd say that means no news is good news." As the words left my mouth, I wasn't sure I believed them. I'd texted Cash to let him know we made it home safely as he'd asked, but he never replied. I assumed he'd fallen asleep, but there was a part of me that was unnerved. He'd seemed a little distant before we left the night before.

That was normal, though, right? It was a hard day, and he was probably just exhausted. I attempted to put the thought out of my mind as I chewed a bite of my toast.

"I haven't even asked how Grandma is," Grace said,

taking a bite of the eggs I'd scrambled for her. "Is she okay?"

"There's not been much change. She did have a few minutes of lucidity the other night. Nicole called me to come, but your grandma was already gone by the time I got there. She thought we were from the church."

"We?" Grace asked. "Did Cash go with you?"

I nodded, taking a sip of my coffee. "He did."

"Grandma would love him if she could meet him," she said. "Like really meet him."

"I think so too."

Grace twirled her fork on her plate, shoving her eggs and toast around more than she was eating them. "Do you think Sam is going to be okay? This mass on his pancreas... do you think it's going to be anything to worry about?"

"I think that no matter what happens, we'll handle it," I said. "Together."

"Cash seemed kinda... I don't know... freaked out last night." Grace chewed her lip.

"I know this news about Sam has him unsettled, and he was very worried about you."

"No, it was more than that," she said. "I think I freaked him out. When you were gone to get coffee, I was still kinda out of it from the meds, and I said some stuff... I basically told him he felt like a dad to me."

My heart twisted. I knew that Craig would have loved nothing more than to have seen his little girl grow up, but if he couldn't be here, he would have picked a man like Cash to take his place. "Did you mean that? Even if you were a little loopy?"

She nodded. "But I don't want to freak him out."

"You told him something that was true to your heart, and I know Cash adores you, regardless of whether or not he and I are seeing each other," I assured her. "I think he was just overwhelmed with all of the emotions from the day." I realized I was also trying to reassure myself. "You know, it's still early in this thing with Cash and me."

Grace looked down at her food. "I know."

"I know you're excited, and I am too." I placed my hand on top of her bare one. "I just don't want you to get your hopes up in case something were to happen."

"Well, it's a little late for that." She laughed. "This isn't just anyone. This isn't that Ryan guy. This is Cash we're talking about. He's already family. I've always secretly hoped you guys would get together."

"I guess the fact that we're already such a big part of each other's lives is what makes this so delicate," I admitted. "Because if anything were to go wrong… well, that makes things complicated."

My phone pinged from the counter, and I stood to grab it.

Cash: Doctor is here and they're taking the tube out now.

"Is that Cash?" Grace pressed. "What'd he say?"

I smiled. "Sounds like Sam is getting the tube out."

"We've got to go," she exclaimed, grimacing as she rose to her feet.

"Give me five minutes," I said. "I've got to throw these dishes in the dishwasher and load up Bradley Cooper. I texted Derek, and he's going to pick him up from the hospital and let him spend the day with him."

"I'll go grab my purse," she said, ambling out of the kitchen.

I pulled up Cash's text and sent one back.

Ella: We're leaving in 5. Any updates on the biopsy yet?

The little bubbles appeared to indicate that he was

typing, but then abruptly stopped. I waited another moment, but a message never came.

"AND HERE I THOUGHT THE BLOODY NODES WERE MY greatest concern." Sam's signature British accent was hoarse, and he sounded exhausted, but he was awake, albeit a little confused. "Are spleens even that important?"

Grace had been catching him up to speed on everything that happened since right before the accident. Cash had greeted us, but left the room to get a coffee once we'd gotten there. He'd kissed me and hugged Grace, yet something still felt... off. I tried to remind myself that he was worn out and on emotional overload—we all were. *Don't be so sensitive, Ella. If he didn't want to be here, he wouldn't.*

"It turns out the spleen is important, but you can live without it. I honestly had no idea," I said, "but when I consulted Dr. Google, it told me it's sort of like a coffee filter for your blood."

Sam chuckled and winced.

"It hurts when I laugh too." Grace reached for his hand, intertwining their fingers.

I watched as he brought her fingers to his lips and kissed them gently. My mama heart was both happy and a little sad watching the intimate gesture. It was obvious from the way he looked at her that he was absolutely captivated by her. It melted my heart to see her being adored the way she deserved, but it was yet another reminder that my little girl wasn't so little anymore.

"I guess we won't be taking you kids to any comedy clubs for a while," I teased.

"Afraid not," Sam replied.

"When do we get to bust you out of this joint anyway?" I asked.

"They said I should be able to be discharged within the week," Sam answered. "He didn't nail down an exact date, but he seemed to feel good about it. I'm a little nervous because he said I'd still need to take it easy, and my house has quite a lot of stairs."

"Don't worry about that," I assured him. "We'll sort something out. Maybe you could stay with Cash or even with us while you get back on your feet."

"What was that?" Cash asked, returning to the room with a caddy of takeaway cups in his hands. He handed one to each of us, keeping the last for himself. "I got some ice chips for you, Sam."

Sam gave a weak smile. "Thanks."

"We were just talking about what to do after Sam is released," I said, taking a sip of my coffee, prepared exactly the way I liked it. "He was saying that he was a little concerned about staying at his house because of the stairs. I said that perhaps he could stay with one of us."

"Right." Cash's smile was tight as a pair of jeans that were a size too small. "I'm sure we can figure something out. By the way, Antoni called to check on you while I was headed down to the cafeteria. He was visiting Nate's family and saw it on the news this morning."

"Bloody hell." Sam grimaced. "My spleen made the news?"

"Apparently," Cash said. "I had a message from someone at the office saying they'd been fielding calls since late last night."

"Shit," I cursed. "I didn't even think to call him."

"I didn't either," Cash admitted. "Everything happened so fast. He didn't know that Grace was the other person in the vehicle so you can imagine he was even more shocked when I told him that part."

"I'll give him a call today," I said. "Why don't we give these two a minute?" I gestured toward Grace and Sam. While I did want them to have some time together, the truth was, I really wanted a moment alone with Cash.

Cash nodded. "Yeah, we can do that." He opened the door and held it for me.

"We'll be right outside," I said, and Grace glanced back at me gratefully. Once the door closed, I took his coffee from his hand and placed our cups on the ledge of the window outside Sam's room, wrapping my arms around Cash. He seemed almost tense at first but then sank into my embrace, resting his chin on top of my head.

"Hey," he whispered, kissing my forehead.

"Hi," I said back.

"How did Grace do last night?" he asked.

"I don't think she slept a lot," I replied. "She was pretty uncomfortable, and I know she was worried about Sam."

"They're pretty sweet together, aren't they?" He peered in through the glass where Grace and Sam were deep in conversation.

"They are," I agreed, looking at them. "I hope I wasn't out of line saying Sam could stay with one of us."

"You weren't," he said, though his tone didn't quite match his words. "We'll make it work somehow."

I nodded, shifting my eyes back to Cash. "Any word on Sam's biopsy yet?"

Cash stiffened and shook his head, but his gaze didn't meet mine.

"Cash, is everything okay?" I asked.

He turned his eyes back to mine, but he still felt distant, disconnected. "What? Yeah, I'm okay."

"You couldn't have gotten much rest last night," I said. "Why don't you let me take over for a while? We'll stay with Sam. You go get some rest."

He looked back to where Sam and Grace were chatting through the glass and then returned his eyes to mine. "Alright. I probably need to catch up with the office too. Just make sure everybody's on the same page about what information we're releasing to the press about Sam."

I smoothed my hands over his chest. "Okay, but promise me you'll get a little sleep."

"I will," he agreed, placing his hand on the side of my cheek, lightly caressing my skin with his thumb. For a moment, I thought he was going to say something else, but instead he pressed a soft kiss to my lips, a longing look in his hazel eyes. "I'll be back later."

"We'll be here," I promised.

He kissed me once more before starting down the hall toward the elevators, and I watched until he disappeared. The space he'd been occupying turned cold, leaving me wondering if there was something more on his mind.

TWENTY-FOUR

Cash

I MADE A COUPLE OF CALLS ON THE DRIVE HOME TO ENSURE everyone at the label was on the same page about Sam's condition and what information we wanted out in the public domain. I also made sure that Grace's name was left out of it. The last thing she and Ella needed were some overzealous fans staking them out. By the time I pulled into my driveway, I felt completely and utterly drained.

I entered through the garage and was met by the usual silence that awaited me. It was something that I'd been used to, but at that moment, the stillness sent prickles of uneasiness down my spine.

The house looked exactly as I'd left it a couple of days before, but it felt emptier somehow. There was suddenly too much space between the furniture, and the walls felt bare. The few memories that hung there felt lifetimes away but at the same time like just yesterday.

This place was supposed to be my refuge from the grief I felt. It was supposed to be a symbol of new beginnings, but sorrow had found me anyway, moving in when I wasn't looking. It permeated the air, leaving nothing behind but the stench of despair.

When I made it to the bedroom, I sat on the foot of my bed and closed my eyes, rubbing my temples with my fingers. The room was dark except for the slivers of light that filtered around the drapes. When I opened my eyes again, I saw that the light had perfectly illuminated Carrie's face in the photograph on the dresser.

I drew in a ragged breath as the weight of the last twenty-four hours pulled me under. I was caught in a vicious current of grief, over losing Carrie, over how close I came to losing Grace, over Sam possibly having cancer... over the fact that I could lose everything I cared about all over again. My body shook as the rapids tossed me further and further from the shore until I was just a dot in a sea of sadness. If just the possibility was enough to bring me to my knees, how would I survive if something were to actually happen?

I'd never lost a child before because I'd never been lucky enough to have a child of my own. But there was something about Grace. When I looked at her, she felt like mine or at least what I imagined that would feel like. I'd always heard people describe being a parent as having your heart beat outside of your body.

Was this what that felt like? When I'd seen her in that hospital bed, it felt like all the oxygen had been ripped from my lungs. I'd have laid down my life if it had meant saving her from pain.

Carrie's picture swam through the deluge of sadness that poured from my eyes as I pressed the heel of my palm into my chest in a vague attempt at stopping the ache that continued to spread. I crawled up the mattress and laid down on top of the comforter, burying my face in the pillow.

Ella's beautiful face tore through the darkness of my mind, but it only made me weep harder because all I could imagine was what would happen if I lost her too. A montage of events that may never happen played on an endless loop, each with a worse outcome than the last.

"I can't do this," I said to the shadows of the room. "God, please help me." My words came out strangled and weak. "I don't know how to do this."

The sound of my phone ringing from my pocket ripped through the otherwise quiet room. I considered not answering it but feared it could be Ella with news on Sam. When I freed the phone from my pocket, I realized it was Delilah's number that flashed across the screen.

Without thinking, I swiped across the device and brought it to my ear, desperate to feel connected to something that felt like home. I tried to say something, anything, but only a warbled sob came out.

"Cash," Delilah's worried voice came through the phone. "Are you alright?"

Once again, no words came from my mouth.

"I just saw the news about that boy you manage," she said. "Oh dear, is he alright?"

"Yes," I managed to choke out. I drew in a couple of sharp breaths, trying to regain some composure. "Grace was in the car with him."

I heard her gasp.

"She's okay." My voice cracked with emotion. "They're both okay."

"You're scaring me," Delilah said softly. "Tell me, dear. What's the matter?"

"It just hurts. Everything hurts," I cried. "And I miss

Carrie. I miss her so much, Delilah. I don't know what to do. I don't know what I'm doing."

"I know, dear. I know. I miss her too." Her voice wavered slightly. "Perhaps Richard and I should come for a visit?"

I thought for a moment about how good it would feel to see Delilah and Richard, but I also knew them being here could make my feelings even more complicated. "No, no. It's okay." I sucked in a deep breath and held it for a few seconds before exhaling. "I'm sorry, Delilah. I'm overwhelmed, and I haven't had any sleep. I just got back from the hospital, and... during Sam's surgery they found a suspicious mass on his pancreas. They're doing a biopsy. It's brought back so many memories. Maybe... maybe I'm not doing as well as I thought I was."

"I know, sweetie," she said. "Some days it breaks my heart all over again. But you know you always have us, right? You don't ever have to go through this alone."

I nodded, though I knew she couldn't hear me.

"I really think we should come for a visit. Even if only for a couple of days."

"I'll be alright," I promised, my breathing slowly growing more even. "I'm sorry. You just caught me during a weak moment. I'll feel better once I get some sleep."

"Alright." She paused, sighing softly. "You know, it's okay to have moments like that. They don't make you weak, dear. They make you human."

I squeezed my eyes shut as I listened to her.

"I love you, Cash," Delilah said. "We both do. Never forget that."

"I love you both too," I whispered.

"Maybe some time away would help?" she suggested. "You can always come here. We'd sure love to see you.

Perhaps you could take a few days off to come visit once things settle down?"

I had to admit, the idea of escaping to their home breathed a little relief into my chest. But I knew that I had to make sure everyone else was taken care of before I did anything else. "I may do that soon."

"I do hope you will," she said.

"I should go and try to get some sleep, but I'll call soon," I promised.

"Alright, dear," she said reluctantly. "Get some rest."

I swiped across the screen to end the call, dropping the phone onto the bed. The despair that had been ravaging through my body slowly turned to numbness, my limbs heavy with exhaustion from swimming against the current. I closed my eyes and succumbed to the waves, letting them pull me under into a deep, dreamless sleep.

A COUPLE OF MORNINGS LATER I WAS IN SAM'S NEW hospital room, gazing outside through the plastic blinds that were drawn open. In the time since he'd been in the ICU, he'd made enough progress to be moved to a step-down unit. He was sipping on a bowl of soup with Grace at his side on the bed and Ella in the chair nearby.

"How's that soup?" Ella asked.

"I don't know if we can call this watery concoction soup." Sam peered inside his cup with distaste. "I'd give anything for some cottage pie about now."

Grace's eyes lit up. "That stuff we had at the pub we went to in Manchester?"

"Mmm." Sam sighed. "That sounds amazing."

"Okay, well, Grace will tell you, the only thing I know

how to cook is a frozen pizza," Ella said. "But I'm sure we can make a cottage pie happen somehow. I bet Katie could figure out how to make one." I could see her eyes looking at me through the reflection in the glass. "And Cash here is pretty handy in the kitchen too." She stood and crossed the room to me, gliding her fingertips along my back. "What do you think? Could we make Sam here a jolly ole cottage pie worthy of the Queen?"

"Hmmm?" I turned to her. "Oh, yes. Sure."

"That settles it then." Ella beamed back at Sam and Grace. "When you get out of here, we'll make you a celebratory cottage pie."

"That would be lovely," Sam said.

"And by 'we,' I mean I'll play the part of sous chef," Ella joked. "My talents include being the world's slowest vegetable chopper and an enthusiastic taste-tester." She looked at me with a grin. I forced a smile in response which caused the joy to fade from her face. My chest tightened as she placed her hand on my arm. I hated myself for making her anything less than happy, but I didn't have happiness in me.

I was drowning inside myself, my heart at war with the sadness that seemed insistent on being present with me every waking second.

Grace flashed Ella a worried look, but before anything else could be said, Dr. Williams rapped softly on the door and pushed his way inside.

"Sam," he said. "How are you feeling today?"

"Better," he replied. "Ready to get out of here."

"In that case, I've got some good news for you." The doctor smiled. "I think I can clear you to leave Saturday, barring any sort of complications. But you're healing well. I don't see any reason you can't go home this weekend. It will take some time for you to regain your strength, but there's no reason you can't do that from home, especially with a little help."

"We're going to make sure he has all the help he needs," Ella spoke up. "He'll have more help than he'll know what to do with. He'll be sick of us before this is all said and done."

Dr. Williams chuckled. "That's perfect. As it happens, I've got more good news for you."

My ears perked.

"I got the results of your biopsy this morning," he said, "and the mass on your pancreas is benign."

Relief flooded Sam's face, and Grace squeezed his hand.

Ella clutched her hand to her chest. "Oh, thank goodness."

"That's wonderful news," I said, but the feeling of despair that had been looming clouded my vision.

"Yes, it is." Sam looked at me and smiled before turning his gaze back to Grace. "We got pretty lucky, you and me."

"The luckiest." Happy tears fell down Grace's cheeks. I couldn't help but remember the many times Carrie and I had waited in hospital rooms and doctor's offices for good news, our eyes full of hope and love. But every time, we were let down.

My throat felt thick, and I could feel my pulse starting to quicken, my breathing becoming more irregular.

I coughed and pulled my phone out of my pocket, pretending to look at the screen. "I uh... I should go call the guys," I said. "They'll want to hear the good news. I should call Antoni too."

Ella looked at me, her brows furrowed, but I couldn't

bring myself to meet her gaze as I made my way to the door.

"I'll be right back." My legs carried me down the hall toward the elevator. I pressed the button, but it merely hummed in reply. I tapped it again impatiently, willing it to come faster. I could feel the waves nipping at my heels, so I followed the signs to the stairwell.

I barreled through the door and only made it down a couple of flights before the sea of emotion took my breath away once again. I leaned against the cool concrete of the wall and slid to the ground, resting my arms on my knees. I drew in jagged breaths, trying to steady myself when my phone rang from my hand.

Delilah's name appeared on the screen, as though she had some sort of alarm system that told her when I was in the middle of a breakdown. I ignored the call and clutched my phone to my chest, trying to regain control of my breathing. I didn't realize how long I'd been gone until a text notification pinged on my phone nearly an hour later.

Ella: Where'd you go?

I stared at the screen and pushed my hand through my hair. I didn't know where I was or what I was doing, but I knew where I needed to go.

TWENTY-FIVE

Ella

I SHUT MY ALARM OFF FIFTEEN MINUTES BEFORE IT WAS supposed to wake me up Saturday morning. I'd tossed and turned before finally giving up, laying in the soft glow of the morning light. I stared at the ceiling, my legs fidgeting under the covers.

Bradley Cooper must have sensed my unease because he'd stayed in bed with me instead of ditching me for Grace. He gave a dissatisfied grunt from the pillow beside me, reminding me that my restlessness had greatly inconvenienced him all night.

Sam was scheduled to go home later that day. Grace was over the moon, and she'd said more than once how excited she was about our little family dinner that was supposed to happen that night. However, I worried we were the only ones looking forward to this time together. Ever since the accident, Cash had been slowly withdrawing.

At first, I'd dismissed it as him being overwhelmed. I thought once things started looking up and he got a little rest, things would go back to normal. Instead, he'd felt more distant by the day. Even when he was in my arms, he felt oceans away.

He stayed each night at the hospital despite Sam's insistence that he go home and get some rest. Cash opted to leave during the day soon after Grace and I got there, trading off to keep Sam company. We were ships passing in the night when I'd thought we were on the same boat.

Bradley Cooper sighed in my ear as though he could read my mind.

"Me too, buddy," I said. "Me too."

I plucked my phone off the nightstand, holding it in front of my face to unlock it. I pulled Cash's name up and considered sending him a text, but what would I have said? I could have told him how much I was looking forward to our dinner together. I could have said that even though I'd seen him every day, I still missed him. But it seemed the closer I tried to get, the more he pulled away.

I scrolled past his name and pulled up my text thread with Liv.

Ella: You up?

Within seconds, the little text bubbles appeared.

Liv: Yep. Chloe was up half the night. You okay?

I laid there for a moment, trying to decide how to answer that question.

Ella: Do you think me and Cash were a bad idea? Be honest.

A moment later, my phone was ringing and Liv's face glowed across the screen.

"Hey," I answered.

"What's going on?" she asked in a hushed tone. "Of course I don't think you guys are a bad idea. Why would you ask that?"

I groaned and exhaled sharply. "I don't know, Liv. Something feels off. He's been so distant ever since the accident."

"Try not to read too much into it," she said. "Things will go back to normal once Sam is out of the hospital. He's probably sleep deprived and has a pretty big emotional hangover after all of this."

I chewed my lip. "I hope you're right."

"Of course I'm right," she insisted. "Cash loves you."

"Wait, what?" I asked. "Did he say something to you?"

"He didn't have to," she said. "It's in the way he looks at you. The way he's always looked at you, really."

"You think so?"

"Are you kidding me?" She laughed. "The man has clearly been smitten with you since the night we all first met. But more than that, I think you understand some of the hardest parts of each other's lives in ways few people can."

"I don't know." I sighed. "I kind of resisted the idea of us in the beginning. I mean, he's basically your boss, he's Grace's boss, and we're all like family. If things ended it could get really weird and awkward. Then, it was like the second we seemed to get on the same page, the accident happened, and he pulled away."

"That was a lot to have happened so quickly, though," she reminded me. "Give it a few days. Sam goes home today, right?"

"Yep," I said. "We're going to the hospital in a couple of hours, but he's supposed to be able to leave by late this afternoon."

"Once Sam gets settled and you've all been able to get some rest, I'm sure Cash will be back to his old self. I can personally attest to how much sleep deprivation can affect a person." She chuckled softly, and I heard Chloe start to cry.

"I remember those days all too well," I said, and then I pictured the way Grace looked at Sam the last few days. It didn't seem possible that the sweet, little baby who had once kept me up for hours on end at night was now a young woman with love of her own. "I'll let you go take care of her."

"Okay. I'll check on you soon."

"Hey, Liv?"

"Yeah?" she asked.

"Hold her a little longer than you need to each day... a little longer than you think you should," I said, a wistful smile on my face. "These days... they go by so fast."

"Yeah," she said softly. "Yeah, they do." We signed off, and I dropped the phone beside me on the bed.

Bradley Cooper nudged my cheek with his nose.

"Are you ready to get up, you little monster?" I asked, turning to face him.

He responded by licking my cheek and nuzzling his snout in my neck.

"I know, I know. I was just saying how fast these days go." I pulled his warm, fuzzy body into mine and rested my chin atop his soft head. "Fifteen more minutes."

———

By the time Sam was discharged, it was nearly six p.m. Cash had gone to get some rest soon after we got to the hospital, but somehow he looked even more exhausted when he returned later that afternoon and asked if I wanted to go grab a coffee from the cart downstairs.

"So, I was thinking," I said on the way back to the room. "Maybe Sam would be more comfortable at your place. He knows you better than he does me, and he might be more willing to let you help him."

"Actually, I think he may be better off at your house." When he looked at me, I noticed the crinkles around his eyes were more prominent. "That way he and Grace would have each other."

I shrugged. "Oh... okay."

"You're a good mom, Ella." He said the words with such sincerity it made my heart ache. "The best. And Sam deserves that right now."

"You're pretty great too, you know? You don't give yourself enough credit," I said, but he wouldn't meet my gaze. I wasn't sure if he'd even heard me, but it didn't matter because he quickly changed the subject and told me he was going to leave the hospital early to pick up some extra groceries and a few things to help make Sam more comfortable. Sam had given him the keys to his house, and he had a list of things to retrieve and bring back to my place.

After Sam, Grace, and I made it home, I got them settled inside before unpacking the rest of the car. They both tried to sneak out to help me, but I shooed them back inside. "You two are still recovering," I'd playfully scolded them. "Get your butts back in the house."

Bradley Cooper rolled out the red carpet for Sam, immediately bringing him a plush lamb chop as a sacrifice.

Once I'd unloaded the car, I joined them in the living room where they had already cued up Netflix and were scrolling through the romantic comedies. *Ah, to be young and in love.* I felt a twinge of hope that Cash and I might be able to regain a sense of normalcy with Sam and Grace both recovering out of the hospital.

Liv's words from earlier that morning had continued to bounce through my mind all day. She was right. A lot *had* happened in a short amount of time. It made sense that he would be a bit overwhelmed. I mean, *I* was overwhelmed. This week hadn't exactly been easy on me either, but I was thankful to have Grace home, and I hoped that with Sam out of the hospital, we might all find our footing again.

"So, I was thinking that Sam could sleep in my room, and I'll sleep on the couch," Grace said, interrupting my thoughts as she flipped through the movie selection.

"In the words of our dear friend Antoni, 'hot damn, no ma'am.'" I narrowed my eyes at her. "You're still recovering too, little miss. You can bunk with me, or I'll take the couch."

"Okay. Oh! What about *Love Actually?*" Grace asked, pausing to point at the TV with the remote in her hand. "Do you think Cash would like that one?"

I chuckled. "You do know it's August, right?"

"So?" She grinned. "It can be Christmas anytime. Besides, it's got Andy Lincoln in it. He's so dreamy." She made a big show of clutching her hand to her chest and closing her eyes.

"Oh, I see how it is." Sam feigned offense. "Already got your eye on another British bloke."

Grace laughed and then clutched her side. "Crap, that hurts."

"I'm sorry, love," Sam said, putting an arm around her and kissing her cheek. "You okay?"

"Yeah." She nodded. "It just hurts to laugh still."

I shook my head. "You guys are so sweet you're going to give me a cavity."

"Do you think Cash would like the movie?" Grace asked.

I heard the sound of a car door shut outside, and Bradley Cooper popped his head up from where he was laying beside Sam on the couch.

"I bet that's him now." I stood up and started toward the door. "I'm going to go help him bring everything in, and then we can ask him."

"Awesome," Grace chirped. "Because I'm starving."

I opened the door as he was coming up the walk with an armful of groceries. "My God, what did you get? You do know I have food here, right?"

"Okay, I might have gone a little overboard," he admitted. "I wanted to make sure you wouldn't have to do a lot of cooking, so I got some prepared stuff from Whole Foods."

I took one of the bags from his hands and followed him into the kitchen, Bradley Cooper zooming in behind us.

"Hey, buddy," Cash greeted, patting him on the head once he'd placed the bag on the counter. He turned his attention back to me. "I also got plenty of snacks and easy to prepare stuff for when you have to be at work."

"You did not have to do all of this," I said, as I emptied the contents of the bag on the counter.

"It's nothing." He waved me off and disappeared outside, returning with two more bags of groceries that I unloaded while he brought in the remainder of Sam's things.

When Cash returned to the kitchen, I had extracted two refrigerated pizzas from the last grocery bag. "Aww," I said. "You get me." I peered into each of the paper sacks to make sure I hadn't missed anything because the ingredients for Sam's cottage pie weren't accounted for. "Okay, I know

I'm not exactly an expert chef, but there don't seem to be ingredients to make a cottage pie here."

"Oh." Cash grimaced. "I'm sorry. I completely forgot."

"I thought we were cooking dinner together?" I pursed my lips. We'd been planning this dinner for days, so it seemed odd he would just forget.

Cash pinched the bridge of his nose. "I know. I'm sorry. I don't know what I was thinking."

"Is everything okay?" I asked.

Before he could answer, Sam meandered into the kitchen. "Thanks for going by my place, Cash."

"Of course," Cash said, reaching into his pocket and handing him the key. "Everything you asked for is in here." He gestured to the large duffle bag on the counter. "I got a few more clothes than you asked for, just in case. And I got the book you asked for."

"Perfect." Sam reached for the handle on the duffle, but Cash stopped him.

"It's heavy, and you're not supposed to be lifting anything." Cash looped the handle over his shoulder. "Where should I put it?"

"Grace's room." I gestured in the direction of her bedroom with my head as Cash's head tilted in a question that hadn't quite formed on his lips. "Since Grace will be staying in my room," I added.

Cash nodded and left the room with the duffle.

"Ms. Claiborne," Sam began.

"Ella," I corrected him with a gentle smile.

"Ella," he repeated, a bashful grin on his face. "I wanted to thank you for all you're doing for me, letting me stay with you, helping me. I don't know how I can ever repay you for your kindness."

"You're very welcome," I said. "We're happy you're here. I want you to make yourself at home."

"Thank you. Truly." He nodded and turned to leave the kitchen.

"Hey, Sam?" I called as he reached the doorframe.

"Yeah?"

"Just… be good to her," I said softly. "You being good to my girl is all the thanks I'll ever need."

He gave me a solemn nod. "You've got my word on that. She's… she's quite important to me, your daughter."

My heart melted into a puddle on the kitchen floor. "I know."

Cash returned and placed a hand on Sam's shoulder. "Your bag is on top of the dresser in Grace's room."

"Thanks, man," Sam said, exiting the kitchen.

"Alright." I clapped my hands together. We may not have been able to make a cottage pie, but I was determined not to let that derail our evening. "So, since we're not cooking tonight, should I pop these pizzas in the oven? Or we could order out. I've got the menu for the Chinese place around the corner here somewhere." I opened a couple of drawers, rifling through them as I barreled on. "Or we could just have some movie snacks. I've got tons of popcorn, and you know I've always got candy lying around here. I guess I should also mention that Grace wants us to have a movie night."

"Actually, I need to get going," he said abruptly.

"Not sure if you're in the mood for a romcom…" I trailed off, his words finally registering in my brain. "Wait… what?"

"Yeah, I'm sorry." He scrubbed his face with his hands. "I've just… I've got a lot I need to get caught up on."

"Okay…" I pressed my lips together as I digested what

he was saying. "But we said we were all going to have dinner together tonight. Grace has been going on and on about it."

His eyes didn't meet mine. "I know. I'm sorry, but I really need to go home and take care of some things."

My stomach felt queasy. *Is he... is he trying to ghost me? Is that what this is?* "Cash, please stay. Even if you can only stay for dinner. I know it would mean so much to Grace, and it would probably make Sam feel more comfortable." *And I need you. I want you here.*

"I can't. Okay, Ella? I can't tonight, " he snapped. His voice came out so sharp that I jumped. This wasn't like Cash at all. I watched as he took a deep breath before speaking again. "We'll do it another night, okay? I have some things I need to take care of."

"And those things don't include me," I scoffed. I regretted the words as soon as they came out of my mouth.

Cash looked stunned, as though I'd thrown cold water on him. "That's not what I'm saying." He kept his voice even. "I've been at the hospital a lot, and I'm behind. I need to get some things done."

"You could do them here," I said bitterly.

He sighed. "Ella, please."

"Fine." I shrugged as though it didn't matter, even though it did matter very much. "Whatever."

I turned toward the fridge and pulled out the pizzas he would not be eating with us.

He crossed over to me and kissed the top of my head.

Every part of me wanted to throw myself in his arms and ask why he was being this way. I didn't understand how he could not need me the way I needed him. But that's not what I said as I carried the pizzas to the oven and pressed the button to turn it on.

"If you need space, fine. We'll manage without you," I spat.

I leaned my hands on the counter and closed my eyes, trying to calm myself. I turned back around to apologize, to tell him I understood even though I didn't, only to find he was already gone.

TWENTY-SIX

Cash

I HATED MYSELF FOR WALKING OUT ON ELLA THE WAY I DID, for not even saying anything to Grace and Sam before I left. But I couldn't. The second I opened my mouth, the geyser of emotions I'd been suppressing would have come to the surface, just as they had the second I got in my car.

The traffic lights and passing cars blurred together through my tears as I made the short drive home, gripping the steering wheel so hard my knuckles turned white. My mind was whirling to the point that I hardly remembered how I'd gotten there when I pulled into the garage.

I didn't get out immediately, opting instead to sit in silence in the darkness. I didn't know whether it was a good or bad sign that Ella hadn't even tried to call or text me after I'd left. She had every right to be furious with me. I'd gone back on my word, but I'd reached my breaking point.

I really had forgotten the ingredients for the cottage pie. When I went to the store, I'd had every intention of staying with Ella that night. But once I was in the house with her, the waves started to rise. Being with her had felt so easy before. Since the accident, all I saw were possibilities. Possibilities that ended with me in a hospital room with her or Grace, or worse, both of them, waiting for the news that my life was over again.

She was thinking about what was for dinner, but I couldn't stop thinking about all the ways I could lose her. I drew in a ragged breath. I needed to think. I needed time to sort through all of the thoughts in my head.

I loved Ella. I knew that. And I loved Grace. But I couldn't seem to reconcile that with my fear of losing them. How could I ever be okay again when there were car accidents, cancers, and God only knew what else that could snatch them from me at any second? I'd survived losing Carrie, but barely. I couldn't do it again. I leaned my head against the leather seat, beads of sweat forming along my hairline.

I had to figure out how to cope with this. Ella deserved better than a man who ran at the first sign of trouble. She and Grace needed someone they could count on. How had I become this person?

The look on Ella's face when I'd snapped at her flashed in my mind, and her words haunted me. She thought that I didn't feel I needed to take care of her, but that couldn't have been further from the truth. I wanted nothing more than to take care of her and Grace—to protect them the way they deserved. But in order to do that, I had to get my mind right.

I needed to call Delilah.

Without thinking, I reached for my phone in the center console and scrolled to her number. She answered on the first ring.

"Cash," she said. "Are you alright? I've been trying to reach you."

"I'm sorry, Delilah. I've just been... I've been really struggling," I admitted. "I haven't answered because I didn't know what to say. I still don't."

"That's okay. You don't have to say anything," she assured me. "I'm here for you, Cash. We can talk about what's got you feeling down or we can talk about something else. Or we don't have to talk at all. I can just sit here with you."

"Maybe you were right the other day." I sighed. "Maybe some time away would do me some good, help me clear my head."

"I've always believed that a change of scenery can be healing," she said. "It's hard for us to see the expanse of the forest when we're sitting amongst the trees."

"Can I come stay with you?" I asked, trying to disguise the break in my voice. "Just for a few days?"

"Of course you can, dear," she said. "You can stay as long as you like. When do you think you'll come down?"

"Tomorrow," I answered quickly. "I'll see if I can get a last minute flight out, and if not, I'll drive."

"It will be so good to see you." Her voice was warm, like a cup of chicken noodle soup when your throat was sore. It instantly soothed my restless soul. "I'll get the guest room ready."

I PRESSED THE LAST OF MY CLOTHES INTO MY SUITCASE, scanning it one last time to make sure I hadn't missed anything. Once I was satisfied that I'd remembered everything, I zipped it up and hoisted it to the floor. I still hadn't heard anything else from Ella, nor had I tried to call her.

What I needed to say was best said in person, so I'd

decided I was going to have the Uber stop by Ella's place on the way to the airport. I'd show up and explain everything as best I could, though, I admittedly didn't know how to do that yet. I'd tell her I needed a few days to recalibrate. I'd be back in a week, and hopefully I'd have a clearer perspective on things. This wasn't a break up, I'd say. This was about me trying to be the man she and Grace deserved. It might not be what she wanted to hear, but she'd understand, right?

The clock on the nightstand showed that it was just after eight a.m., and the Uber was supposed to pick me up at eight-fifteen. I rolled my suitcase through the house, turning the lights off as I went, making sure I'd left nothing plugged in that wasn't supposed to be. I propped my suitcase by the door and was starting toward the kitchen to get a bottle of water when the chime of my doorbell echoed through the house.

I stopped in my tracks. Did Uber drivers normally ring the doorbell? Every car I'd ever called had only honked the horn from outside.

"One second," I called as I padded to the door and turned the dead bolt. When I opened the door, Ella was standing there, her eyes red rimmed and her hair piled in a messy bun on top of her head.

My eyes widened. "Ella... what are you doing here?"

"I hate what happened last night. I hate the way we left things," she said. "You wanted to go home, and I wasn't listening to you. That shouldn't have been a huge deal, but I made it one. I overreacted because I wanted to be with you. Because all week it's felt like you were pulling away from me, and I thought that if I could keep you there, I could somehow make that feeling go away. " She dabbed at her eyes with the pads of her fingers. "I should have been

more understanding. I should have told you what I was feeling, but I was selfish."

"Ella, you weren't being selfish," I began, but she cut
me off.

"No, I need to say this." She looked at me with tears
pooled in her eyes. "I'm in love with you, Cash. I know I
was scared at first, but I was only scared because the last
time I felt this way it was for the man I knew I wanted to
spend the rest of my life with. I've leaned on you hard these
last few weeks, too hard probably. But at a time when everything in my life was confusing, you were the one thing that
made sense."

"You didn't lean on me too hard," I said. "I wanted to
be there for you."

"I didn't stop to think about what you may be going
through," she continued. "I didn't consider that this was so
different for you because you aren't just getting me in this
relationship. You're getting Grace too. I realized the accident probably reminded you of that. The next thing you
knew, we were together all the time, and I was relying on
you the way a wife relies on a husband. It was too much too
soon, wasn't it?"

I shook my head, trying to think of the words to say
what I needed to say.

"I didn't stop to think…" Her eyes fell to a spot behind
me, and she trailed off just as the Uber pulled to a stop in
front of my house with its sign illuminated on the dash. She
looked at the car that waited on the curb and then back to
me as she registered what that meant. "Are you… are you
going somewhere?"

I squeezed my eyes shut briefly before opening them
again. "It's not what it looks like."

"No?" she asked. "Because what it looks like is you were

about to skip town without so much as an explanation or a goodbye." She choked back a sob, turning to head down the walkway, but I reached for her hand and stepped in front of her.

"Ella, wait. That's not what was happening. I was going to come see you on my way to the airport," I explained.

"The *airport*?" she exploded. "Are you fucking kidding me right now, Cash? Gee, thanks for stopping by as you hightailed it out of town. You didn't think to call or send me a text or a fucking telegram to let me know you were going to leave?"

"I was going to tell you," I said.

"Oh yeah?" she asked incredulously. "And what exactly were you going to tell me?"

My throat was thick, and I could feel the waves pulling me under. They took my breath and my words away.

"That's what I thought." Her face crumpled as she turned away from me.

"Ella, wait," I croaked out. "Please."

She whirled around to me with tears streaming down her face, her blue eyes turned to ice. "You know, Grace told me what she said to you. That you felt like a dad to her." Her voice was frayed around the edges, as though the pull of a tiny thread might cause her to completely unravel. "Her dad never would have left her. Not if he'd been given a choice."

I felt like I'd been punched in the gut.

"We're done here," she spat, delivering her final blow. "Have a nice trip or whatever."

The waves pulled me down further and further until I couldn't breathe. Ella was gone.

TWENTY-SEVEN

Ella

MY HEART POUNDED SO HARD I FELT IT IN MY FINGERTIPS, pulsing against the steering wheel as I started back toward home. Cash was really getting on a plane to God-knows-where, leaving Nashville, leaving *me*, without so much as an explanation. He hadn't even bothered with a half-hearted break up text. Hell, even Joe Jonas left Taylor Swift a shitty twenty-seven second voicemail. Did I not even deserve that much? Because I know damn well that my daughter did. She deserved so much more.

I deserved so much more.

A horn blared at me, wrenching me from my thoughts as I attempted to get in the turning lane and accidentally cut someone off. I needed to pull over. Hadn't Grace and Sam just been in a freaking car accident? I needed to not be reckless.

I drove a little further until I found a coffee shop with a relatively empty parking lot. My fingers gripped the steering wheel as I carefully pulled into the lot and cut the engine. At least the shop would lend me a cover story for where I'd been when I returned home with coffee and breakfast for Grace and Sam.

Tears fell from my eyes as I let out a scream that would have surely frightened any passersby if I'd had my windows down. Fury and sadness danced around inside me in some sort of deranged tango that made my entire body tremble. Where on earth was he going? How could he end things without at least talking to me first? It was the first time I'd let someone in since losing Craig, and he of all people knew what a big deal that was. How could he just *leave*?

Was he going to some tropical location with sandy beaches and sparkling oceans, leaving us behind to grieve his absence? That didn't sound like something he would do.

What was I going to tell Grace? I couldn't break her heart like this, especially not while she was still recovering. I had to shield her from this pain a little longer. I had to somehow pull myself together for her. I couldn't let her and Sam bear witness to me having a total meltdown after what they'd just been through.

I pictured my sweet daughter who'd already lost enough for a lifetime, and my blood raised to a boil. Grace would be losing the man who'd become a father figure to her, but she'd also be faced with a really uncomfortable professional situation. Would she feel she needed to quit her job? She loved her job. She loved him.

I was hurt. No, fuck that. I was *pissed*. Okay, I was hurt too. How could he do this to me? To *us*? Hadn't he told me he loved me on the phone the day of the accident? Maybe it really had been a heat of the moment thing. But that didn't feel right either. *We have something special, something real… right?*

Liv and Derek knew Cash well, and they had seen the connection between us. They'd each told me on different occasions that they thought Cash had felt something for me for a long time. If that were true, why would he just leave when we'd finally found our way to each other?

My mind spiraled to what this split would do to our family of friends. Would they feel the need to choose sides? Would Grace and I lose more than Cash because of this?

Rage burned inside me.

"I hate him," I said out loud to absolutely nobody. "I hate Cash Montgomery."

Except I didn't hate him. Not even a little bit.

Sure, I was furious. But I was also of the belief that it was possible to love people even when we didn't like them very much. Even when we were pissed off and they'd hurt us. At that moment, I definitely didn't like him.

But I loved him.

I tilted the rearview mirror so that I could see my reflection. My eyes were swollen, and my face was splotchy. *You've got to keep it together, Ella.* I took a few deep breaths in an attempt to center myself. *You don't get to fall apart right now.* I pulled my purse onto my lap from the passenger seat and rifled through its contents for my makeup bag.

Sweet Jesus, I look like the sad heroine from a Nicholas Sparks movie. One where there definitely wasn't a happily ever after. All I needed was a good thunderstorm to come along so the rain could mix in poetically with my tears. *And scene.*

Does Nicholas Sparks ever tell stories about women who don't need a man any damn way? If not, he should.

Grace and I had managed all these years without me having a man around, even if that wasn't part of our plan. We had each other, and we had Liv. It was always us against the world. I didn't *need* a man. But I wanted Cash.

My breath caught in my throat as I dabbed some concealer on my face in an effort to hide my emotions. I realized that was a lot to ask of a bottle of Maybelline. I swiped on a sheer lip gloss. *Maybe she's not having a total emotional breakdown. Maybe it's Maybelline.*

I sighed as I tossed my makeup bag back in my purse and prepared myself to go inside the coffee shop.

I wanted to know where Cash was going, but more importantly I wanted to know *why*.

"Mom," Grace's voice pulled me from my thoughts early that evening.

"Yeah, sweetie?" I popped my head out of the fridge where I was deep in organizing mode. After I got home, I cleaned the baseboards, scrubbed the bathrooms, vacuumed, dusted, and even gave Bradley Cooper a bath. I had to do something, anything to keep my mind busy, because the second I slowed down, the floodgates threatened to open again. "Are you guys hungry?"

"No," she said, eyeing me suspiciously. "Are you okay?"

"Of course," I answered, not meeting her eyes as I grabbed myself a bottle of water and twisted the cap off, letting the refrigerator door close. "Why wouldn't I be okay?"

Bradley Cooper stood nearby, hoping I would retrieve something from the fridge for him as well.

Grace surveyed the room with pursed lips before turning her eyes back on me. "Because you're cleaning."

"So?" I asked, taking a swig of my water.

She raised her brow. "So… you never clean."

"I do too."

She snorted. "Only when you're stressed, upset, or pissed off."

259

She knew me too well. "It's been a stressful week. Besides, Bradley Cooper has never seen the house super clean before."

"You're cleaning for the dog?"

I gasped, feigning offense. "Don't talk about your little brother that way. He's sensitive."

She leaned down to where Bradley Cooper stood and scratched his head. "Our mom is crazy."

I propped my hand on my hip. "Grace Eloise Claiborne, can I get you something?"

She laughed. "No, I was just wondering if you'd talked to Cash today. I sent him a text to see if he was coming for dinner since he had to go home last night."

And there it was. I turned away, busying myself with wiping down the countertops. "Yeah, he called while you were laying down earlier. He had to, uh, go out of town real quick." *So quick that he didn't bother to tell us about it.*

"Out of town? Where?" she asked.

Shit. I kept my back to her as I scrubbed the sink. "Um, some sort of work thing." *Double shit. Ella, you idiot. You know she literally works with him.*

"A work thing?" she repeated. "I should text him and see if there's anything I can help with."

"No ma'am," I said a little too quickly as I spun around to face her. "I mean, you're supposed to be recovering. You and Sam both need to be resting." The last thing I needed was her contacting Cash before I'd even figured out how to break the news to her.

"Fine," she said with a sigh.

I tried to keep my tone casual. "Besides, you should enjoy this time with Sam before you go back to school."

She shrugged. "I guess you're right."

"Of course I'm right. I'm your mother." I smiled at her.

Or at least I thought I did, but my face seemed determined to betray me.

"Are you sure you're okay?" she asked.

"Yeah," I replied. "I guess I am pretty stressed. I have a bunch of stuff I need to get caught up on at the bakery."

"But didn't Aunt Liv fill in while you were at the hospital with me and Sam?"

"She did, but there's still a ton of administrative stuff to do," I said. That wasn't entirely true. Katie, as always, had made sure everything had been taken care of. She'd even set up some interviews for the following week with some prospective employees. But I needed a cover to get me out of the house so I could think. "I was thinking I might go in for a couple of hours and do a few things. Maybe I'll call Derek and see if he could come hang out with you guys." I couldn't ask Liv. She'd see through me in a heartbeat, and I didn't know how to tell her yet.

She rolled her eyes. "Mom, we don't need a babysitter."

"I know that," I insisted. "But you're both still recovering. Should anything crazy happen, I want someone here who can help you. Besides, neither of you can drive while you're still on painkillers, and I'm pretty sure Bradley Cooper got his license revoked because he doesn't have opposable thumbs."

"Okay, fine," she said. "Call Derek." She left the kitchen with Bradley Cooper on her heels.

I grabbed my phone off the counter and called Derek's number.

He answered on the second ring. "Hey, Ella. Everything okay?"

"Yeah," I answered, trying to maintain an air of perkiness to my voice so as not to give myself away. "Everything is totally fine. I was actually calling to ask a favor if you're not busy."

"I'm not busy at all," he said. "I'm just doing some reading."

"What book?"

He laughed. "The manual for the new camera I just bought."

"Nice," I said.

"So, what's up?"

"Would you by any chance be available to come hang out with Grace and Sam for a couple of hours? I need to run a few errands, and with them both still recovering, I hate to leave them alone. You know, just in case they need anything," I explained. "Besides, I know Bradley Cooper would love to hang out with you."

"Of course," he said. "I'd be happy to. I'll be there in say, half an hour?"

"Perfect," I replied. "Thank you. Seriously. You're the best."

"Don't mention it," he said. "I'm happy to help."

We ended the call, and I leaned my head back, squeezing my eyes shut in an attempt to keep my emotions locked inside. I needed to think, but I also needed to be with someone who loved me.

I knew exactly where I needed to go.

AFTER DRIVING AROUND LOST IN THOUGHT FOR ABOUT AN hour, I pulled into the parking lot at Richland Place. I sighed as I cut the engine. My mom may not know I was there, but I would know. And at that moment, I needed her.

A summer storm was brewing, making it look much

later than it actually was. I normally preferred the sunshine, but on that night I didn't mind that the weather matched my mood—swirls of clouds and emotions on the verge of giving way to torrential downpours.

Thunder echoed in the distance as I walked toward the building and went inside. I waved to the receptionist who was on the phone as I crossed the lobby toward the elevator. It was the very same path Cash and I had taken the night he'd come with me to visit my mother a little over a week before. As I got on that same elevator, I wondered how everything had gotten so messed up since then. It felt like we'd lived a thousand lifetimes in a matter of days.

I keyed in the code, and the elevator lurched upward.

I felt a little selfish for visiting without Grace because I knew she'd want to see her grandmother, but I needed this moment for myself. I needed to figure out how the hell I was going to tell my daughter that Cash had left us.

Who was I kidding? I needed this moment to figure out how to process it all, how to come to terms with the fact that the moment I'd gone all in was the moment Cash had decided to fold.

Before Cash, the only person I'd ever brought with me to visit my mom besides Grace had been Liv. Watching my mom's mind slowly disintegrate, having a front row seat to losing her piece by piece, was something I struggled with.

To go from having a mom I could talk to about anything, to having one who didn't recognize me anymore was a heartbreak unlike any I'd ever experienced. Being vulnerable about it wasn't something I did often with people who weren't Grace or Liv, but I'd felt comfortable with Cash. I felt I could trust him, but I'd been wrong.

That's not true. Despite what had happened, I knew I hadn't been wrong to trust him. But what *had* gone wrong?

The elevator came to a stop on the third floor, and I started toward room 3012. Nicole was coming out of the room as I approached.

"Hey, Ella," Nicole greeted, looking around me. "Just you today?"

My eyes watered at the edges as I forced a smile. "Just me."

Her face softened as she seemed to read the words nestled inside my expression.

"How is she today?" I asked.

"Today's been a good day," she answered. "She seems less agitated than usual. I'm glad you're here." She placed a hand on my arm. "And she will be too."

"Thanks, Nicole." I nodded and entered my mom's room to find her seated in her armchair with the television playing at a low level.

"Hey, Mama," I said.

"Hello, dear," she replied, looking up at me with bright eyes. "I wasn't expecting any visitors. Are you from the church?"

"No, Mama." I shook my head. "I'm not."

She smiled through her puzzled expression. "How can I help you, dear?"

I sat on the loveseat near her. "I know the things I'm about to say aren't going to make any sense, but I just needed you to hear them."

Her eyes squinted as though she were trying to figure out what on earth I was talking about.

"I don't know what to do, Mama." I'd barely opened my mouth, and my eyes were already swimming with tears. "I found someone. Someone I saw a real future with, but he's gone. He left, and I don't even know where he went."

She studied me intently, her lips pursed.

"I love him, and what makes this even worse is that Grace loves him too," I cried. "But he left. He left us both. All these years, I've tried to give Grace everything I could. The one thing I couldn't give her was her father back. After Craig died, I honestly never thought I'd find someone I loved the way I loved him, someone who could stand in his place and not pale in comparison. Someone who could be the dad Grace still deserved."

My mom leaned forward, absorbing my every word.

"But I did find that." My voice broke, and I took a shallow breath. "I found all of that in Cash. And I know that Grace is basically an adult now, but a little girl never stops needing her mom and dad. I know that because I still need you. And I miss you and Daddy so much."

I watched as her eyes filled with tears.

"I try to be Super Mom. I know I can do everything on my own, that I don't need anybody." I said with a sniffle. "But I wanted him. You and Daddy would have loved him. You would have felt he deserved us because he did. I don't know where we went wrong... where I went wrong. Mama, I wish you could tell me what to do." I buried my head in my hands, my shoulders shaking as all of my heartache and shattered pieces poured from my eyes.

I wept so hard I struggled for air, choking my words out. "I don't know how to tell Grace. How... do I tell her... that he's gone? That he just left us."

"Sweetheart." I startled when I looked up to realize Mama had moved to sit beside me on the loveseat. She smoothed her hand over my hair, her eyes filled with such warmth. "Those who love us never truly leave us."

I watched her through wide eyes as she reached for my hand, taking it in both of hers.

"The people who are meant to stay in our lives will

always find their way back home." She patted my hand. "Those that can't, they'll never be far. They'll be right here." She placed her hand over her heart. "And they'll stay there forever."

I stared at her in stunned silence as my mind tried to make sense of what was happening.

"I'm so sorry, dear. I've gone and gotten all teary-eyed." She dabbed at the dampness that slid down her checks. "It just hurts my heart to see you so sad."

"Thank you, Mama," I managed to choke out as she squeezed my hand. We sat quietly for a moment, and for a few seconds, I felt like I had my mom back, until she lifted her hand from mine.

"You remind me of someone, but I can't place who," she said, a puzzled expression returning to her face. "My memory… it's not very good these days."

I nodded, a rush of sadness swallowing my heart.

"James will be here soon." She gave me a friendly smile. "James is my husband. You'll like him." She paused for a moment, tilting her head to the side. "I'm sorry, dear. Did you say you were from the church?"

Just like that… the moment had passed, and it was too much. It was all too much.

"I love you, Mama," I whispered as I stood, leaning to kiss the top of her head. "I need to go."

"It was so kind of you to visit," she said. "Please come back."

"I will." I forced a smile. "Soon." I started toward the door, and I barely made it outside her room before I fell apart all over again. I darted past where Nicole was on the phone at the nurse's station and got on the elevator, willing it to go faster.

When I finally stumbled outside the building, I was met

with a steady downpour. I didn't bother to run to my car to avoid the onslaught of rain. Instead, I let it wash over me. Every drop represented the hopes I had for the future— hopes that once seemed so solid but had dissipated into nothing.

There would be no pretty Nicholas Sparks ending. Cash wouldn't be standing there waiting for me in the rain, waiting to tell me what a mistake he'd made. Those things only happened in the movies. In reality, I was left with nothing but my memories and a wet face as a reminder that Cash and I had happened at all.

I texted Derek when I got in my car to let him know I was on the way back, that he could go ahead and leave if he wanted to. I pretended it was under the guise of not inconveniencing him any longer than necessary, but the truth was, I didn't want to be seen. I just had to pull myself together enough that I could get past Grace and Sam. I'd tell them I got stuck in the rain and needed to take a shower. And I'd stand under the stream and cry until I had nothing left.

As I made the short drive home, I realized I was no closer to figuring out how to tell Grace that Cash was gone. I was no closer to understanding how someone I felt this much for could choose to leave us.

My mother's face appeared in my mind. I thought about her and the ways my dad kept her going while he was alive, and I wanted that too. But I felt more alone than ever.

By the time I pulled into my driveway it was dark and the rain had slowed to a sprinkle. I took a deep breath before getting out of the car and made the short walk to the door. When I approached the front stoop I realized Derek was sitting there waiting for me.

"Hey," I said, as he rose to his feet. "Thank you again

for staying. I feel bad taking up your evening. Are Grace and Sam okay?"

"Yeah," he answered. "They're in the kitchen eating some dinner."

I nodded. "Good. I know Bradley Cooper loved having you here."

He studied me through concerned eyes. "Is everything okay, Ella?"

"Of course," I said too quickly.

He leaned against the wall. "Something dawned on me while I was here."

"Oh?" I asked. "What's that?"

"Where's Cash?"

I shifted uncomfortably.

"Grace mentioned he'd gone out of town for something really suddenly," he continued. "She said he left last night without telling her goodbye, and she texted him to ask if he needed help with anything, but he hasn't responded to her at all. I think that's weird."

I groaned inwardly. *Dammit, Grace.* "I'm sure he's just busy."

"Look, Ella, I don't want to overstep, but I guess I'm going to." He moved closer to me. "You look like you've been crying, Cash is nowhere to be seen, and Grace hasn't heard from him."

My mouth was so dry that my tongue pricked at the roof of my mouth when I swallowed.

Derek's eyes searched mine. "Ella, where is Cash?"

That was all it took for the dam to break.

I told him everything.

TWENTY-EIGHT

Cash
___

I RENTED A CAR AFTER I LANDED IN CHARLESTON. I NEEDED to drive and clear my head. I let Delilah know I'd landed but that I'd be arriving later.

Ella's words seeped into my blood, tiny little weights pulling me under the waves. *Her dad never would have left her. Not if he'd been given a choice.*

She was right. I didn't have to know Grace's dad to know he wouldn't have done what I did. He wouldn't have left Grace or Ella if he'd had anything to do with it. I doubted Ella would believe me, but I didn't want to leave them. I only wanted to be better for them, but the truth was, I didn't know how.

When Ella said she was done, I didn't try to fight it. How could I? She needed someone who could be there for her and Grace, someone she could really depend on. I thought I could have been that man, but when I saw the ghost of Carrie and what we went through together, I was reminded of how quickly I could lose it all. I didn't think I could survive it again.

Ella was right to call it off. She deserved someone whose first inclination wasn't to run. Still, her words sliced through my core. I could drive all day and never get away from them.

I found myself retracing many of the same steps Carrie and I had taken together around the city in an effort to feel near her... as though somehow she could tell me what to do.

First, I stopped in for some coffee and macaroons at our favorite place and sat near the window people watching, just like we used to do. Sitting there, I could almost see Carrie's reflection in the glass out of the corner of my eye as though she were right across from me. Almost. But as soon as I blinked, her image disappeared.

I watched as couples came in, hand in hand, and left with coffees and boxes of pastries. One of them came in with their daughter who looked a little younger than Grace. A lump formed in my throat as I saw the man pull the woman close and kiss her tenderly. The young girl rolled her eyes, and her parents took that as an opportunity to sandwich her with kisses on either side of her cheek.

I sipped my coffee to find it now tasted sour, the bitterness I felt intermingling with the taste of the toasted praline roast. When I stood to leave, I took one last glance at the family, and I wondered if they knew just how lucky they were.

I walked down the street to the used bookstore Carrie had loved. My chest ached as I ran my fingers along the spines of hundreds of stories, the way Carrie once did. I wondered if any part of her still lingered amongst the pages housed there. Even after all this time, I wondered if there was a book that lived on those shelves that Carrie had touched. I closed my eyes and tried to connect with her there, yet somehow she felt further away than ever. That realization made the walls feel as though they were closing in on me, so I left in search of more echoes of Carrie.

As I got in the car, Grace sent me a text to ask if there was any work she could help me with, but I didn't have the heart to respond. I knew it was only a matter of time before Ella told her what I'd done. She wouldn't want anything to do with me, and she certainly wouldn't want to work with me. I shoved my phone back in my pocket and drove some more.

Even though I could go to a Target store anywhere, I stopped at one while I was there because that's what Carrie and I used to do after our date nights. We'd go to dinner, and afterwards she rarely wanted to go to a movie or to a bar for drinks. Instead, she wanted to roam the aisles of Target. The bright colors inside the store seemed dimmer, and everywhere I looked there were more couples and families. Their presence seemed to taunt me, heartbreaking reminders of what would never be.

Finally, I ended up at Folly Beach. I parked and walked along the water's edge the way Carrie and I used to do and headed up to the pier. It was unusually quiet, and it felt like the sunset was putting on a show just for me. Vivid pinks gave way to shades of peach, the same color of Ella's dress the night of Liv and Jax's wedding. My chest tingled as I pictured her that night... the night it all began, even though I knew that my attraction to her had begun long before that.

I watched as the colors faded into darkness, and I thought about what a metaphor that gorgeous sunset had been for my time with Ella. In such a short time she had filled my life with color, but in her absence everything felt grey.

My phone rang from my pocket, and I suspected it was Delilah wondering where I was. When I brought my phone in front of me, I was shocked to see Derek's name on the screen.

"Hey, Derek," I answered.

"Where are you?" Derek's voice was tense.

How does he even know I'm not in town? "What?" I asked.

"I talked to Ella. She told me everything." Derek was the most even-tempered of all the guys of Midnight in Dallas. He rarely got mad, but he sounded *pissed.* "What the hell, Cash? Where are you?"

"She talked to *you?*" I didn't mean for my words to come out as accusatory as they did. "I'm sorry. I didn't mean it like that. I'm just shocked."

"Well, who was she supposed to talk to? It's not like *you* were there," he fired back. "She asked me to come over and hang with Grace and Sam while she ran some errands. When she came back, she looked like she'd been crying."

It felt like he'd punched me in the face.

"So, what gives?" he asked. " Where are you?"

I paused for a few seconds and sucked in a deep breath. "Charleston."

The line went quiet for a moment. "Okay. Why didn't you just tell her that? I'm sure Ella would have understood if you wanted to go see Delilah and Richard."

"That's not entirely why I came."

"So, why did you?"

"I don't know, Derek. Alright?" The emotion exploded out of me. "The accident thing and Sam's cancer scare really freaked me out. It hit too close to home. Losing Carrie was…" I didn't have to finish the sentence because Derek knew. He and the guys had all been there for me through it. "I love them. The possibility of losing a spouse is bad enough, but a *child*?"

"Let me get this straight," Derek said. "You didn't want to risk losing them, so you just *left*? You didn't think to, I don't know, tell Ella what you were feeling instead of abandoning them when they needed you?"

"I wasn't abandoning them," I insisted.

"What do you call what you're doing right now?" he asked.

I had no defense because I knew he was right. I had abandoned them.

"This isn't you, Cash." Derek's voice softened. "You're not the guy who leaves when things get tough."

My chest ached. "Maybe I am."

Derek sighed into the phone. "So, what's your plan? Are you going to alienate yourself from everyone who cares about you? Because the only way to keep from losing people is to leave everyone you love."

Her dad never would have left her. Not if he'd been given a choice. Ella's words echoed in my mind again and grabbed at the edges of my heart, trying to pull me under.

My voice came out as a hoarse whisper. "I don't know, Derek. I don't know what I'm doing."

"You need to figure it out," he said gently.

"She hates me," I replied. "You should have seen how upset she was. She was furious with me."

"She's hurt, Cash," Derek said. "I don't know. Maybe I'm a hopeless romantic, but I think love is always worth fighting for."

I opened my mouth to speak, but no words came.

"Just think about it, alright?"

I nodded even though he couldn't hear me and ended the call.

I closed my eyes and begged Carrie to tell me what to do. I tried to imagine what she would say if she were there.

My questions were met with an unyielding silence, and the waves crashed around me.

"HOW ARE YOU DOING, SON?" RICHARD ASKED AS I WALKED through their front door. He gripped my hand in a firm handshake and clapped me on the back.

"I'm sorry it's so late," I said.

"Don't you apologize for a thing, dear," Delilah's warm voice sounded like a cozy blanket on a cold day as she rounded the corner into the foyer. "Richard, take his suitcase to the guest room, will you?"

"Woman, give me two seconds to look at the boy, would you?" Richard teased, giving my shoulder a squeeze.

"Oh, I can do that," I insisted as Richard reached for my suitcase.

"Nonsense." Richard waved me off, hoisting my rolling bag off the ground. "Gives me an opportunity to show Delilah here that these ole muscles still have a little mileage left in 'em."

"Oh, Richard." Delilah shook her head. "You hush now." Richard disappeared through the foyer and up the stairs with my suitcase as Delilah took my face in her hands.

"Cash, it's so good to see you." She pulled me into a hug, holding on a little longer than usual. "We've missed you."

"I've missed you too," I said as she pulled back and looped her arm through mine.

"Come on. Let's go sit in the living room and talk." She smiled at me as she guided me beyond the foyer to the den that was decorated in shades of brown and tan with dozens of framed photos on the walls. The scent of banana bread and fresh cut flowers mingled in the air. "Can I make you some tea?"

"No thanks. I'm okay." I took a seat at the end of the tufted beige sofa, and she sat beside me.

Richard wheezed a little as he returned down the stairs, and I instantly felt horrible for letting him carry my suitcase, even though he hadn't given me much choice.

"I've been telling Richard he needs to go to water aerobics with me," Delilah commented, taking note of Richard's heavy breathing.

He scoffed as he ambled over to the matching recliner, slowly lowering into it. "The only thing that could possibly be more boring than that is going with you to one of your luncheons. I'd rather gouge out my eyeballs."

Delilah rolled her eyes. "It's good for your heart."

"This ticker is top notch." Richard patted his chest. "It just runs a little slower than it used to is all."

Delilah turned her attention to me and placed her hand on my knee. "Now, tell me, dear, how are you?"

I hung my head, trying to figure out where to start. "I met someone."

"I knew it." Delilah's face softened. "It's Grace's mom, isn't it? I told Richard I had a feeling."

I nodded, the corners of my mouth curved downward.

"That's great news, son," Richard said with a smile. "So, why the long face?"

"I'm afraid I've messed things up," I admitted. "I don't know if they can be fixed."

"Well, I doubt that." Delilah's tone was tender and kind. "I reckon there's nothing that can't be fixed with a little love or a lot of duct tape. That's what my mama always told me."

I sighed. "I don't know. I think it might take more than that."

"Tell us what happened, dear," Delilah said.

"Isn't that… I don't know, isn't that painful for you?" I questioned. "For me to ask you for advice about someone who isn't…" I trailed off. "I just don't want to hurt either of you."

"You know we love you as if you're our own." Richard leaned forward in his chair. "Part of loving you means we want you to be happy. We want you to have someone you can share your life with."

"That's right," Delilah agreed. "And Carrie wanted that too."

At the sound of her name the volcano of emotions that had been bubbling inside me spilled out. I told them everything. I explained how my attraction for Ella grew over time and how we connected the night of Jax and Liv's wedding. The last few weeks we were together played in mind as I relayed every detail.

They listened intently as I described what happened inside me after the accident. I told them what it felt like to see Grace in that hospital bed, and looks of recognition came across both of their faces. They knew exactly what it was like to watch their child helplessly from the sidelines when she was hurt.

Delilah patted my knee, and Richard looked over at me with concern in his eyes when I told them about Sam's cancer scare and what that had done to me.

"I didn't know what to do. I just knew I needed to get away and clear my head." My voice came out strangled. "I thought maybe I could get my mind right and be the man they deserved, but what if I'm just not capable?"

"Of course you are, son," Richard said.

"All day I've been looking for Carrie." I scrubbed my hand down my face. "I went to all of her favorite places because I needed to be close to her. I needed to feel her. But how can I ever truly move on if I'm always searching for her? If I'm always waiting for the other shoe to drop, for the next tragedy to come and take away everyone I care about?"

Delilah studied me for a moment. "Cash, I'm going to ask you a question, and I want you to answer honestly. I don't want you to worry you'll hurt us with your answer." I nodded, and she continued. "With all that you know now, and with all of the pain you had to endure from losing Carrie, do you ever wish you hadn't met her?"

I winced, shaking my head vehemently. "God, no. Of course not."

"Delilah." Richard gasped. "What are you getting at?"

Delilah kept her gaze steady on me.

"I'd do it over again in a heartbeat," I choked out. "I'd give anything for another minute with her."

"Sweetheart, you're being given a second chance at happiness right now. Ella and Grace are your second chance." She gave me a wistful smile and placed her hand on mine. "You suffered a great loss, Cash. Many people go through life for decades without knowing what that kind of earth-shattering loss feels like. That kind of loss… it changes you. But your fear of losing them isn't there as a warning to make you pull away. It's there to remind you to hold on tight, that love and hope are always worth it. You didn't want to leave Ella and Grace. You wanted a guarantee that you'd never know what it feels like to lose them.

In doing that, you've let them know what it feels like to lose you."

My shoulders shook, and I buried my head in my hands.

"I still search for her too, you know," Richard spoke up. "Sometimes I swear I can still feel Carrie with me, especially when I sit out on the back deck in the evenings with a cup of coffee, the way she always loved to do when she was here. I miss her constantly, but I still have hope because I have Delilah. And I have you, Cash, and anyone else you bring into our lives."

"I'll never stop loving Carrie," I whispered.

"Of course you won't, sweetheart." Delilah dabbed at the corners of her eyes. "You can miss Carrie but still want to build a future with Ella. Carrie brought you so much happiness, but Ella and Grace will too. Just when you think you don't have room for more love, your heart always finds a way. That's the amazing thing about love—it's infinite."

"What if they can't forgive me?" I asked.

"I think they can because I believe they love you as you love them," Delilah answered. "I've never met Ella, but I've spoken with Grace many times, and that girl adores you. But I think you've got to be honest with them about how you feel."

"Let the dust settle for a day or so," Richard suggested. "Give Ella a moment to catch her breath, then talk to her."

"I think you need a moment to catch your breath too," Delilah said to me. "And I think there's one other person you should talk to while you're here. I think it might help you find some peace with everything."

I closed my eyes and sighed as she pulled me into her embrace. As much as it hurt, I knew she was right.

I needed to go see Carrie.

TWENTY-NINE

Ella
───────

THE NEXT DAY PASSED, AND I STILL HADN'T TOLD ANYONE but Derek about Cash leaving. I hated lying to Grace when she asked if I'd heard from him, but I couldn't stand the thought of hurting her. I knew I had to tell her eventually, but I wanted to buy an extra day or two of peace for her after all she'd been through since the accident.

She and Sam were both feeling a little better, which meant Grace was ready to get back to work. She was just like me—she hated to sit still. But I needed her to be still, at least for just a little while longer.

I busied myself by doing every little thing for Sam and Grace, despite their insistence that they could do most anything on their own. Playing nurse to them eased my mind and gave me something to focus on besides how hurt I was. Bradley Cooper followed me around, picking up on my mood. He gave me extra snuggles and kisses as we fell asleep at night to the soundtrack of the evening news and Jimmy Fallon.

Cash still hadn't tried to contact me. Not that I expected him to.

Despite not really being a romantic, I'd still been hoping for that magical Nicholas Sparks ending. But hadn't I had enough experience with loss to know there was a reason those endings happened in books and movies? They were nice to think about, but real life was a lot more complicated.

I did have to go to work at the bakery the following day, but I called to check on Grace and Sam every couple of hours. They were moving around much more easily and didn't need a lot of help. That meant Grace's barrage of questions as to Cash's whereabouts were only going to increase.

When it was closing time at the bakery, I realized we'd been so busy that I'd barely seen Katie all day. Once I flipped the open sign over to closed, she'd said she was exhausted and headed out. I was worried about how over-worked she'd been, but I'd scheduled several interviews for the rest of the week on top of the ones Katie had already set up. I hoped we'd be able to find her some relief soon.

As I got in my car to head home, I noticed a text from Grace.

Grace: i texted cash earlier about work. still haven't heard from him. weird. you heard from him today?

I couldn't put this off any longer. I needed to figure out what I was going to tell her. I needed to talk to Liv. If anyone could help me make sense of what I was feeling, it was her. I fired off a quick text to Grace.

Ella: Not today. I'm sure he's just busy. Are you and Sam okay? I need to make a couple of pit stops on the way home.

The little text bubbles popped up immediately.

Grace: we're good. :) just watching reruns of the walking dead.

Ella: OK. Be home soon.

As I made the drive out to Liv's house, I thought about the last time I'd been there with Cash when we saved Liv and the kids from the mouse. It was the day after I'd had a meltdown about the washing machine. When he hadn't freaked out after that, I knew he didn't spook easily. He didn't seem the slightest bit put off by seeing me be so emotional and vulnerable. If anything it seemed to bring us closer.

My eyes burned with tears, and I turned the radio up loud and let them out to the sound of a sad Taylor Swift song. This time, it wasn't the kind of crying that shook me to my core. It was the quiet, resigned cry of a woman who felt completely lost.

Halfway to Liv's house, I thought maybe I should have called first, which wasn't something we ever did. We'd always had an open door policy, but with the addition of the kids and Jax in her life those boundaries, or lack thereof, now felt blurry. That thought caused the tears to come a little harder, but I knew if I called I'd lose my nerve and try to put off telling Grace for another day. And I couldn't do that.

By the time I pulled into Liv's driveway, my eyes were red, my cheeks were wet, and I felt defeated. I didn't even try to disguise it as I started toward the front door. I still had a key, and I almost used it, but then thought better of it and knocked instead.

A couple of seconds later, Jax appeared at the door with a shocked expression on his face. "Ella, are you okay?"

"I'm sorry to show up like this, but—" I started but he cut me off.

"Are you kidding me? Come here." He chuckled softly

and pulled me into a hug. "You can show up any way you want, anytime you want."

The gesture made a lump form in my throat.

"Liv was just trying to get Chloe to eat her dinner," he explained as he led me through the house to the dining room where Liv sat with Chloe while Jonathan sat nearby drawing on a large sketchpad. Mama sauntered through the room and looked up at me with her accusatory yellow eyes.

"Look who's here!" Jax's voice was chipper as he announced my arrival to Liv.

"Hi," Jonathan greeted me.

"Ella." Liv took one look at my face and she knew. That, at least, brought me some comfort.

Jax had already moved to the other side of the table. "Why don't you let me take over so you and Ella can talk?"

She nodded and stood, crossing over to me. "Let's go talk on the deck," she said as she curled her arm around me, steering me toward the back door. She stopped on the way to grab two wine glasses and a bottle of pinot grigio from the fridge before we stepped outside.

"I'm sorry." I slid onto the bench of the picnic table as Liv poured the wine and sat across from me. "I should have called."

"Hey," Liv reached for my hand. "Since when do we have to call first?"

I rested my elbow on the table and my head in my hands. "I don't know, Liv. I don't know how everything got so fucked up."

"What's going on?" she asked.

I took a big gulp of wine. Then, I told her everything from the beginning. I started with the night of her wedding and told her about the washing machine, the day we'd been at her house, the way he'd been there for me the night we'd visited my mom, what happened after Grace and Sam's accident, the morning he'd left, and every moment in between. By the time I'd finished she'd moved to my side of the table and placed her arm around me. I leaned my head on her shoulder, and we both cried.

"Oh, Ella." Liv leaned her head on top of mine. "I'm so sorry. I can't believe he left like that. That doesn't sound like him."

"I know." I sniffled and took a sip of my wine. "The more I think about it, the more it doesn't make sense. At first, I was so... angry. But now I just feel broken."

"Why didn't you tell me when he left?" Liv asked softly, her concerned green eyes focused on me. "I would have come right away."

"I don't know." I sighed "I wanted to tell you, but I didn't know how. Especially after I hadn't told you we were seeing each other to start with."

"Look, I know we didn't get to really talk about what happened at Sunday dinner," Liv said. "And I'm sorry I blew up like that. I shouldn't have. All of this is just as much on me. Every time you called I had to cut the conversation short. The truth is, I guess I'm struggling with this new dynamic too. Don't get me wrong, marrying Jax and having Jonathan and Chloe... it's everything I ever could have wanted. But even the things we want most in the world come at a cost."

Wasn't that the truth? Knowing what it was like to love Cash Montgomery had certainly come with a price—the price of what it felt like to lose him.

"I don't know how I got here, Liv," I cried, feeling fresh tears form in my eyes. "I feel like everyone is moving on to the next phases of their lives, but I'm being left behind. Grace is grown up now as evidenced by the fact that her very sweet, British boyfriend is currently staying at our house. And she looks at him the way Craig and I looked at each other at that age."

Liv kept her arm around me as I spoke.

"My mom's condition is getting worse. I can't even recall the last time she remembered me. You've got Jax now and a whole new family of your own that I'm not a part of. Cash doesn't want me anymore." My chest heaved as I wailed. "My grandmother had Alzheimer's, and my mom has it, and I'm probably going to have it too. My mom had my dad to remind her who she was all those years, but who's going to remind me of who I am when I've forgotten? I'm going to be completely and utterly alone."

I wept with my head in my hands, my entire body shaking.

"Ella, look at me," Liv said.

I turned toward her, and she cupped my face in her hands. "You are never going to be alone. Do you hear me? And if you do get Alzheimer's one day, you better damn well believe I'll be there to remind you of who you are. Jax may be my husband, but *you* are my person. You are the sister I never had, my very best friend. You are my family."

I threw my arms around her, and we stayed like that for a moment. Even through my sadness, the world suddenly felt like it had been set upright again.

"I don't know what the future looks like for you and Cash," she said in my ear. "But our future together will always be bright."

"When we're old and in the nursing home, can we pull the fire alarms to get the hot firefighters to show up?" I smiled through my tears.

She laughed. "Obviously."

We sat quietly for a moment before I spoke again. "I

haven't even told Grace yet," I admitted. "I don't know how. I lied and told her he had a work emergency, which was pretty fucking stupid considering she works for him. It's only a matter of time before she figures out that I'm bluffing."

"Grace is strong," Liv assured me. "I think you've got to rip the bandaid off and be honest with her."

"I still can't believe he's gone."

"I'm still not convinced that it's over," Liv said.

"I mean, he left. How much more over can it get?"

"What if he did get a little scared?" Liv asked. "He should have communicated that to you, but especially after the accident and Sam's cancer scare, I could see how his response might be to kind of freak out and run. What if he realizes what a mistake this was and wants to make things right?"

"I don't know, Liv." I shook my head. "What if that's his response every time things get scary? I don't know if I could risk being hurt again."

"You once told me that love is a risk no matter how you slice it. Love isn't about choosing who you think won't hurt you. It's about choosing who's worth hurting for." Liv recited my own words to me, advice I'd given her back when she wasn't sure if she should take a chance on Jax.

I pretended to be offended. "Using my own words against me."

"No, that's not what I'm trying to do at all," she promised. "But I just think about what happened with me and Jax. If you'll remember, I hurt him pretty badly too. I know the circumstances are different, but I can't help but wonder what would have happened if Jax hadn't given me another chance. I wouldn't have the beautiful life I have now."

She had a point, but Cash hadn't even attempted to call me. "I guess I'll cross that bridge if I ever come to it. For now, I've got to figure out how to tell Grace."

"I think you tell her exactly like you told me," Liv said, "but no matter what, I'm going to be there for you. For both of you. It's always been us, and it always will be."

She squeezed my hand, and for the first time since Cash left I felt a sense of calm. Maybe my relationship with Cash would never be okay. But somehow, I would be.

THE NEXT MORNING, GRACE PADDED INTO THE KITCHEN where I was having coffee while Bradley Cooper scarfed down his breakfast.

"Morning, sunshine," I said as she pulled a mug down from the cabinet. "Need any help?"

"I've got it. Really, I'm feeling a lot better," she assured me as she carefully poured coffee into her cup. "Still sore and I can only use one arm, but overall I feel pretty good."

"I'm so glad. I hate seeing you hurting." I watched while she maneuvered around the kitchen, pouring cream into her coffee. I knew I needed to tell her about Cash. I could keep waiting for the right moment, but the reality was that it was going to hurt no matter when I did it.

Liv was right. I needed to just rip the bandaid off.

"I'm worried about Cash," Grace said, taking a seat across from me at the table. "I know you said I needed to rest, but I texted him a couple of times to see if I could help him with whatever work he's doing, and he never replied. The more I think about it, the way he left the other night was weird, don't you think? This isn't like him."

It's what everyone kept saying, and deep down, it's what

I felt too. None of this felt like Cash. "Sweetheart, we need to talk about something."

She raised her brow at me. "I don't like the sound of that."

"I haven't been completely honest with you." I took a sip of my coffee and cleared my throat. "You're not wrong about the way he was the night Sam was released from the hospital. He left suddenly because we had a bit of an argument. He'd been acting distant since the accident, and he said he needed to go home and take care of some things. Admittedly, I got a bit frustrated because we'd planned on having dinner together. I knew how much you were looking forward to it, and I pressed the issue."

"I mean, I was looking forward to it, but it was okay." Grace tapped her fingertips along the side of her coffee cup.

"I know," I said. "So, early the next morning I went to his house to talk. I didn't like how we left things, and I wanted to apologize." I braced myself for the words I would say next—the ones I knew would break Grace's heart. "When I got there, I found that Cash was leaving to go to the airport."

"Where was he going?" she asked.

"I don't know," I admitted. "I said it was a work thing because I honestly didn't know how to tell you. I didn't want to hurt you, but you deserve to know the truth."

"None of this sounds right," Grace said, shaking her head. "Did I scare him off when I told him he felt like a dad to me? Was this my fault? Is that why he won't text me back?"

"Absolutely not. This is between me and him," I explained. "He's probably not responding to you because he can tell by your text messages that you don't know what happened yet. He's probably being respectful of both of us. I may not understand why he's doing what he's doing, but I know better than to think he would ever intentionally hurt you."

"Why do you think he left?"

I sat thoughtfully as I replayed my conversation with Liv in my head. "Everything happened so quickly. Sure, we'd known each other a long time, but the actual dating part was still new. I think the accident and what happened with Sam was probably a lot for him to swallow, and it likely brought up a lot of unpleasant memories for him." My throat tightened. "He probably realized he wasn't ready for this kind of relationship yet."

"But he loves you. I know he does," she insisted. "He never said so, but he didn't have to. It was obvious. He can't walk away from you like that. Away from *us*." Her eyes burned with a mixture of hurt and anger.

"Sometimes you don't know you aren't ready until you've already arrived, and I'd rather him realize that sooner than later." I reached across the table for her hand. "It's better for us to end it now than months or even years down the road."

If our relationship was too much for him, I wish he'd have said so. But no matter how upset I was, I knew he'd never have purposely hurt either of us. I wasn't blameless either. I'd been so upset that I flew off the handle without truly giving him the time to verbalize his thoughts.

Grace's mouth was set in a hard line. "I can't believe him."

"I know you're disappointed. I am too, but try not to let this one thing ruin how you see Cash. He's been very good to you," I said. "People make mistakes."

I winced at my own words, at the realization that maybe that's what I'd been to him… a mistake.

She chewed her lip, her eyes clouding over. "Are you okay?"

"I'd be lying if I said I wasn't hurt, but I'll be okay." I forced a smile. I knew it was true—I would be okay. I had everything I needed, even if I still wanted Cash. "Listen, I don't want this to affect your job or your own relationship with Cash. I know you're hurt, and I am too, but I do know he loves you. I don't want you worrying about whether or not you having a relationship with him will upset me because it won't. Cash and I are adults, and we'll be okay. The most important thing to me is that *you're* okay."

She seemed to contemplate this for a moment before she finally nodded. "Are you sure you're going to be alright?"

"I'm absolutely positive," I promised. "I don't want you worrying about me. I'm going to be just fine. After all, I still get to come home to Bradley Cooper every day."

The dog's ears perked at the sound of his name.

Seemingly satisfied with my answer, she rose from the table. "I need to get out of the house today."

"You and Sam may be feeling better, but neither of you are supposed to be driving," I reminded her.

"I know," she said, "but I was thinking maybe I would call Derek and see if he'd be up for grabbing lunch with us or something. Maybe we could go somewhere with a patio so we could take Bradley Cooper."

I smiled. "I like that idea. I'm glad you like spending time with Derek. He's pretty great, isn't he?"

"He's kinda like the big brother I never had."

"Remember when you had a crush on him?"

"Ugh." Grace grimaced and covered her face with her hand. "Don't remind me. That's so embarrassing."

"I've got to keep you humble somehow," I teased.

"Gee, thanks," she said sarcastically as she picked up her coffee and leaned down to kiss my cheek. "I love you, Mom. Have a good day at work. Tell Katie I said hi."

"I love you too, honey," I replied. "Have fun today."

She sauntered out of the kitchen, leaving me alone with my thoughts.

I tried to keep my mind from wandering to Cash, but all of my thoughts seemed to lead back to him. I wondered where he had gone and if he was okay. I thought about how much I missed him and how long that feeling would last.

And I wondered, wherever he was, if he'd even thought of me at all.

THIRTY

Cash

I LISTENED TO DELILAH AND RICHARD'S ADVICE AND TOOK A moment to catch my breath. The day after our conversation, I spent a lot of time sleeping. After the turmoil I'd gone through since the accident my mind had simply shut down.

The following day, I spent some time with Richard and Delilah. We poured over photo albums, and they told me stories about Carrie, some of which I'd heard dozens of times before. They even told me a few things I didn't know about, like how when she was little she carried rose petals that had fallen off the bush outside to her kindergarten teacher every day because she thought they were beautiful. In those hours, Carrie came alive to me. Once I let go and stopped trying to feel her, I realized she'd been there all along.

I told my in-laws more about Ella and Grace and even Bradley Cooper. It meant the world to me when they said they hoped to meet them one day.

I hoped they would too.

When I woke up the next morning, I was ready to go see Carrie. It felt like I'd been putting myself back together like a jigsaw puzzle, shades of grey fading out into beautiful, bright colors, and Carrie held the last piece.

I stopped by the florist and picked up a bouquet of pink peonies, Carrie's favorite, and drove to the cemetery. As I turned in the parking lot, I remembered arriving the day of her funeral and the way the palls of vibrant flowers looked juxtaposed against the dreary autumn sky. She'd requested that no one wear black to her service, so everyone was dressed in shades of pink—her favorite color. Even though she was gone she still managed to light up the world around her.

I parked the car and got out, winding my way through the headstones, a journey I made often after she died. I walked until I reached the big evergreen tree that sheltered her, and I saw the shimmering granite stone that let me know she was there.

"I brought you some flowers," I said, gently placing the bouquet on top of the headstone. I looked around, noticing I was the lone mourner in that corner of the cemetery, so I took a seat on the grass. Beads of sweat formed along my hairline as a result of the unforgiving August heat and my own nerves.

"I miss you, Carrie." I closed my eyes for a moment, listening to the birds chirp around me, hoping I might catch a whisper of her. "That makes what I need to talk to you about so hard." I sucked in a shallow breath. "I met someone. I feel like you probably already knew that. Maybe it's crazy or maybe it's wishful thinking, but I wonder if you somehow had a hand in me meeting her. You always told me you wanted me to move on and be happy one day. I remember how many times you wanted me to promise you I would, but I couldn't. For so long, I couldn't see a future in which you didn't exist. I think that's why I resisted the idea so much. I was going about it all wrong. A future without you in it was never possible because you're part of me."

I wiped at the tears that fell freely from my eyes. "You'd like Ella and Grace. They both know what it's like to lose someone they love. Ella lost her husband when Grace was a little girl, so they've been through this before. I know they'd help me keep your memory alive, and if you ever come across a guy up there named Craig, you should get to know him. I think you'd like him.

"I just need you to know that I will never stop loving you. I'll never stop missing you. What I feel for Ella and Grace doesn't change that. And because I've known what it feels like to lose you, I'll never take a single second with them for granted if they give me another chance. I don't know what to do, what to say to make things right with them. I wish you could tell me what I should do."

I kissed my fingers and placed them on her headstone before rising to my feet. "I love you, Carrie. I always will. I'll come back again soon."

With a heavy sigh, I turned and started the journey back to my car. Carrie was a part of my story. She was imprinted on every page in the book of my life. But I was finally ready to begin a new chapter.

A slight breeze rustled around me, and my phone rang from my pocket. I almost didn't answer, but I heard Carrie's voice clear as day in my mind. It said, *You wanted a sign. Here it is.*

I extracted my phone from my pocket and saw Grace's name flash across the screen.

My heart pounded in my ears as I swiped across the screen to answer. "Grace…"

"I'm going to say this, and I need you to listen," she began, and I heard her voice waver. "I don't care that you're my boss. Right now, I'm not talking to my boss. I'm talking to my friend, the guy who has felt a lot like a dad to me. You leaving sucks. It really sucks, but I forgive you. I know you didn't ask for forgiveness, but it doesn't matter because I forgive you anyway. Because this isn't like you." She barely took a breath as she barrelled on, much like her mother had the morning I left. "Things got weird after the accident, and I don't know why. I don't know if I scared you off or what happened, but I know—"

"Grace, no," I said, cutting her off. "This wasn't your fault. It had nothing to do with you."

"Then what is it?" The hurt in her voice was palpable, and I made a solemn promise to myself to never be the reason she hurt ever again. "Why did you leave?"

"I got scared," I admitted. "The accident and what happened with Sam knocked the wind out of me. They reminded me how quickly I could lose everything I love. Seeing you in that hospital bed shook me to my core, Grace."

"But I'm fine," she said.

"At that moment, all I could see were the millions of possibilities that could cause me to lose you or your mom," I explained. "And it scared me."

"You were scared to lose us, so you *left* us?" Grace snorted. "That doesn't make any sense."

"I said I was scared. I didn't say I was smart."

Grace's soft sigh came through the phone. "So, where did you go?"

"I came to visit Carrie's parents," I confessed. "I needed to clear my head, but I didn't know how to tell you or your mom that. I barely understood what I was feeling at the time. But Carrie's mom helped me realize that the fear I had of losing both of you wasn't a warning sign telling me to shut down to keep myself from being hurt. It was a reminder to love you both every second I have with you. And I failed at that."

"You only fail if you don't try again," she said gently. "You can try again."

"I'm so sorry. Can you forgive me?"

"I already did. I love you, Cash. Of course, I forgive you."

"I love you, Grace," I said, my voice breaking. "I love you so much, honey. And I'm going to be here for you as long as you want me to be."

She paused for a moment. "What about Mom? I know you love her too."

"I do," I said, "but I don't think she's going to want to talk to me right now, and I understand that. I hurt her a lot when I left."

"You just have to tell her what you told me."

My chest bloomed with hope. Would Ella give me a chance to explain? "Grace, I want to, but I don't know if she'll even agree to see me."

"Oh, she'll see you." She got quiet for a moment, and I could practically hear the wheels in her head turning. "You leave that part to me."

THE NEXT AFTERNOON, I PACKED UP MY SUITCASE AND rolled it into the foyer where Delilah and Richard were waiting for me. After talking with Grace, I decided to cut my trip short and booked an earlier flight home. I didn't know if it would work, if Ella would even give me the time of day, but I had to try to get her back.

"It sure was good to see you, son," Richard said, clasping his hand on my shoulder. "Are you sure you won't let me take you to the airport?"

I shook my head. "The Uber will be here in a minute. That airport traffic can be kind of crazy. There's no sense in you getting out in it."

"I'm so glad you came." Delilah placed her hand on the side of my face. "And I'm glad you talked with Grace."

I didn't know what plan Grace was cooking up in her head, but she seemed confident Ella would see me. "Me too."

"You will always have us, dear." Delilah said. "We're your family."

"I know." I pulled her into my embrace. "I don't know what I would have done without you."

"You had all the answers you needed." She placed her hand on my chest. "Right in here. They were there all along."

"You're going to get Ella back," Richard assured me.

"I hope so," I said, a flurry of nerves rising in my stomach.

"I know so," Delilah insisted. "And one day, when you're ready, I want you to bring her and Grace to meet us. You can even bring Bradley Cooper."

"I would love that," I said. In my mind's eye, I could see myself walking through their front door again with Ella and Grace by my side. The vision felt so real it could have been a snapshot. I didn't want to get my hopes up, but I prayed that vision would become a reality.

Richard peeked out the front door. "Looks like your Uber's here." He pronounced it 'youber,' and I stifled a laugh. "Let me take that suitcase out to the car for you."

"I've got it." I tried to stop him, but his reflexes were quick. He snatched it before I could stop him.

"Richard, you're going to throw your back out," Delilah said, shaking her head.

"I've got it," he insisted.

Delilah rolled her eyes. "At least use the rollers."

"Mind your own business, woman." He stuck his tongue out at her before rolling my suitcase to the waiting car.

I watched the way Delilah's eyes followed Richard as she chuckled. "I swear that man will be the death of me." If Ella and I were lucky, we'd be like them one day. I hoped we'd be together long enough to drive each other crazy. "Let us know when you land, will you?"

"I will," I promised. "Thank you, Delilah. For everything. I don't know what I did to deserve you and Richard, but I'm so thankful for you both."

Delilah's eyes misted. "You get on out of here before you make me cry." She stepped up on her toes to kiss my cheek. "We love you, son. Never forget that."

I gave her one last hug. "I love you too."

"Now, get," she said, shooing me out the door. "I don't want you to miss your flight."

I got in the Uber and waved as the car pulled away. When we got to the edge of the driveway, I turned back and watched as Richard pulled Delilah into his arms. They may not have been my family by blood, but they were my family by love.

And love was all that mattered.

"So, to the airport?" the driver asked, making small talk. "Where are you headed?"

As I watched Richard and Delilah disappear from view, I thought of Ella and Grace. "Home. I'm headed home again."

THIRTY-ONE

Ella

"HELLO, MY LITTLE CHICKEN CUTLETS," ANTONI GREETED as he sauntered over to our table at Rosepepper Cantina. "Sorry I'm late." He made his way around the table passing out kisses to Liv and Katie.

Liv had organized a night out under the guise of finding out how things had gone for Antoni meeting Nate's parents, though, I suspected she really did it to cheer me up.

"We ordered you a margarita," Katie said, pointing to the vacant spot beside me.

He clutched his chest. "You know the way to my heart."

"Hey, sweet cheeks," he said when he got to me, kissing the corner of my mouth. "Where's Grace tonight? How's she feeling?"

"Better. She and Sam went to see a movie with Derek," I answered as he took his seat beside me. "So, how was Nate's family?"

"Yeah," Liv said. "Remind me again where they live?"

Antoni raised his brow. "Honey, they live in Valentine, Nebraska."

"I don't think I've heard of that place before." Liv took a sip of her cocktail.

"Exactly." He leaned in as though he were telling us a secret. "Population: twenty-eight hundred. But honey, this place was God's country. It felt so good to kind of unplug a little bit. I mean, I'd never want to live there because I need to be within a ten mile radius of every minor convenience at all times, but it's sure fun to visit."

"What was his family like?" I asked. It felt good to see Antoni so happy, even if I was a sad sack at the moment.

"His mama and daddy are sweet as strawberry pie," he purred. "I swear to God his mama is basically M'Lynn from *Steel Magnolias*, and his daddy looks like Clint Eastwood. I see where Nate gets his good looks from." He paused to take a swig of his margarita. "We went kayaking together. Even his cute little granny went with us. Her name is Mildred, and if Shirley McClain and Betty White had a lovechild, honey, it would be her. She's ninety-one, but she could out row every single one of us. We were thick as thieves by the end of the weekend."

"That's so sweet." I may not ever get to meet the people Cash considered family, but I loved seeing the way Antoni sparkled talking about Nate's family.

Katie laughed. "Sounds like a great time."

"It was. And I've come bearing news." Antoni paused dramatically before thrusting his left hand out at us. "I'm engaged!"

I looked down to see a gorgeous diamond-studded platinum band wrapped around his ring finger.

Liv shrieked and grabbed his hand. "Oh my God! It's gorgeous, Antoni."

"It's beautiful," Katie echoed, leaning in to take a closer look.

"Wow," I said. "That's wonderful news, babe." My throat constricted, and my eyes clouded over. "I'm so happy for you."

And I was. Antoni deserved every ounce of happiness, but I couldn't stop my mind from wandering to Cash and the moments I'd naively let myself hope for. If I couldn't get a happy ending of my own, I was thankful I got to watch two of my friends get one.

"Thank you." Antoni pulled his hand back and admired his ring. "We're so happy. I know we've only been together a few months, but honey, when you know you know."

Except when you thought you knew, but it turned out you didn't know at all.

Liv flashed me a sympathetic glance.

"So, what's new with you, ladies?" Antoni asked.

Liv shrugged. "I've seen every available episode of *Paw Patrol.*"

"I've been discovering the world of internet dating," Katie added.

Antoni pursed his lips. "When is Dallas going to pull his head out of his hairy ass and ask you out?"

"We're just friends," she insisted, but I caught the wistful look in her eye. I recognized it because I felt it too.

Liv burst into laughter. "Wait, how do you know if his ass is hairy?"

Antoni chuckled. "Honey, whenever they have wardrobe changes at awards shows, those boys will drop their drawers without warning, and the next thing you know, you're staring at a full, hairy-assed moon.

"I get to go home to Bradley Cooper every day," I said,

shifting Antoni's focus to me as I sucked down my margarita.

"Hold the phone, Lady Gaga." Antoni whipped around to face me. "You can't just name drop like that and not show me the receipts."

I pulled my phone out of my purse and found one of my favorite pictures of Bradley Cooper.

He took the device from my hands. "Honey, you need to get your eyes checked because *this* is a dog."

"Yep." I smiled. "My dog."

"Look at that cute little nugget," Antoni said as he studied the picture. "Let me guess, you named him that just so you could say you're going home to Bradley Cooper to fool suckers like me."

"That's correct." I laughed. "If you swipe over there's a few more pictures."

"He is adorable, Ella." He moved his fingers across the screen, making schmoopie faces as he did. He came to an abrupt stop, his mouth gaping open. "Is this our own Cash Mongomery with your dog?"

Shit. I hadn't been able to bring myself to delete those photos he'd sent me the day he took Bradley Cooper out while I was at work. In fact, I'd spent more time than I cared to admit staring at them.

"I knew it," Antoni exclaimed, slamming his fist down on the table. "I saw the way he looked at you at Liv's wedding. It's about damn time is all I have to say."

My gaze fell to my lap. "Well, it's kind of complicated."

Katie's eyes widened with concern. I hadn't had a chance to tell her yet. "No…"

I frowned. "We had started seeing each other, but things didn't quite work out."

Antoni placed his arm around my shoulders. "What happened, honey?"

I gave Antoni and Katie the *Reader's Digest* version of our relationship, unable to make myself relive it all in detail again.

Katie reached for my hand across the table. "I'm so sorry, Ella."

Antoni shook his head. "I just... I don't get it. This isn't like him."

I sighed. "That's what everyone keeps saying."

"And I have no doubt in my mind that man is in love with you," Antoni said. "I don't know, honey. Call me crazy, but I don't think your story is over."

"It sure feels over to me," I muttered.

"How did Grace take it?" Katie asked.

"She handled it pretty well," I admitted. "I kind of got the feeling she might try to talk to him, but if she did, she hasn't told me. And I think I'm okay with that."

"Is that... weird for you?" Katie's brow furrowed with concern.

"She and Cash have a relationship outside of the one I had with him. I don't want her to feel she can't maintain that if she wants to," I said. "I'm sad because I guess I really saw a future for us, but it just wasn't meant to be. It might be a little awkward for a while, but I don't want this to affect anyone else's relationship with Cash. I don't want us to be the reason Sunday dinners get weird."

Liv snorted. "That's Luca's job."

"Exactly," I said. "Besides, even though this didn't turn out the way I hoped it would, I still care about him. I want him to be happy." Even if it wasn't with me.

My gaze dropped to my margarita as I twirled the straw around the glass.

Liv caught my eye, and sensing my mood, she changed the subject. "Antoni, we've got to tell you about the latest Luca debacle."

Katie nearly choked on her cocktail. "Brandi?"

"With an i," Liv and Katie said together.

Antoni leaned in, listening intently as Liv and Katie regaled him with the details of Luca and Brandi's sexcapades at our Sunday dinner.

As they talked I found my mind wandering back to Cash. I wondered where he was and if I'd crossed his mind. I wondered if he missed me the way I missed him.

I even let myself wonder for a moment if Antoni could be right—if maybe, just maybe, our story wasn't over.

"So, what did you think about Sydney?" I asked Katie after we'd finished closing up for the day. "I think she had potential. And I *loved* that Jacob guy."

"I agree," Katie said. "I liked both of them a lot, and I kind of love that they don't have a ton of experience. It means they're malleable."

"And both seemed eager to learn," I added. We had wrapped up four interviews, and we both felt optimistic. The new selection of candidates felt so much better, and the last person we interviewed had some great ideas for some low-cost lunch items to add to our menu. "And I love how much initiative Sydney had. She came in with pie charts, spreadsheets, and everything."

Katie laughed. "Right? She makes both of us look bad."

"I think we need someone like that," I said. "We need to be able to relax a little bit."

"Yes." Katie untied her apron and tossed it on the counter. "Yes, we do. And it couldn't come soon enough with the renovations being almost done."

"Big Earl said this morning that we're about two weeks out. We have another crop of interviews tomorrow, but if they don't dazzle us, I think we found two really good ones today."

"Now, we just have to find a barista," Katie added before pausing a beat. "Ella, I'm really sorry about Cash."

I shrugged. "It's alright. I mean, it isn't, but it will be. *I* will be."

"Of course you will," she said gently. "But you're allowed to be hurt. You're allowed to not be strong all the time."

"Trust me, I've had my moments," I admitted. "Last night I ate an entire sleeve of Oreos in the bathtub and cried."

"It's all about balance," Katie teased. "Look, I know this didn't go down the way we all thought it would, but I'm proud of you."

I snorted. "For what? I can eat an entire sleeve of Oreos in my sleep."

She shook her head and smiled. "No, silly. For putting yourself back out there. I know that couldn't have been easy because it never is. For what it's worth, I imagine that after you've had the kind of love you shared with your husband it was probably pretty hard to let yourself believe in that kind of love again, but you did. You gave it a chance, and I think that's pretty brave."

"Thanks, Katie Bug," I said, pulling her into a hug. "I appreciate you. More than you know."

"Ditto," she replied. "I'm wiped out, so I'm about to head home unless you need anything."

"Nope," I said. "Get some rest. I'm about to head out too."

"Good night," she called as she disappeared through the door to the kitchen.

I decided to text Grace before I left.

Ella: Hey honey. Want me to pick up something for dinner?

Almost immediately, the text bubbles appeared.

Grace: actually, i'm having dinner with lexi. she came and picked me up. i let bradley cooper out to pee before i left tho.

Ella: Did Sam go with you?

Grace: he's having dinner with one of his friends. we're going to pick him up on the way back.

Ella: OK. You and Lexi be safe.

Grace: we will. :) i won't be home too late. promise.

I sighed with my entire body. *Guess it's just me and Bradley Cooper tonight.* I finished locking up, turned off the lights, and started toward the back door to leave. As I flung the door open to the outside, my phone pinged with a text.

Derek: Hey. Are you busy?

Ella: Not unless you call going home to have dinner with my dog 'busy.'

Derek: Good. I could really use your advice on something. It's kind of important. Would you be available to have dinner tonight?

I was overcome with gratitude for the offer so I didn't have to sit at home alone and wallow in my feelings. Plus, I wanted to do anything I could to help Derek.

Ella: Sounds good. Where should I meet you?

Derek: I'll swing by and pick you up in half an hour.

Ella: Perfect. Where are we going?

Derek: You'll see. :)

Ella: But I need to know what to wear!!!

I swear, boys didn't understand how much thought went into things like that.

Derek: Something nice-ish? Not crazy fancy.

Boy directives were so weird.

Ella: You could just tell me where we're going.

Derek: And ruin the surprise? It's a really cool place. I promise you'll love it.

Ella: A surprise? Fiiiiiine. See you soon.

What kind of surprise was this anyway? I thought he needed advice?

I didn't have much time to overthink it because I had to get home and hunt down something to wear. As I started toward home, doing a mental tour of my closet, I realized I was thankful for the distraction.

By the time I pulled into my driveway I noticed the clouds thickening in the air and heard the sound of thunder in the distance. When I stepped out of my car I smelled the scent of rain in the air, a silent warning that a storm was coming.

THIRTY-TWO

Cash

I ROLLED UP THE SLEEVES OF MY WHITE BUTTON-DOWN AND ran my fingers through my hair. Taking a deep breath, I glanced at my reflection in the bathroom mirror at Carrie On Records one last time. I shook out my hands in a futile attempt to shake out my nervous energy.

Grace and I were meeting Ella for dinner, and I was going to get the chance to try and win Ella back. I walked out to the front of the office where Grace was waiting for me, holding the bouquet of white tulips I'd gotten for her mother.

"How do I look?" I asked timidly.

"You look great," she answered. "There's nothing to be nervous about. It's just mom."

"What time is she meeting us at Moto?" I took the flowers from her hand, and she smoothed the hem of her yellow sundress.

"They'll be there at seven," she replied as we made our way to the door. "But we should get there a few minutes early so we can get a table."

"Wait." I furrowed my brow. "They?"

Grace's eyes went wide. "*She* will be there at seven. Sorry. I don't know why I said that."

I narrowed my eyes on her as she started toward my car. "Grace..."

"Yeah?"

"Your mom does know about this dinner, right?" I asked, jogging ahead to open the passenger door for her. "She knows she's meeting us?"

"Of course," she said. "Don't worry. She'll be there."

I rolled my neck from side to side, trying to release some of the anxious tension as I rounded the car to the driver's side door. The sky was darkening, signaling the arrival of a late summer storm. A couple of random raindrops splattered against the windshield as I started toward the restaurant.

"How did she seem when you talked to her?" I asked for what felt like the millionth time since she said her mom was willing to talk about things over dinner.

Grace giggled. "I already told you. She was ready and willing to talk to you."

"I know, but maybe I should have called her first?" I asked, second guessing myself. "It just feels weird that this will be the first time we've even talked since everything happened."

"No, it's not weird," she said quickly. "She thought it would be better that way. You know, talking in person."

I nodded. "Right." I still felt strange about it, but I chalked it up to how nervous I was about seeing Ella. I couldn't help but feel hopeful that we would walk away from the conversation differently than we'd arrived. That she would give me another chance to show her I could be the man she deserved.

Grace had suggested we go somewhere that was meaningful to us, but the truth was, every moment I'd spent with Ella meant the world to me. Part of me wished I could have gone to her house and talked with her there, but Grace had insisted that meeting for dinner was what Ella wanted.

She probably preferred to be on more neutral territory, somewhere she could easily leave should she realize that this wasn't what she wanted. That *I* wasn't what she wanted.

My stomach churned at the thought. What if she didn't take me back?

"Grace, I need you to know something," I said as I drove. "No matter how this turns out, I'll always be here for you, okay? But if your mom doesn't want a relationship with me, I need to know that you will support her and be on her side, no matter what. Can you promise me that?"

"She's going to want to get back together with you," she insisted. "I know she will."

"But if she doesn't," I said, "I don't want you to hold that against her, okay? I hurt her, and that is my burden to bear."

Grace's mouth turned downward. "She's going to forgive you."

"I need you to promise me, Grace," I said again.

She sighed. "I promise."

I hated to even think about the possibility that I would walk away without Ella, that she wouldn't be able to forgive me. But I knew my actions had consequences, and I was prepared to accept whatever they were. I was just grateful she was willing to hear me out.

The closer we got to the restaurant, the darker the skies became, and I hoped that wasn't a bad omen. We drove the rest of the way in silence as I mentally tried to calm my nerves, rehearsing everything I would say to her. I'd thought it through over and over again in my mind. There were a million things I wanted to say, but they were all a longer version of the same thing... that I loved her and Grace, and I would spend my life showing them if she'd let me.

"We're here," Grace said, rubbing her palms together as the sign for Moto came into view.

My stomach flopped around like a fish on dry land as I found a parking space.

"We better get in there before it starts raining," Grace urged. "Are you ready?"

I closed my eyes and took a deep breath.

She reached over and placed her hand on my arm. "It's going to be okay."

I placed my hand on hers and nodded. No matter the outcome, I'd been given the gift of a second chance. As the waves ripped around me, tugging at my heart, I was reminded that they were never there to take me down or pull me under.

They were there to teach me how to swim.

THE WIND WHIPPED AROUND US AS WE APPROACHED THE front door of the restaurant, and I noticed a familiar figure walking toward us.

Thunder rumbled, causing the ground to tremble slightly beneath my feet. "Is that... Is that Derek?"

"Shit," I heard Grace curse as my eyes gravitated to the figure that fell into step beside him. Her hair fell in soft waves around her face, and her blue, floral dress held her tight—the way I longed to. She was breathtaking.

Ella's eyes landed on mine, and I watched as a mix of emotions flooded her face in a matter of seconds. First, there was a look of surprised recognition, followed by an almost happy half-smile. But all of that gave way to a look of startled confusion. She certainly didn't look like she was expecting me.

Grace shot me a nervous glance as Derek and Ella approached.

"You're early," Grace said to Derek.

Derek gave her an apologetic smile. "I'm sorry. I was trying to beat the storm."

Judging from Ella's face, the storm had arrived.

"Does anyone want to tell me what's going on?" Ella asked, throwing up her hands and then setting her fiery gaze on me. "Did you put them up to this?"

Derek's eyes grew big as saucers. "Uh-oh."

"No," Grace answered, stepping in front of me as though she could shield me from her anger. "This was all my idea."

"I thought you said she knew?" I asked incredulously.

Grace spun around to face me. "Okay, so that wasn't entirely true."

My heart plummeted in my chest. If Ella didn't know about this dinner plan of Grace's, chances were she also had no interest in hearing what I had to say. In fact, from the looks of it, she probably didn't even want to see me.

I pushed my hand through my hair and sighed. "Grace, what's going on?"

"*Knew what?*" Ella's nostrils flared, and she crossed her arms looking from me to Derek and then back to Grace. "Grace Eloise Claiborne, you have some serious explaining to do."

"I know," Grace said, taking a step toward her mom. "I

asked Derek to help me get you here so you and Cash could talk."

Derek attempted to back away slowly, but Ella caught him out of the corner of her eye. "Don't even think about it."

"Sorry," Derek muttered.

"I wanted to surprise you." Grace smiled meekly. "So… surprise?"

"This isn't the kind of thing you surprise someone with," I said gently. "She deserved to know."

"Exactly, Lindsay Lohan." Ella scoffed. "This ain't the *Parent Trap*."

"To be fair, it did work in that movie." Grace gave her mom a hopeful smile. "If it's good enough for Disney, it's good enough for us, right?"

"You're on thin ice, little lady," Ella warned. "You're lucky your arm is still in that cast and I still feel sorry for you. Why didn't you tell me, Grace?"

She shrugged. "I don't know. I guess I was afraid you wouldn't come if I told you why you were coming."

Ella narrowed her eyes. "You tricked me. And you tricked Cash. I understand that you want us to be together, but you can't force this kind of thing, sweetheart. I think it's best if we all just go home." She took another look at me, and I saw the tears pooled in her eyes. "I'm sorry… about all of this. I had no idea. I know you needed space." She turned away as a light rain started to fall.

My throat tightened, and I worried the storm really had been a bad sign. "Ella, wait."

"No, mom," Grace said, starting after her. "He wanted to talk to you. He came because he thought you were willing to talk to him. I was the one who told him not to call you, and I stupidly set this whole thing up, which I see now was maybe not the best idea. But I was afraid you wouldn't want to hear him out."

"Because I'm such an unreasonable person?" Ella said over her shoulder.

"Because I know how hurt you are," Grace insisted. "I've heard you crying in the bathroom every night, and I know we're out of Oreos. I just knew that if you gave him a chance to explain, you'd understand—that you guys could work it out and get back together."

"Grace, let me take it from here," I said, bypassing her and jogging to catch up with Ella. "Please wait." I grabbed her hand and turned her around as the rain fell around us. "I'm so sorry. I'm sorry for the way I left, for hurting you, for not just telling you what I was feeling."

She looked up at me through a mix of tears and raindrops. "And what is that exactly?"

"The accident and what happened with Sam... it all took me back to what happened with Carrie and how quickly I could lose everything that matters to me in this world. I got scared, and I ran," I admitted. "I went to see Delilah and Richard, and they helped me realize that fear wasn't a warning to leave. It was a reminder of all the reasons I should stay. It scared me because I don't want to be without you and Grace a single second of my life."

Her eyes pleaded with mine. "How do I know you won't get scared again?"

"I'll definitely get scared. I'm terrified now, to be completely honest, but that's because I have something to lose." I tucked a piece of hair behind her ear, cupping her head in my hands, not even caring that we were getting soaked. "Since Carrie died, I felt like I didn't really belong anywhere, but you and Grace make me feel like I have a home again. You've both given me a second chance to live the life I always wanted. I may not always get it right. I may not show up perfectly, but I'm not going anywhere." I gazed into her eyes and saw my whole world. "I'm in love with you, Ella, and I'll spend the rest of my life showing you if you'll let me."

She placed her hands on my chest, and for a moment, I felt all would be right in the world.

Her hands dropped to her sides, and her gaze fell to her feet, taking my heart along with it. "I don't know if I can."

She could have kicked me in the stomach and it would have hurt less. "Oh... I understand. It's okay. I... I get it." I swallowed hard and withdrew my hands. "I understand."

Her eyes rose to meet mine, and a slight smile stretched across her face. "You see, I've already promised myself to Bradley Cooper, and I don't know how he'd feel about playing second fiddle to another man."

Slowly, her words registered in my mind, and I felt my heart beating hard against the walls of my chest. "I think he could be bribed." I closed the distance between us and kissed her, wrapping her in my arms as the rain fell in sheets around us.

"I love you too," Ella said, breaking our kiss. She looked down and tugged at her dress that was practically shrink-wrapped to her body. "I got my Nicholas Sparks moment!"

"Who's that?" I asked, wiping the water from my face. "Is that another actor I don't know?"

She laughed and kissed me softly. "Don't worry. There will be many more movie nights ahead where I can teach you everything you need to know."

Derek and Grace cheered from where they stood beneath the awning of the restaurant.

Grace squealed and ran toward us, and I enveloped her and Ella in my arms. "I love you both so much." As I kissed the top of Grace's head, I was overcome with emotion. Those feelings that had overwhelmed me before came rushing back. The waves nipped at my heels, but this time I wasn't afraid.

Because I knew there would never be a storm we couldn't weather together.

THIRTY-THREE

Ella

Three months later...

"I PROMISE THERE'S NOTHING TO BE NERVOUS ABOUT," CASH said as he pulled the SUV into Richard and Delilah's driveway.

I exhaled sharply, bouncing my knee. Being stuck in a car for hours had done little to calm my anxiety. "I really hope they like me."

"They're going to love you," Cash insisted.

"Delilah said that between me and Cash she already feels like she knows you," Grace piped up from the back seat.

Bradley Cooper gave a yip of approval from Sam's lap.

Grace was finished with school for the semester, so after spending some extra time with my mom, we'd decided to take a road trip to Charleston. The bakery was fully staffed which afforded me the ability to take a few days off to enjoy some time together. We even stopped for a night in Gatlinburg to see the Christmas lights and give us all a break from being in the car.

"It'd be impossible not to love you," Sam said in his adorable British accent. "You're sensational."

"Did you hear that?" I nudged Cash with my elbow. "I'm sensational."

"You are," he agreed. "And I know Delilah and Richard will think so too." He pulled to a stop and parked the car. "Ready?"

I squeezed his hand. "Let's do it."

We got out of the car and unloaded the few gifts we'd brought along with our luggage, rolling our suitcases up the walk as Bradley Cooper scampered ahead to the front porch.

I held my breath as Cash rang the doorbell. A few seconds later, the cutest little older couple I'd ever seen flung open the door.

"There they are," the man who I knew to be Richard greeted us. "Get on in here." He pulled Cash into his embrace while Delilah found her way to me.

"Ella, sweetheart." She enveloped me in her arms. "It's so good to see you. I've been waiting a long time to hug your neck. How was the trip?"

"It was great," I answered.

"We stopped last night to see the Christmas lights in the mountains," Grace said as Delilah made her way over to her.

"That sounds magical." Delilah kissed Grace on the cheek. "How are you, sweetheart? I take it this handsome young man is Sam."

"How do you do?" Sam asked, extending his hand.

Delilah playfully pushed away his hand and pulled him into her arms. "I'm a hugger. You'll get used to me."

"I'd be delighted," Sam said.

"Isn't he precious?" Delilah asked as she reached for Cash, and Richard came over to me.

"You didn't tell me how pretty these girls were, son." Richard said, squeezing Grace and me. "Have mercy. And this British fella is quite handsome too." He patted Sam on the back.

I smiled. "It's so nice to finally meet you."

"And this little guy must be Bradley Cooper." Richard crouched down, sending the little dog into a frenzy. He twirled in circles, his tail whipping back and forth.

"Oh goodness." Delilah cooed as Bradley Cooper flopped on his back in front of her, begging for belly rubs. "He's the cutest little thing."

"Let's get you all settled," Richard said, taking my bag from me. "Dinner will be ready in just a minute. I hope you're hungry."

"Starving," Grace replied. "Something smells good." And it did. It smelled warm and inviting like roasted turkey and homemade cranberry sauce.

"Delilah's been cooking up a storm for two days. Come on, young man. I'll let you help me. I'd like to have a chat about your intentions with Grace." Richard talked animatedly as he and Sam rolled the suitcases down the hall. "You know she'll be our granddaughter one day, once Cash makes it official."

"He's always looking for an excuse to exercise those muscles, isn't he?" Cash chuckled. "I'm going to put the presents by the tree." He squeezed my hand before carrying the gifts into the living room.

"Don't mind Richard," Delilah said, placing her arms around me and Grace. "I promise he won't scare the boy too badly." She led us to the dining room where a feast suitable for twenty people awaited us. "I hope Bradley Cooper likes treats. I found a recipe online for some homemade peanut butter doggie biscuits."

My heart melted. "Delilah, that's so sweet of you. You didn't have to do all of this."

"Oh, I loved doing it." Delilah's smile was so warm that it reminded me of my own mom. "It feels good to have people to care for. And yes, Bradley Cooper is people to me."

At the mention of his name, Bradley Cooper wiggled his butt so fast it became a furry little blur.

The dining table was covered with a fancy red table cloth. Not that you could see much of it for the mountain of food Delilah had prepared. A roasted turkey, macaroni and cheese, mashed potatoes, green beans, fried apples, rolls, cranberry sauce, three pies, a pitcher of tea, and two bottles of wine were placed beautifully across the table. It was a gorgeous feast that looked like it had come out of a Hallmark movie. Or *Harry Potter*.

"You've really outdone yourself, Delilah." Cash's eyes were wide as he came into the dining room. "Everything looks delicious."

"I told you she'd been cooking up a storm," Richard said, entering the room with Sam on his heels. "Come on, everybody. Let's eat."

We all sat at the table with Delilah and Richard taking their places at either end.

"Wow, what a beautiful spread," Sam said, awestruck.

Bradley Cooper circled the table, already hoping for a handout.

Richard passed one of the bottles of wine down the table as Grace poured her tea.

When I handed the bottle to Delilah, I noticed her eyes were misty.

"Delilah, are you okay?" I asked.

"I'm more than okay, sweetheart," she answered. "I'm just... It's been a long time since there was so much life at this table. It feels good. I'm so happy you're all here."

Delilah's eyes met mine, and I reached for her hand. "I'm happy too."

AFTER DINNER, DELILAH AND RICHARD SPOILED US WITH gifts. Their faces lit up brighter than the twinkly lights on the tree as they watched Grace unwrap the sterling Tiffany bracelet they gave her along with a cupcake Christmas ornament and a basket of shimmery, scented lotions.

They got me a beautiful cashmere scarf and Grace and I fluffy robes that matched. Sam received a set of gourmet teas and coffees along with two holiday-themed mugs. Cash opened a new luggage set with an invitation for all of us to spend spring break with them. Even Bradley Cooper got a new stuffed toy that he happily gnawed on beneath the Christmas tree.

"I love it," Delilah exclaimed, holding up one of her gifts, a burgundy chenille throw blanket. "It's so soft. Thank you."

"I'll get a lot of use out of this." Richard examined the new grill set we'd given him. "Especially when you all come back for spring break."

"I'm glad you like it," Cash said, standing to clean up the wrapping paper that now littered the floor.

"Now, what do you say we dig into those pies Delilah made?" Richard asked, rising to his feet.

"I say that's a great idea," Grace chirped as she and Sam trailed behind him toward the dining room.

"Cash, do you mind helping Richard slice the pies?" Delilah asked. "I'd like a moment alone with Ella. You know, for some girl talk."

"Of course," he answered, flashing me a smile before leaving the room with Bradley Cooper on his heels.

My stomach fluttered, and I smoothed my hands over my jeans. What could she want to talk to me about?

Delilah moved to the Christmas tree and found a small envelope with a tiny box on top. "I have one more thing to give you."

My face softened as she sat beside me on the couch. "You've given me so much already."

"This one isn't from me. It's from Carrie."

I couldn't help the puzzled expression that veiled my face.

"Before Carrie passed away, she said she wanted to leave something for the woman he'd spend the rest of his life with. She didn't want to leave it with Cash because she knew how much the idea upset him at the time, so she entrusted it with me." She handed me the card-sized envelope and the box. "She said I'd know who it belonged to, and she was right."

I looked down at the envelope, reading the inscription that was written in cursive:

To the woman he loves next...

"But..." I trailed off as I ran my thumb over the black ink. "We're not married. We're not even engaged yet." It was something we'd talked about, and I knew it would happen one day. But I wasn't in a hurry. I knew our hearts belonged to each other, and that was all that mattered.

"I know," she said, placing her hand on my knee. "But,

Ella, I've always known it would be you. From the second he mentioned your name after you first met, I knew you'd be the one. He just didn't know it yet. After I got to know Grace, I was only that much more certain. I could have waited to give it to you. I could have saved it for the day you two do get married, but something told me now was the right time. Go on. Open it." She gave me an encouraging smile.

I slid my finger between the folds of the envelope, broke the seal, and pulled out a small pink card with peonies on the front. I swallowed hard as I opened it to see the same flowery script inside.

To you,

Cash gave me this for our first Christmas together. It's been worn a lot, but it's filled with years of love and happy memories. I'm passing it on to you with the hope that you'll fill it with even more.

Love him enough for us both.

Carrie

Tears pricked at the corners of my eyes, and my stomach did cartwheels as I looked down at the box in my hands. I pried open the top to reveal a gold heart pendant with a pearl at the center. "It's beautiful."

"I know it meant a lot to her for you to have it," Delilah said, her voice breaking. "And I want you to know how much it means to me to have you in our lives too."

I closed the box and held it tight as I wrapped my arms around her. "Thank you, Delilah. This is… thank you."

She kissed my cheek. "You're welcome, sweetheart. I know these last few months have been hard on you. Grace and Cash have been keeping me filled in about your mother's health, and I'm so sorry to hear that she's been unwell. But I want you to know you have family here, Ella."

Gratitude swelled in my chest. My mom's Alzheimer's

had been getting progressively worse, and her slow decline was getting harder and harder to watch.

"I'd never try to take your mother's place, but I hope you know I'll be there for you and Grace too." Her eyes were so sincere, they reminded me of my mother's. "I'll be your mother-in-love."

I laughed through my tears. "I'd really like that."

"Dessert is served whenever you two are ready," Cash said, sticking his head into the room. He took one look at our faces and immediately grew concerned. "Is everything okay?"

Delilah laughed. "Yes, of course." She patted my knee. "Why don't I give you two a moment?"

With that, she excused herself, giving Cash's arm a squeeze as she passed him.

He made his way over and sat next to me. "What was that about?"

I didn't speak for fear that I'd never be able to stop the waterworks from coming. Instead, I opened the box for him to see.

His eyes flashed with recognition and then confusion. "But how…"

I opened the card, and his hand covered his mouth when he saw Carrie's handwriting.

After he read it, he looked back at me, astonished.

"Can I put it on for you?" he asked.

I nodded, and he gently took the pendant from the box as I gathered my hair in my hand. The cool metal hit my chest, and I placed my hand over it. I held it close to my heart as I made a silent vow to the woman I would never meet. *I will, Carrie. I promise.*

Epilogue

CASH

Five months later...

I watched as Ella and Derek twirled little Jonathan and Chloe on the dance floor as the song "Stand By Me" played. Liv and Jax danced nearby, smiling and likely grateful for the moment alone together. It was a warm, spring evening in Nashville. Liv and Jax had transformed their property into a magical, matrimonial wonderland for the perfect sunset ceremony and reception. They'd spared no expense in making sure Antoni got all the glitz and glamour his heart desired for his and Nate's big day. I was sitting at the bridal party table with Dallas who had been sulking since Katie had walked in with a date.

"Cash Montgomery, you better get your ass out here," Antoni said as he and his groom floated by me. "Even Luca's crazy ass is dancing!"

My eyes landed on Luca who was dancing alone, drink in hand, and shook my head. At least he hadn't tried to bring another woman he didn't know.

"You heard the man." Grace propped her hand on her hip as she approached.

"Wouldn't you rather dance with Sam?" I asked, looking for his mop of red hair amongst the crowd.

"I'm asking you." She held her hand out to me. "Besides, this is our song."

"Well, I can't say no to that." I let her pull me to my feet and lead me out onto the floor.

"They look so happy." Grace and I swayed back and forth together, watching as Antoni and Nate waltzed past us.

"Almost as happy as Nate's parents." I laughed as I spotted the two people I knew to be Nate's mom and dad sitting at a table nearby openly weeping with the biggest smiles on their faces. The two had told everyone within earshot how lucky they were to have Antoni joining their family.

"I don't know," Grace said. "I think Antoni's dad might give them a run for their money. I didn't think he was going to make it down the aisle." Antoni's dad had cried through the entire ceremony, beaming with pride as he watched his son and new son-in-law say their vows.

"It was pretty sweet." The whole thing had made me a little misty-eyed as I imagined Grace up at the altar one day.

"I'd like that to be us one day." It was as though Grace were reading my mind. "Someday, when I get married, I want you to walk me down the aisle."

My heart swelled in my chest, and I feared I'd be joining the running for the most emotional parent at the wedding. "Grace, it would be the greatest honor of my life." I cleared my throat, seizing the opportunity I'd been waiting for. I thought I already knew the answer, but my palms started to sweat. "With that in mind, I have a favor I'd like to ask of you."

"What's that?" she asked.

I took a deep breath. "You know I love your mom, and I love you. You two are everything to me."

Her eyes lit up, and her mouth stretched into a grin. "Are you about to ask me what I think you're about to ask me?"

"I'd like your permission to ask your mom to marry me."

"Yes," she exclaimed, throwing her arms around me. "Yes, of course."

I held her tight and saw Ella smiling at us from where she danced with Derek and the kids. "I already went and visited your grandmother. I know she doesn't quite understand what's going on, but I wanted to ask her. It was important to me that she knew I'd always take care of you and your mom."

"She would have approved." She gave me a wistful smile. "Do you already have the ring?"

"I do," I replied, thinking of the little velvet box in my jacket pocket. I'd gotten it last August, right after Ella and I had gotten back together because I knew then I wanted to spend the rest of my life with her. I'd been holding on to it, waiting for the right moment.

"When are you going to ask her?"

"Tonight," I answered. "After we get home." I'd moved into Ella's home earlier that year. I already stayed there most of the time anyway, so it felt like the natural next step. My old house had never quite felt like home, but Ella's house did, and it was important to me that Grace always had that place to come back to.

Grace's eyes misted over. "Are you serious?"

I nodded. "Tonight's the night."

Before either of us could say anything else, the song changed to an upbeat tune, and Ella approached.

"My dogs are barking," Ella said, kicking her heels off and picking them up. "Speaking of dogs, we better get home to Bradley Cooper. He's not used to going this long without a potty break."

"Yeah, we better hit the road," I agreed, and Grace's smile grew.

"What's got you all smiley?" Ella asked, grabbing her daughter's hand and pulling her close for a hug.

"I just love weddings," Grace replied, glancing over at me. "They make me happy."

"Is Sam bringing you home, or do you want to ride with us?" Ella asked.

"Sam will bring me home," she said quickly. "You guys go ahead. Don't wait up."

"You two be careful driving home." I kissed the top of Grace's head.

"We will," she said before whispering in my ear. "Good luck."

Ella and I made our rounds and said goodbye to everyone before heading out, the music fading the closer we got to the car. She breathed in and looked up at the night sky that was filled with stars.

"Love is in the air," she said, slipping her arm around me. "Tonight was perfect."

"Almost perfect," I said as we approached the car.

"Almost?" she asked, looking up at me. "What could possibly make it more perfect?"

I pulled her close and kissed her softly, thinking of the little velvet box residing in my pocket. "Going home with you."

Acknowledgments

The quote at the beginning of this book from the amazing Dolly Parton is one that's stuck with me since September the 11th of 2020, the day I lost my sweet Granny. The following month, I began my publishing journey, and nothing could have truly prepared me for the love I received. The #bookstagram community showed up for me in ways I never could have imagined. You have been the wind in my sails these last few months. The messages you've sent me after reading *Home Is Where You Are* and your enthusiasm for *Home Again* have truly kept me afloat. There aren't enough words to tell you how thankful I am for each and every one of you.

To the Indie Author community, thank you for welcoming me into this wonderful family. Special love goes to Lauren H Mae, Eve Kasey, Mia Heintzelman, JL Stiles, and Andrea Nourse (and the Indie Author Book Club).

To Elle Maxwell, you are magical. Thank you for bringing Ella, Cash, and Bradley Cooper to life.

To Mrs. Ross, you're still my favorite teacher.

To Neal, for making me the best writing playlist. (In case anyone was wondering, it's full of sad songs because that's all I can write to.)

To Ali, Brooke, Sydney, Andree, DeYuna aka Dee, Carina, Gaby, and Suzanne... I love y'all.

To Kia, thank you for always believing in me. Love you.

To Jen, I love you FOR-EVA. I refuse to wait till 2025, so hurry it up.

To Kate, I truly couldn't do life or write books without you. I love you to pieces. Are you moving to Nashville yet?

To Lauren aka Wonder Woman, I sure got lucky when you decided to work with me as a critique partner. You've helped me grow as a writer, and you have had my back from day one. Your friendship means the world to me, and I feel pretty damn lucky that I get to watch all of this magic unfold in your life. You deserve every bit of it. I'm so proud of you.

To Nicole, my SSMATBMDBFFAATE, my medical consultant, you know I would be lost without you. I'm so lucky to have you as one of my best friends. Love you.

To my Mama, Daddy, and brother Matthew, I love you all special.

To my Granny, who I miss every single day.

To my husband, you make it possible for me to live my dreams. I am blessed beyond measure. Love you and our babies more than anything. (Even if you don't like cats.) Can we go to Target?

To every person reading this who is grieving, no matter where you are on your journey, just know that you are not alone. Sending all my love to you.

Melissa Grace is a freelance writer whose work has been featured in publications like *Medium, Thought Catalog,* and *The Mighty.* She resides just outside of Nashville, Tennessee with her husband and five (yes, five) fur children, including her dog, Cash. This is her second novel.

Learn more and stay in the loop about Melissa's future projects, including the next installment of the Midnight in Dallas series at www.melissagracewrites.com.

Find her on social media:

- facebook.com/heymelissagrace
- twitter.com/heymelissagrace
- instagram.com/heymelissagrace
- goodreads.com/melissagrace
- bookbub.com/authors/melissa-grace
- amazon.com/Melissa-Grace/e/B08LMS2237/ref=dp_byline_cont_pop_e-books_1